David, –
reading th
enjoyed writing them.
Ralph

To Glory
and
Beyond

✛

By Ralph Reaves

PublishAmerica
Baltimore

ISBN: 978-4489-1450-0 (softcover)
ISBN: 978-1-4489-9098-6 (hardcover)
PUBLISHED BY PUBLISHAMERICA, LLLP
www.publishamerica.com
Baltimore

Printed in the United States of America

CHAPTER 1

Andy Butler lays the book on the grass beside him, and watches the young girl riding up the slope toward him. She rides like a Comanche, pushing herself and her horse to the limit. The buckskin on white, paint horse, is laboring to dig his way up the soft loam to the caprock.

The girl with ash blond braids and bluebonnet eyes is leaning forward, nudging the stallion in the ribs with her spurred boot heels, and speaking encouragement into his ear.

So beautiful, he thinks. *So much like her mother, but a lot of me in her too.* Nancy, her mother, would never have pushed a horse like that. She had too gentle of a spirit. She would probably have gotten off and led the horse up the bluff.

"Hi Dai," the girl shouts, swinging down from the panting horse. Her spurs jingle merrily as she walks over to her father. "Thought I'd find you up here." She picks up the book from the grass, glances at the cover. "Is this her diary?"

He nods, his eyes looking out over the valley below, but not seeing the beauty of the silver mesquite grass, bluebonnets, horsemint and Mexican blanket that once enthralled him.

"I thought you'd put all this behind you. Why now?" she asks.

He ignores her question. "Do you remember her at all, Annie?"

She flips through the pages, shrugs. "Sometimes I think I do, but I was so young, maybe I've just created her in my mind from the diary and what you and Jjajja have told me."

Jjajja is the half Creek Indian, half Negro woman who Annie knows as her grandmother, and whom Nancy had adopted as her surrogate mother. The name Jjajja is derived from an African word for grandmother.

She lays the book down reverently, strokes the cover with her fingers. "Let her rest in peace, Dai. She's been gone from our lives for ten years now. Don't put the past between you and Ilsa. She's been a good wife to you and a good mother to me. She loves you so much."

He shrugs, "I love Ilsa too, and it wasn't meant to put your mother between us. I just happened across it this morning…"

"And decided to come up here on the mountain to read it," she finishes for him.

"It's not like that, Annie. When I found it in my old sea chest I decided to put an end to it once and for all. I brought it up here to burn it."

The pain in Annie's eyes makes him look away. "Oh Dai, don't burn it. It's my only legacy from her."

"But you said it; its very existence puts a wedge between me and Ilsa. I don't want that. It's just that, well, reading Nancy's diary is like visiting her grave. Can you understand that? Does Ilsa understand that?"

She places her finger on his lips. "I understand it quite well, and so does Ilsa. She knows mother's memory will always be precious to you, but you need to keep Ilsa number one in your life."

"Even before you?"

"Even before me," she says with a smile.

She puts her foot out for a leg up, and he boosts her into the saddle. "Where you headed?"

"I thought I'd ride out to the escarpment camp, and see how the boys are coming with the branding."

"See how the boys are coming with the branding, or wiggle your fanny in front of Yoni?"

"Oh Dai, I don't wiggle my fanny in front of anybody. You know Yoni thinks of me as a little sister." She leans down for a kiss. "Why don't you ride out there with me?"

He shakes his head, "No, I believe I'll stay here for a while, and then go on down and see what's for supper."

"I'll probably eat out at the camp," she responds. "In fact, I'll probably stay out there tonight if that's okay."

He knows his daughter, and he knows that if he told her no, she'd probably figure out a way to make it happen anyway, like claiming a loose shoe on her horse, or something equally ridiculous. Every good cowboy carries a couple of extra shoes, a tack hammer, short handled shoe pullers/hoof trimmers in his saddle bags and a few horseshoe nails in his, or her, hat band, and can pull and replace a shoe in fifteen minutes.

While his daughter rides across the caprock on her way to the escarpment, he picks up the book. It falls open at Nancy's last entry, and her ring, the scrimshaw ring he gave her as a boy, falls out.

Sunday, April 2ⁿᵈ, 1865

Good morning my wonderful husband, I feel so good today. IT'S SPRING AND EVERYTHING IS BEGINNING TO BLOOM.

I will be riding up to the mill today. It's Sunday, so no one will be working, but I need to check on some work that was done on the roof last week. It's still a little cool, but I think I'll take a swim down to the honeysuckle cave, just to see if it's still there.

Annie has pestered me to go ever since she found out I was going. She says, "Go mommy, pease, go mommy." She's such a firecracker. She's so much like you in so many ways. Mama says she looks just like me, but I see a lot of you in her. She's a very stubborn little girl—now, I wonder where she gets that?

I hope you don't mind that I named her after you, you and Mama, Andrea Lula. Jacky is the one who started calling her Annie, and I like that,

7

since Ann was my mother's name. So in a way, she's named for all three of you.

I miss my sweet Missy. It's not that I mind riding Berty. She's a good mule, but I loved my horses so much. It just broke my heart to sell them. I guess we'll have lots of horses out in Texas though.

When you get home (can't wait, can't wait) maybe we can start working on a little brother to, as you sailors say, take the wind out of Annie's sails a bit.

Well, my dear, I need to close. I need to get on up to the mill before it gets too late.

I love you. Please hurry home now that peace has come.

The letter was written on the same day that Nancy was killed by Andy's avowed enemy René Labeaux; written right after he, Andy, escaped from the Union prisoner of war camp at Point Lookout, Maryland.

Retribution had come to Labeaux, but there was no joy in it. It didn't bring her back to him.

Ten years. Has it really been ten years? He runs his fingers through his hair, hair turned prematurely gray by the ravages of Point Lookout.

Ten years. He lays the book on the grass beside him, stretches out on the soft mesquite grass, and tucks the saddlebag under his head as a pillow. As he watches the scudding gray clouds thicken and build against the mesa, he thinks, *hmmm, maybe it'll rain; good, we could use some rain,* and then his mind wanders to a different time, and a different place.

******

The old mill stands the same, as if the war had never passed around it. The slow water moves under the wheel, and it creaks as it turns.

Andy lifts Annie down from Barak's back, and together they walk to the wooden cross in the grass near the dogwood. She's so little she has to reach up to hold his hand.

He stands silent for a moment, letting his pain and sorrow settle in him. His whole life lies buried there under that dogwood, the only real happiness he'd ever known, and it was so short.

He reaches up, plucks a creamy white blossom from the tree, and studies the crimson edges. Nancy's quiet voice comes to him. *They say that Jesus' cross was made out of dogwood, and ever since He was crucified, the blossoms have been cross shaped, and the red on the tips is the blood from His hands, feet and head.* He can envision her eyes smiling at him from the wet tangle of golden hair around her face.

He presses the blossom to his lips, and then places it gently on the ground at the foot of the cross. His heart swells in him, and the tears flow freely down his cheeks as he reads what's carved into the crosspiece.

I WILL GO AHEAD OF YOU AND PREPARE A PLACE FOR YOU

"Good bye, my darling," he whispers.

******

Lula stands with her arms folded, watching as Andy secures the load on the packhorse with a diamond hitch. Her mouth is a thin, grim line. Her stomach is so uneasy she's afraid she might throw up. He's been after her for a week now, ever since he returned to Leary Plantation after the death of Labeaux, trying to convince her to leave Mississippi, and go to Texas with them. Now she can't put it off any longer. He's loading the packhorse, and her son Jacky is waiting in the gig with Annie.

Oh Nancy, Nancy, her mind cries, *how can I leave my baby out deah at dat ol' mill wid nobody to care fo' her, and look aftah her grave.* She shakes her head. *No, I cain't leave. My John be restin' in dis Leary soil, my baby, Nancy, out to de ol' mill. I cain't leave.* She gives Jacky a pleading look, and he returns a sympathetic smile.

Andy strolls up to her, puts his arm around her shoulder, kisses her on the temple. "I understand Mama Lula. In a way, I wish I could stay too, but now Jacky and I are both wanted men. We'll be safer in Texas; besides, that's where my home is, that's where the ranch that would have mine and Nancy's is." He mounts Barak, and trots past the gig. Jacky raises a hand in farewell, and jigs up the pony. Her heart is about to break.

Annie scrambles over the seat of the gig to the back, and leans out, her arms outstretched. "Jjajja, Jjajja. No!! Unca Jacky, don't leave Jjajja. Jjajja, come Annie," she screams.

Lula's fist flies to her mouth, and a sob escapes her throat. *What am I thinkin'? Nancy's gone, but Annie still needs me.* She rushes to the back of the gig, and grabs Annie's tiny hands.

"Wait, Unca Jacky, wait for Jjajja!!"

Lula scrambles up into the gig beside Annie, the sobs wracking her body. Annie pats her on the cheek. "Don't cry Jjajja, I don't let Unca Jacky leave you."

They cross the river at Natchez, take the Vidalia road to the Black River, drop southwest to Alexandria, south to Lake Charles, and cross the Sabine River at Orange, Texas. They struggle their way through the Big Thicket, fighting blood-sucking mosquitoes, marshes and bayous. As they continue west, they begin to leave the thick forest; and then one evening Andy tops a hill, and stretching endlessly before him is the rolling Texas prairie. He spurs Barak back to the gig, lifts Annie onto the saddle in front of him, and then turns, and rides back to the top of the hill.

"Look Annie, Texas."

She squeals, stretches out her little arms, and cries, "Tesas!"

Jacky drives the gig to the top of the hill. He just sits, and nods his head, satisfied. Lula gets out of the gig stiffly, looks out across the waving grass. *So big, so dry, no rivah, no bayou.* She shakes her head in desperation.

Nine days later, the trail-weary travelers sit on the bluff overlooking the Frio valley. Below them the Frio River flows over a granite floor and around huge boulders. The stately cypress trees stand at the water's edge, their knees sticking out of the shallow water. Back from the river's edge, spreading pecan trees shade the profusion of wild flowers. In little parks, dogwood and Mexican buckeye add to the color with their creamy white and rose-colored blossoms.

Andy has dismounted. Barak is standing close by cropping the succulent mesquite grass shoots. Lula sidles up beside him; Annie lifts her arms silently to him, wanting to be held in his arms.

"It be real purty, Andy," Lula says softly. "I jes wish my Nancy could have seen it."

"All I ever wanted was to share it with her." His voice is barely audible.

She points out across the valley. There is a large stone and log house near the confluence of the river and a small creek. It seems to be two separate cabins joined by a covered dogtrot. From the house a dirt track leads across a stone bridge to the barns and corrals. "Dat our house?"

Andy shakes his head, "No, that's the Macgregor place; my cabin is at the foot of this bluff, in the brush. You can't see it from here. I don't know what kind of shape it's in after all these years, but I do know it's not big enough for this family now. We'll have to see if I can put you and Annie up with the Macgregors. Me an' Jack may be able to stay at my place."

Ilsa Jenkins is in her side yard scattering grain out to her hens. Her twin boys, now eight years old, are playing with a litter of black and white puppies in the smoke house. She raises her hand to push a wisp of straw yellow hair into the bun on the back of her head. She shades soft green eyes to get a better look at the caravan coming down from the bluff. Her heart hammers against her ribs.

Sure, he's changed; he's not the same carefree boy of nineteen who drove a herd of cattle out of this valley five years ago, to deliver them to the Confederate army. His hair is almost white now, and he has aged considerably, but it's him, no doubt about that. Her hand goes from her brow to a tentative wave as they approach.

"Andy?" There is a quaver in her voice.

"Hi Ilsa, you staying in the Macgregor's house now?" He swings down from the big gray horse.

"Yeah, Brian joined the Texas Rangers, and Colin and Becky went back to the Ohio. They just couldn't stay in Texas, their sympathies being with the north the way they were. Brian comes around occasionally. He stays here sometimes, but we pretty much traded property, and he stays in my old cabin, across the river, when he comes."

Andy just nods. "I'm kind of surprised you didn't go back to your folk's place at Fredericksburg."

"Nope, I've stayed here." What she doesn't say is, *I've been waiting for you to return.*

"Is my place livable?" he asks.

She just shakes her head. "Not without some fixin' up. We had a bad flash flood couple o' years ago, washed away most of your shack. The water came all the way up to this place, and we had to camp out on the mountain for a few days, but it dit'n do too much damage. This is a sturdy ol' house." She glances lovingly at the big log and rock home.

Andy waves his arm out toward where the others are waiting by the gig. "I brought my family from Mississippi." He motions for them to come forward. "Ilsa, this is my mother-in-law, Mama Lula and my brother-in-law, Jack Leary. That little scamp in the smoke house with your boys and the puppies is my daughter, Annie. Annie, come out here!"

Ilsa smiles, and extends her hand to the tall Negro woman. *Could Andy have married a colored girl?* "Proud to meet you, my name is Ilsa. Those rascals by the smoke house are Yoni and Fritz."

The little girl scampers up to her father, giggling, holding a squirming black and white puppy in her arms. "Mine!" she announces.

Well, if the little girl with the platinum curls and bright blue eyes is his daughter, she don't rightly look part Negro, not that it would matter. "Ya'll come on in the house now. I'll start some supper. Jack, you like beef steak?"

Jacky's face breaks into a big grin. "Yes'm, I like just about anything, but steak sounds mighty fine."

Lula takes the extended hand. "Anyting I can do to help?" She likes this young woman in spite of the fact that there was obviously something between her and Andy before he married her Nancy. She can tell it in the way the girl looks at Andy. There was love there once.

"No ma'am. You just go in that back bedroom and rest. It'll be a little while before I can have it ready. In fact, you can just take all your stuff back there. That'll be yours and Annie's wing now. That'll be your new home."

Tears well up in Lula's eyes. *New home? How'd all dis come about?*

Six years ago she was mistress of a fine plantation house, and the companion of a loving plantation owner. Then the war came, and John was killed at the battle of Memphis. The war was lost. Nancy was killed, and she was reduced back to the slave quarters where she began as a girl. Now, here she is in a strange land, among strangers. *I jes be getting' too ol,'* she thinks. *I should be restin' under de sod at Leary point next to my John. I got no business out in dis wilderness. I be too ol' t' start ovah.* The tear breaks over, and rolls down her cheek.

This doesn't escape Ilsa. She rushes forward, and throws her arm around Lula's shoulders. "Oh, Mama Lula, you're just tired, honey. Everything's gonna be alright. You'll see." She looks up pleadingly at Andy.

He comes over, and puts his arm around Lula. "Come on Mama Lula; let me help you get settled."

When he comes out of the back bedroom, Ilsa is sitting at the table with a cup of coffee. She hands it to him. "She gonna be alright?"

"Yeah, she's asleep now. The last couple of years have been hard on her. Her husband and Nancy, my wife, were both casualties of the war."

"Nancy was her daughter?" she asks.

He sips the coffee. "Not her birth daughter, but they couldn't have loved each other any more if she had been. Nancy's real mother died when she was just a little girl, and in her mind Lula became her mother."

"And the boy?"

"Nancy's father and Lula." He looks up, and shrugs. "It happens. Legally he couldn't marry her, but in the eyes of God they were man and wife."

Ilsa smiles, "I can certainly see why. She's beautiful."

He nods, "Thanks for being so kind and takin' 'em in like this."

She reaches across the table, and lays her hand on his. "This is your ranch, Andy, and they are your family."

He looks at the hand on his, a ranch woman's hand, small and gentle, but strong; strong enough to milk a cow or wring a turkey's neck. He lifts it, and squeezes it gently. "It's good to be home, Ilsa, but I'm packing a lot of freight right now. The war took a lot out of me, and away from me. I'm afraid it's gonna take a while to heal."

As he continues, his eyes stare into space, as though his mind is a thousand miles away. "You know, I once told Hawk that life was like a wild mustang, and that I was gonna saddle it, and bridle it, and ride it to glory." He looks up into her eyes helplessly. "I did'n break it, though; it broke me. It threw me to the ground, and stomped on me; broke me into a thousand little pieces. I lost everything, Ilsa, everything."

She looks sadly into his eyes for a moment, and then her voice is soft and loving. "For I know the plans that I have for you, declares the Lord," she quotes, "plans for welfare, and not for calamity, to give you a future and a hope."

A smile starts slowly on Andy's lips, and then widens into a grin. "Jeremiah, twenty nine, eleven. I did'n know you knew scripture."

"Lots o' things you don't know, smarty pants." She pauses, and then continues in the same loving voice. "When Lucky disappeared, and then you rode away, and dit'n come back, I read that verse to myself over and over. It's the only thing that kept me goin'."

He studies the chapped knuckles and chipped fingernails. Life has been hard for her, too; no man, no help keeping a home, and raising two boys.

She pulls her hand away self-consciously, and folds it in her lap. "Andy, you dit'n lose everything. You still have this ranch, and you have a wonderful, beautiful daughter. You've just ridden to the back side of glory, that's all. I know you're still grievin', honey, but I'm here, and I'll be here to help you pack that freight, and pick up the pieces, whenever you need me."

"We got any cattle left in the brush?" She knows he's just changing the subject.

"Yeah," she says brightly, "they're pretty scattered, but they come back to the escarpment during the freeze up. An old friend of yours is a frequent visitor here."

He gives her a questioning look.

"That ol' lead steer you took to Mississippi with you. You know, the one with the twisty horn and scarred eye."

He laughs. "You mean Beast? He's still around? That ol' moss back, I'd like to see him."

"You will. He generally leads a herd in after the first snow up on the Llano Estacado. They pretty much stay up on the escarpment, but they come down to the river to water."

"What about Blue?" He's almost afraid to ask about his old cowpony, his first horse and second love.

"She's down at the corral. She's got a long-yearling colt beside her, good lookin' horse colt, piebald paint. He'll make a fine stud someday, I think."

He gives her a weak smile. He'd cared for her once, before Nancy; maybe he can again.

"Think I'll wander down that way, and say hi to her."

"Dinner'll be ready in about an hour." She smiles, but when he turns his back she bites her lip. *He's hurtin' real bad. He's gonna need my strength, and when he does, I'll be here. I'll always be here.*

He steps up to the corral rail; the big horse colt has his head between Blue's flank and side. She looks up, sees Andy, and with her back hoof, gently kicks her greedy colt away from her teat. She trots over to the rail, and puts her nose out to him. She chuckles softly down in her throat, the way she used to.

For a minute he is almost overwhelmed. He rolls his head back onto his shoulders, and looks at the clear sky, blinking the tears away. She nuzzles him in the chest, and tucks her nose under his arm.

He hugs her nose to him, and scratches her under the chin. "Hello ol' girl; yeah, I'm back."

For the first time in a long time he feels a sense of well being, of being back home. "Maybe between you an' me an' Ilsa we can put me back together again."

The colt, angry about his dinner being interrupted, races by, and kicks the corral next to Andy. He is a handsome colt; buckskin on white with a white face and one brown eye and one so light blue it looks white. "Uh-oh," he says to Blue, "you threw a white eyed colt. You know the old sayin.' Never trust a thin lipped woman or a white eyed horse."

The house is quiet now. Her wing is a good thirty feet from the other wing, the one that will now belong to Mama Lula and Annie. She can hear her boys breathing heavily in the next room, but she can't hear anything from across the long dogtrot living room, which separates the two wings.

Andy and Jacky have gone up to Brian's cabin for the night. She gets out of bed and walks to the window, and looks out across the moonlit expanse. There is a light showing at the window of Brian's cabin. She sees a shadow pass by, and senses that it's Andy. She fingers the ribbons holding her gown together, and an old memory comes unbidden to her mind.

She remembers the night the wolves came. If there ever would have been a time that she would have welcomed him to her bed, that would have been the night, but he wouldn't have it. No, not Andy Butler.

******

She lay restless in her bed, unable to sleep.

She rose to check on her babies, then went to the fireplace, and sat on the hearth to stare into the dark lonely room, and think. She felt an uneasiness in her soul.

She had heard wolves in the woods behind her cabin earlier. She had heard wolves before; she had even seen one that her husband, Lucky, shot, but tonight they frightened her. She tried not to think of her predicament, but her mind kept pulling at the threads of reality.

Lucky had been missing for more than three months. She knew, now, that he would never come back. He'd either been killed out there somewhere, or maybe just run off. She was fifteen years younger than him, and she suspected that he'd never really been happy being a family man. He was a woods runner, happier out there than by his own hearth.

A feeling of despair crept over her. Whether he was dead or just gone, she was alone. Oh, she could count on the others at first, but eventually even that would dwindle, and she would be all alone to raise her boys.

It was odd, her feelings toward Lucky. She felt a sense of loss but no real sadness. She honestly believed that she cared for him. She certainly hadn't minded being his wife. He was a good provider. She hadn't even minded giving him her love whenever he required it.

Sometimes she thought that their age difference was too great. They really had nothing in common, not even the boys.

She recalled something he said once: "When they're old enough to go hunting with me, they'll be sons to me; until then, they're yours." Now it was too late, they'd never be his.

Her mind rambled over events since he'd slapped her on the behind, and said simply, "goin' huntin." That was the last time she'd seen him.

A few days later, Andy had come by with a side of beef, and said he was worried about her and the boys. It struck her as strange at the time that he would be worried about her. He was a busy man—well boy really—and Lucky was known to stay out hunting for a week or better. Somehow, even then, he knew that Lucky would not be coming back. She'd have to ask him about it when she saw him.

Funny how much of the past three months included him; he had become very much a part of her life, stopping by every couple of days to check on her, and see if she needed anything.

A wave of loneliness washed over her, and she wished she had someone to talk to. She wished it was morning and Andy was here eating breakfast in his hungry way, and laughing with the boys. How they loved him. She felt a pang of guilt. She should have wished that it was morning and Lucky was back.

She stood, and started back to her room. Her spine turned to ice as the night silence was shattered by the howl of a wolf. It was so close. He had to be right outside of the cabin. She took a step, and then froze in fear. *They are right outside the door.*

One began snuffling, and scratching at the door itself. She threw a hand over her mouth to stifle a scream.

The wolves found the meat hanging from the porch rafter, and were tearing at it viciously. When that was gone, she thought, they would get in; somehow, they would get in. She was terrified. They began snarling and growling, fighting over the meat. One slammed against the door, shaking dirt from the doorjamb.

The sound of a gunshot, and a wolf screaming in pain barely registered in her stunned senses, and then there was a series of shots, and the sound of brush breaking as the wolves retreated into the woods.

"Ilsa, are you okay? Ilsa, open the door, it's me," Andy's voice shouted.

She stood shaking, still stunned for the moment. She couldn't make her legs move. Andy's fists drummed on the door. "Ilsa, open up."

She shook off the stupor, and rushed to the door, throwing off the bar. When she saw Andy standing there, she broke into hysterics. He held her in his arms, and kissed her hair.

"It's okay now," he whispered, his mouth against her ear, "I'm here."

"Oh, Andy," she sobbed, "don't leave me, please don't leave me. I was so afraid." She started to shake and her knees gave way. He scooped her up in his arms, and carried her to the hearth. When he sat her down, she clung to him.

"It's okay now," he said soothingly, "they're gone. I ran 'em off."

She choked back her sobs, and seemed to get control of herself. "Will you stay here tonight?" she pleaded.

He didn't answer right away, and her eyes got the same terrified look they had held a few moments before.

She clutched at his arm. "Don't go back to your cabin tonight, stay here. Please, don't leave me." She began to cry again, softly this time. "Stay with me."

"I'll stay," he said. "I won't leave you."

She released the hold on his jacket, and changed from a terrified, lonely woman to an excited little girl. "I was so afraid," she chattered. "I dit'n know what to do. I just knew they would get in." She stepped away from him, and the firelight filtered through her thin nightgown, and accented her silhouette beneath. She noticed his glance, and turned toward the shadows of the bedroom. "I'd better go check on the boys."

He watched the movement of her hips under her gown as she hurried away, and remembered how warm and firm she felt when he danced with her at the big fandango at Hawk's place.

"I'd better go put Blue to bed," he called out, "I won't be long. I'll just put her in the barn with your milk cow."

She came back to the door with fear in her eyes. "Don't leave," she pleaded.

He went to her at the door, lifted her chin, and looked into her eyes. "I will be right back. I will not leave you."

At the barn, he couldn't get the image of her—standing with the fire behind her, glowing through the fabric, showing the outline of her body—out of his mind. Absent-mindedly, he pulled the saddle and bedroll, and threw some corn in the stall for Blue.

When he entered the cabin again, Ilsa had left the bedroom door ajar. The yellow glow of a candle flickered by her bed. He went to the hearth, and dropped his bedroll on the floor in front of the fireplace. She had banked the fire, and the coals glowed softly. It brought the image of her standing there in the glow to mind again.

Ilsa lay in bed staring at the ceiling, listening to Andy moving around in the other room. She wondered if he needed anything before he went to sleep. She turned over, and watched his shadow as he moved about. Then she caught her breath slightly when she saw the shadow at her door, and heard the soft jingle of his spurs as he came into the room.

She had known he would come, and she knew that she wanted him to, but now that it was happening, it frightened her a little.

"Ilsa," he whispered, kneeling beside her bed, unsure of himself.

She reached up, and touched his cheek. "It's alright," she assured him.

He stroked her hair and bent to kiss her, stopped, and looked into her eyes.

"Ilsa, I—."

She hushed him with her lips on his, pulled his hand down to the neck of her gown. He fumbled with the ribbons holding the gown together. Her hand went up, and helped him untie them. Her eyes searched deep into his. *Here I am,* they said, *alone in the world, and yours for the taking. It doesn't matter if you take my love tonight, and ride away in the morning. I have no one else to turn to and I need someone so badly.*

He kissed her lips, chin and bare throat. Then, abruptly, he stood, and turned his back to her. "I can't do this."

Her voice was soft. "What is it?"

"Lucky," he answered.

There was despair in her voice, "Oh Andy, Lucky's not coming back; he's probably dead."

He knelt beside her, took her hand in his. "Ilsa, what if we did this, and then Lucky showed up? Could we live with what we'd done? Could we all live in the same community? Could you and me see each other every day, and be okay with what we'd done?"

Her eyes smiled, soft and gentle, but she pulled her gown together, and retied the ribbons. "I s'pose not."

He kissed her lightly again and pulled the quilt up around her chin. "Goodnight," he whispered.

And then he rode away to the war, and he hadn't returned with the others, and Lucky never returned, and she was left alone, as she knew she would be.

CHAPTER 2

Calvin Aloise Mahone, Pug to his friends, is waiting outside the Secretary of State's office. He's been in the office many times. During the recent war, variously called the Civil War, the War Between the States, the Rebellion or the War for Southern Independence, depending on who is doing the calling, he was the Secretary's personal bodyguard. The Pinkerton Detective Agency had been given the contract as National Security Service. Then, just before Lincoln was shot, they had lost the contract, and he had returned to private citizen and detective again. Now, unexpectedly, he's been summoned to the Secretary's office.

"Secretary Seward will see you now," the Secretary's secretary says.

Pug picks up his green bowler derby and enters the office. Inside he recognizes Secretary of War, Edwin Stanton, Secretary of the Navy, Gideon Welles and Major General Benjamin Butler. He bows his head slightly to them.

"Hello Pug. You remember Secretary Stanton and Secretary Welles."

He nods again and mumbles in the affirmative.

"And Congressman Butler?

Yes, he remembers Butler; possibly the most hated Union officer by the south. Beast Butler he's called. He responds with a single word, "General."

"How've you been Pug? How's the detective business?" Secretary Welles asks.

"It's alright, sir."

"Well, we're sorry that Pinkerton lost the National Security contract. Things were much better when you were watching our backs."

Mahone nods grimly. "Yes sir, you know how I feel about that, if we'd been there, Mr. Lincoln wouldn't've been assassinated."

Seward nods, but doesn't respond.

"How's Pinkerton treating you? Your pay okay? You happy there?" Stanton asks.

Pug nods, "We're the biggest detective agency in the country now. We stay busy." He's wondering silently what this is all about. He's a poker player and he senses that it's time for him to bet on his hand. A grin breaks across his homely face. "Of course I could always use a raise in pay."

Welles speaks up. "Pug, we four know you to be a man of discretion, a man who can keep his mouth shut. Can we depend on you not to repeat anything you hear in this room today?"

"Yes sir, of course."

Congressman Butler gets up, walks across the room, opens the office door, looks out at the secretary's desk and then closes it again. "As you may be aware, President Johnson is in favor of leniency for the major leaders of the rebellion. We already have most of them, including General Lee and the rebel pirate Rafael Semmes, in custody to stand trial for treason; there are a few more out there on the loose however, whom we would like to have brought in. We were wondering if you'd like to work for us."

"For the government?" Pug asks.

Stanton steeples his fingers in front of his lips, and stares at Mahone. "Not exactly, you would be working for an independent organization, an organization that would not have anything to do with the government directly."

Congressman Butler speaks up. "Let's just say that there are people in high places who want justice done and they're willing to pay a man, a man like you, to bring them in." He raises his left eyebrow questioningly.

Pug laughs out loud. "You want me to be a bounty hunter. Dead or alive?"

Butler smiles knowingly. "We wouldn't want you to put yourself at risk trying to arrest them, if they could be brought in alive to stand trial all the better, but—." He shrugs.

"How much bounty on them?" Pug asks.

"No bounty, the organization would pay you a monthly salary of one hundred dollars."

"And expenses?"

Welles looks to the other three for affirmation. Each of them nods.

"And daily expenses—within reason."

Pug stands up and puts his hand out to Welles. Somehow he senses that Welles is the ringleader here. "When do I start?"

Butler hands him a sealed envelope. "No particular order, it's a short list." he smiles.

Outside, Pug opens the envelope. Inside he finds four one hundred dollar bills and a list with four names on it.

Lieutenant James Waddell—Commander CSS Shenandoah

First Lieutenant William Whittle—Executive officer—CSS Shenandoah

Lieutenant Commander Andrew Butler—Commander CSS Alamo

Julius Principe—Confederate spy.

******

Mahone is a good detective, very thorough. It has taken him a full three months digging into government records and files to gather information on his fugitives. He opens the first file and scans his notes:

Waddell, James Iredell—born 1824, Pittsboro, N.C.
Commander of the Confederate cruiser Shenandoah.
Considered to be a pirate by the Federal government.
Continued to sink the artic whaling fleet after the end of the war. Surrendered the Shenandoah to the British government rather than take his chances with the United States government.
Believed to be living in the London area of England.

Whittle, William C.
Executive Officer CSS Shenandoah
Son of Commodore William Conway Whittle of Virginia.
Graduate of U.S. Naval Academy class of 58.
Last known whereabouts London, England.

He writes the numerals 3 and 4 on the jackets of the files and places them in his safe. These will have to wait until he has dealt with the other two. He will take them in order of availability not necessarily priority.

He opens the next file:

Julius Salvador Principe
Born 1845, Charleston, S.C.
Actor. Confederate spy.
Known aliases: Major Jason Prichard, U.S. Army (Artillery); Julia Principal, supposed wife of Delaware businessman and Union Officer Harvey Principal, Washington socialite. It is believed he got much of his information at social gatherings in and around Washington, Baltimore and Philadelphia while playing the part of a lonely wife looking for companionship. General Wilfred Barnard actually got him into a bedroom and partially undressed before the General was knocked unconscious, his personal papers and money stolen, and Principe made good his escape.
Escaped Washington after the war as Sally Prince with Feldstein Theatrical Tour Group.
Last seen on stage in Nashville, Tennessee.
Master of disguise.

Here Mahone scribbles: Interesting character!! Am I looking for a man or woman?

He puts the folder aside, and picks up the last one.

Andrew Jackson Butler

Believed to be from either South Carolina or Georgia, somewhere along the Savannah River.

Commander of the Confederate cruiser Alamo, also Staff Officer to Rear Admiral/Brig. Gen. Rafael Semmes.

Known aliases: Juaquin Donavan, Irish-Mexican seaman. Captured aboard the blockade-runner Giraffe. Butler/Donavan escaped from Point Lookout prison camp. General Semmes says he was sent out as a dispatch rider just before the surrender.

Wanted for piracy on the high seas, treason, escape from a Federal prison and questioning in the death of Federal Land Commissioner René Labeaux, Natchez, Mississippi.

Married to Nancy Leary of Leary Point, Mississippi.

He scribbles: Could be the most dangerous of the four. Best place to start seems to be Leary Point or Natchez, Mississippi.

He holds the folders in each hand as if he's weighing them, drops Butler's folder on his desk, and marks a big numeral 2 on the jacket. He holds the Principe file in the air. "Okay Mister Principe or Missus Principal or Miss Prince, whoever you are, you'll be the first to go down."

******

The walk from the big house, across the ford, to the cabin where Andy and Jack are staying isn't a long walk, maybe five minutes. Ilsa's made it thousands of times. She's always tried to keep the cabin clean for Brian for whenever he happens to come in, and now that Andy is staying there, she wants it to be clean for him. She has brought a basket with clean linen and a soft pillow, which she made with Cottonwood lint, to put on his bed.

She has also brought a coffee pot, coffee grinder and a bag of coffee beans, just in case they want to make coffee before they come to her house for breakfast.

They have ridden up the canyon to visit Andy's old friend and partner, Chico Garza. Andy hadn't known about Hawk and Dolores's little girl, let's see, she would be about two years older than Andy's daughter now, anyway, Andy wanted his Annie to meet her and play with her. They should be gone most of the day. That will give her plenty of time to clean the cabin before she goes home to do her own chores.

As she is straightening up the room she finds a leather-bound book lying on the floor next to the bed. It is branded with the word TEX, and the ranch brand hB~. She picks it up and sees that it is hand written. It must be Andy's diary. She looks around the room guiltily. She knows she should just put it back but she sees her name and begins to read:

After I left the Queen of Scots, our original three grew to include Chico's sister, Dolores, and little brother Carlos, Lucky Jenkins, his wife Ilsa, their twin baby boys, and the Macgregor family. The stout Macgregors they are called, and the joke in central Texas is, that they can plow a forty-acre field in a day with either of them pulling the plow. The older brother, Colin, has a wife and two children. Brian is just a little younger than me. Neither are actually cowboys. They ran a blacksmith shop in Goliad, and had a small place they tried to farm.

Lucky isn't much of a cowboy either. In fact, the only cowboys in our group are Hawk and Chico. I guess if you had to put a label on Lucky you'd have to call him a woods-runner and hunter. As long as there's game in the brush, the community will never go hungry.

Ilsa is his second wife. His first wife was Ilsa's older sister. When she died right after their marriage, he went back to the same German family, in Fredericksburg, and married Ilsa. She's a lot younger than him, a good fifteen years I'd guess. The age difference doesn't seem to bother her though. She seems happy enough.

Hawk and me have built a shelter like an Indian wickiup near the cave where the Spanish and Comanche shrines are. The Macgregor's are building a nice log house for the five of them on a knoll near where the creek flows into the river. Chico and Carlos threw up a lean-to affair for his family near the canyon.

Our various places are scattered, but close enough for mutual assistance and protection in case of Indian raids.

It is now coming on fall, and the wild cattle will be coming down from the Llano Estacado, the Staked Plains. Hawk, Chico and I plan to go onto the plateau, round up a small herd, and hold them on our range through the winter. Any calves born on our range will imprint this area as their home range, and even if they stray next year, they will return to this range. At least that's the plan. If it works, in four or five years, we should have a pretty good herd carrying the hB~ brand.

Today is Thanksgiving and next week is Dolores's birthday. Tonight we're having a real fandango. Lucky brought in a nice fat white tail doe and a couple of turkeys. Colin made some genuine whisky bawtha (water of life) or so he calls it. Becky Macgregor has made some pecan pies. Dolores made Mexican biscochitos, and Ilsa is supplying sauerbraten, German potato salad and German pastries. Man, that woman can cook.

Colin is playing his bagpipes while Lucky will accompany him on his fiddle. Carlos thinks he will add his part with a willow flute. It ought to be a real boot stomper.

Chico says it is a tradition in their family for Dolores to dance a special Mexican dance for her birthday. She's been flirting with me for over a month now, and tonight I just may try to steal a kiss.

Ilsa remembers that time, before Andy left to go to the war, before Lucky left her to raise their sons by herself. As she reads, it all comes back to her as if in a dream, as if she is reliving it.

******

"Hey Chiquita, you gonna dance for me tonight?" Andy called to Dolores as she helped lay out the table.

"Si, amante. I'm going to make you a very special dance." She answered by swishing her full skirt around her legs, showing an ample amount of calf.

After their Thanksgiving dinner, Colin pumped up his bagpipes to a screeching wail, and Lucky tried to keep up with him on the fiddle.

When Hawk finished a dust-raising dance with Ilsa he came over to where Andy and Chico were standing by the homemade-whiskey jug. "Whooie!" He panted. "That German gal is one handful of woman. Why don't you go get aholt of her fer the next dance young sprout?"

Andy smiled at no one in particular. "Naw, Dolores promised me a special dance. Maybe later."

Dolores had disappeared into the Macgregor house, and now made her grand entry, clicking castanets. She strutted across the yard, grabbed Andy's hat, and jumped into the bed of the buckboard. Chico strummed his guitar in time with her clicking heels and castanets. She tossed her long dark hair, and began a slow dance around the brim of the hat. Steadily the pace grew. The castanets clicked. Her heels clacked, and Andy felt a tightness in his chest. Suddenly Hawk let out a Comanche yell, and jumped into the wagon with her. He began clapping his hands in time with the guitar, and dancing around her as she danced around the hat. It was surprising how good he was. When they finished the dance, Hawk scooped her up in his arms, and they collapsed into the bed of the wagon, laughing.

"Dolores, I think you promised me the first dance." Andy said, reaching over to give her a hand up.

She jumped down next to him. "Si, my young horse-colt, so I did." He took her into his arms, and they began to sway to the music. She laid her cheek against his shoulder, and he nuzzled her ear with his lips. "Dolores, I think I'm falling for you. I want to kiss you."

She laughed. "Ah, you are a frisky colt."

He guided her over into the shadows, tilted her head back, and placed a kiss on her lips. They were soft, and returned the kiss, but then she whirled away from him, and went back out into the light. Hawk saw her, grabbed her around the waist, and whirled her around.

"Andy, would you like to dance with me? Lucky is busy with his fiddle." Ilsa asked smiling.

Andy smiled and shrugged. "Sure, Ilsa." And he whisked her out into the dance area for a rousing polka.

As the party wore on into the night, Andy drifted away from the crowd, and ambled off toward Colin's barn to relieve himself. He'd had a few swigs from the uiske beatha, and he felt like he needed to get away from the dancing for a while. When he reached the barn he heard soft laughing inside and low voices. At first he thought maybe Brian and Carlos had snitched a jug, then he recognized Dolores's laugh. He threw open the barn door, and there was Hawk and her lying in the straw in each other's arms.

His mind exploded in rage. "What are you doing?!" He rushed across the floor and kicked Hawk away from her. "She's my girl! Whada ya think you're doin'?"

Hawk jumped up into a defensive position. Andy swung, and hit him in the mouth.

Hawk fingered his split lip. He just stared at Andy.

"Dolores?" Andy sobbed.

Dolores stood up, brushed the straw off of her skirt. "Andy, I never said I was your mujer. I never said I was anybody's mujer."

Andy was humiliated. Not only was his girl being unfaithful, now she was denying that there was anything between them.

He reached down and pulled off a spur. His first swing caught Hawk across the chest, tearing his shirt. Little beads of blood appeared where the rowels passed.

Hawk pushed Dolores aside and sidestepped another swing; he felt sorry for the kid, but dang it, this was going too far. "Cool down kid; somebody's going to get hurt. Let's talk about this like a couple of men."

Andy answered by making another pass with the spur. Hawk's jab caught him square on the chin. A flash of red went through his brain, and he just lay there, only half conscious. When he raised his tear streaked face, Hawk and Dolores were gone, and he was alone with his misery. He knew he couldn't go back to the party, and he didn't want to be in the wickiup when Hawk returned, so he saddled Blue, and rode up onto the escarpment.

It was a beautiful night. There were a million stars out, and the fragrance of damp sage, cedar and juniper was as it can only be in Texas after a light shower. He built a fire of mesquite branches, and sat hunched over in his misery. He wiggled his sore chin tenderly with his thumb and forefinger.

He'd have to ride out tomorrow. He couldn't go back, not now. The thought of leaving this place made the tears sting his eyes again, and as he pulled his blanket up around him, he wept. He wept softly, but he wept.

He woke to the sound of a mockingbird's wondrous repertoire, and then the answer from another off in the brush, to Blue's soft snort as she grazed nearby—and to the smell of coffee boiling.

He jumped to his feet, his fists balled.

"Now wait a minute!" Hawk said, scrambling back away from the fire. "I didn't come out here to finish last night. I came out to apologize. Honest, I didn't know you felt that way about Dolores."

Andy hung his head. "I guess nobody knew it, but me."

Hawk poured a tin cup of coffee, and handed it out to Andy. "You know, Dolores is such a flirt, she does it without thinking about the consequences. She don't mean to hurt nobody by it. Heck, she even flirts with Colin and Lucky. Truth is, me an' her, well, we been sparkin' each other for a spell now."

Andy's jaw dropped. "You mean she's your girl?"

Hawk gave an embarrassed nod. "Wal, yeah, I guess you could say that."

"Oh, Hawk, I'm sorry I made such a fool outta myself. Dolores must think I'm a real idiot."

"No, it's okay. I think she learned a lesson last night. I know I did. I'm gonna make a honest woman out of her, finally."

Andy shook his head. If he felt humiliated last night, he felt doubly so today. "I don't know what to say." He stammered. "I guess I should leave, maybe go back to La Vaca, see if I can find a ship."

Hawk's face registered genuine shock. "Leave? No. What about yore place?"

Andy smiled. "It ain't really my place. You an' Chico just gave it to me because——." He just shrugged.

"Because we wanted you as our partner." Hawk finished. "When Dolores and me goes to Bandera to get hitched, I's gonna draw up a deed. It's yours. If you don't still want me for yore partner, well, that's okay, but that place is yours."

Andy swallowed hard. "I ain't never owned nothin' in my life Hawk. I love that wickiup an' cave an' creek. First time I seen it, I knew I didn't want to ever live nowhere else." He stuck out his hand. "If you'll still have me as a partner, I want to be yours."

As the weeks passed, he and Hawk and Chico rounded up their cattle. The community pitched in, and built Hawk and Dolores a cabin near Chico and Carlos's lean-to.

Christmas came, and he cut a small juniper tree and decorated it with the little red apples of the manzanito brush, blue berries from cypress and small gourds which he carved, and placed small candles inside, and hung from the tree branches. It was the first Christmas tree he had ever had in his life.

He was proud of his little home. After Hawk moved out, he had cleared the brush away from the cave, and widened the entrance with a pick-ax. He formed a dogtrot from his wickiup to the cave using willow poles and cow hides, and built a stone basin around the pool at the back wall of the cave. It made a natural cool-room to hang meat in. He left the shrines as they were except to repair them.

He'd never been happier, and never lonelier. For the first time in a long time, he thought of the little girl in Mississippi, his first sweetheart, Nancy Leary.

Ilsa closes the book and places it back next to the bed. It seems like a lifetime since those good times, more than a lifetime, a hundred years. Now Andy has returned, a haunted, broken man, and Lucky will never return. She's known that for years now. Of course she can only speculate as to what might have happened to him. She knows down deep that he was good man. He would never have just walked away from her and the boys. Some terrible thing had happened to him out in the brush, but what could it have been?

******

Lucky slung his powder horn and shot bag over his shoulder, and cradled his old Kentucky rifle in the crook of his arm like a baby. It was an old flintlock, seventy-five years old, but he loved it. He kept it in mint condition, and refused to hunt with anything else.

He slapped Ilsa on the backside and vaulted the cedar-rail fence around their yard. "Goin' huntin." He said simply.

Ilsa smiled, and continued to broom the bare yard. She knew she was being taken for granted again, but she didn't really mind. Lucky was a good provider, better than good; they had something different on the table every night. She did wish that she'd get more than a whack on the fanny when he left though.

He stood stone still for a couple of minutes, and watched the whitetail buck in the clearing ahead. The deer raised his head from browsing, and tested the air with his nostrils. He sensed that all was not exactly as it should be, and also stood absolutely motionless.

32

Lucky was too far for a good head shot, and so consequently too far to be detected. The deer watched and listened for a few minutes, and then went back to feeding.

Lucky moved his hand slowly to his powder horn, and filled the flash-pan. Ever so slowly he moved backward, keeping the cover of the Mesquite between them. It took nearly an hour to circle the clearing and get into a better position. He wasn't even sure the deer was still there, he had lost sight of it when he moved back into the trees. He moved to the edge of the woods, being careful that his soft moccasins didn't crack a twig or rustle dry leaves.

The Buck was still there. It was moving slowly towards him, its tail flipping nervously. Even as he watched, his woodsman's eye took in the faint movements all around him, a string of ants moving across the narrow path, and disappearing again in the undergrowth, an armadillo rooting at a mound of soft dirt, a woodpecker tapping noisily on a tree nearby. The deer raised his head, and stared across the clearing.

Now, was the automatic response, and the Kentucky rifle jumped to his shoulder, and belched flame and black smoke. Too late, his eye looked past the deer, and caught the movement on the other side.

Comanche! The hair on the back of his neck bristled. In an instant the smoke encased him, and he couldn't see the deer or the Indian.

He turned, and started to run through the trees, reloading as he went. When the reloading was done, he crashed through the thickest of the Mesquite and Chaparral. The thorns ripped his clothes and skin, but, on foot, he could move through places that would be difficult for a pursuer on a horse to follow.

He tried to angle away from the settlement, but didn't want to get up onto the escarpment, where there was less cover. *God, don't let'em find Ilsa and the boys.*

He was at the base of the mesa, south of the river now, and the thick bosque of the river was giving way to sparse cedar, juniper and cactus. He crouched behind a thick clump of cactus, and waited. He knew he couldn't get away now. He might just as well wait here, and make a fight of it.

The Comanche had no trouble following his trail, and the thick brush slowed them only a little. When they appeared, they were riding slow, laughing, obviously enjoying his attempts at getting away. They knew that soon he would tire, and it would be easy to ride him down.

He stepped out from behind the cactus, and fired. The ball took the lead Comanche right between the eyes. Again the smoke enveloped him, and he used the cover to move to a fat Juniper. He popped the ball from his mouth into the muzzle, rammed it home with the ramrod. The Indians seemed confused, it had taken seconds only for him to shoot, move, reload, and take aim again. In this short time, the Indians hadn't moved. The second shot flipped another of his pursuers backwards over the rump of his horse. This seemed to activate them, and they charged toward his Juniper screaming their Comanche war-yell.

He stepped out swinging his rifle like a club. The butt struck the skull of the horse, sending it sprawling in the dust, throwing its rider over its head. He was on the trashing body, stabbing with his Bowie knife, before the Indian stopped sliding. He turned just in time to thrust his knife into the throat of a second pony, sending pony and rider to the ground.

Took enough of 'em with me, was his last thought, before a lance sliced through him, pinning him to the ground. His name held true though, and he was dead when hit the ground.

The enraged hunting party landed on his lifeless body, and began to hack and rip it to pieces. They had paid a dear price for this afternoon's fun. They tied what was left of his body behind a horse, and drug it up onto the escarpment, and then left it for the buzzards and wolves.

Blue danced nervously away from the dead deer on the ground. She didn't like the smell of blood around it. Andy tried to hold her steady while he studied the scene. He didn't like it either, shot through the head, and then left untouched. He scouted around the meadow, and found the tracks of unshod ponies. He wasn't surprised to see Indian sign. They all knew that eventually it would happen. What surprised him was that they shot a deer, and then just left it for the buzzards.

He followed the pony tracks into the thick brush, and up toward the mesa. *Well, at least they were heading away from the settlement.*

When he came to the scene of the battle, and saw the two dead Indian ponies, he dismounted, tied Blue to a scrub oak, and began to scout around. He almost missed the old Kentucky rifle. The stock had shattered on impact with the pony's head, and flown into the brush, but the barrel lay in the rocks only a few feet away.

He picked it up. "Lucky's old flintlock." He said aloud. There was no doubt. There probably wasn't another one like it in Texas.

He followed the Indian trail until he lost it in the scree. He pushed his hat back, and looked up toward the caprock of the escarpment. They were moving fast. In fact, it looked like they were traveling at a full gallop. No point in trying to pick up the trail up on the escarpment. The sign was old, at least a couple of days. They would be up on the Staked Plains by now.

It was very puzzling. Obviously Lucky had killed the two horses, but his body wasn't anywhere around. There was plenty of blood on the rocks and grass, but that could have belonged to the two dead ponies, or any dead or wounded Comanche that were carried off. It looked like he had either escaped, or been captured. If he was captured, they would eventually kill him, a long and horrid death.

Hawk looked up from his chore of shoeing Buck when Andy rode into his yard. He wiped the sweat out of his eyes with the rough leather of his gloved hand, straightened up painfully. Buck had always been one to rest his weight on Hawks back while he was being shoed.

"Que tal, amigo." Hawk spoke. "How's things up to your place?"

Andy just nodded. "You seen Lucky?"

"Not for a day or two. Why?"

Andy reached under his fender-skirt, and pulled out the broken flintlock. Hawk took it, looked it over. "Lucky's. Where'd you find it?"

"Down by the mesa. Lots of Injun sign, like there'd been a real fight up there. Couple o' dead Injun ponies too. No bodies, Lucky's or Injun."

"Wal, you wouldn't o' found no Injun bodies. They'd o' hauled 'em off."

"Yeah, that's what I figgered. You reckon he got away?"

Hawk shrugged his shoulders. "No sé. I guess if'n he did, he'll be showin' up here soon enough."

"Reckon we'd oughta go lookin' for 'im?"

"Wouldn't do no good. If they'd o' killed 'im there, you'd o' found his body. If they got 'im, they'll take 'im back to their camp, and let the squaws torture 'im. If'n he didn't get away, he'll be dead by now anyhow."

"I think I'll ride over to his place, and poke around some," Andy said, "see if Ilsa knows anything."

Hawk nodded. "Yeah, you might could take her a side o' beef. If he went huntin' they might be low." He was thoughtful for a minute. "Maybe you oughten to tell 'er what you found just yet."

The ride down to the Jenkins's place from Hawk's was about three and a half miles. It gave him plenty of time to contemplate as he kept one eye on the trail and the other on the brush.

As he rode toward it, he could see the little spiral of smoke coming from the stone chimney. Ilsa was in the fenced yard with her two little boys. When she saw him, she ran to the fence waving, a big smile on her face. She always seemed to be genuinely glad to see him.

"Hi Ilsa. Lucky around?"

She gave a little pout. "No, he went out huntin' a few days ago." She didn't seem concerned, and he knew that she was used to Lucky staying in the woods for two or three days. The truth was he wasn't comfortable around her and the boys. He liked to be alone.

"You need anything? Some beef?"

She grinned. "No, I have beef." Then she laughed. "One of yours I think. I made some sauerbraten, you know, that German dish you like so well. Will you stay and have supper with us?"

He swung down from Blue's back, and flipped the reins around the fence rail. "Sauerbraten? You bet. Hot potato salad too?"

"Of course. I just had a notion you'd be ridin' up, hungry."

"Now why would you think that? It's been a week since I came by for any o' your cookin'"

She grinned. "That's why, because it's been over a week." She watched with pleasure as he wolfed down the sauerbraten. She liked to watch him eat. He had an appetite like her German father and brothers.

He looked up, and caught her looking at him. "What?"

She shrugged. "Did you save room for some pecan pie?"

He groaned. "Oh, Ilsa, what are you tryin' to do, make me fat?"

"You could use a little more meat on your bones. But don't worry you won't get fat eatin' once a week."

"I eat. I just don't stuff myself but once a week."

Two days later, he roped a young cow, and drug her bucking and plunging to the Jenkin's place. "Ilsa! Hello in the house. Ilsa, you around?"

She stuck her head out of the smoke house. "Over here." She called.

"Hey, I brought you a fresh heifer. I believe the wolves got her calf. She really needs to be milked."

She smiled, but the normal good humor was not there.

"You okay?" The minute he asked it, he wished he hadn't.

"Lucky ain't comin' back," she said simply. "Somethin's happened to 'im. I can feel it"

He didn't know what to say. He led the heifer over to the smoke house, and tied her to a mesquite tree. "You'll probably have to tie her hind feet to the fence to milk 'er. She's a little wild."

"Maybe he just got tired of us, and took off. He dit'n really like bein' married I don't think."

"He did'n get tired o' you Ilsa. I don't know what happened to 'im, but he did'n just take off. He might come waltzin' in here tomorrow with a deer over his shoulder, and some cock-n-bull story about losin' his rifle an' havin' to kill the deer with his pocket knife."

"Losin' his rifle?" She searched his face. "You know somethin,' don't you?"

He let out a long sigh. "No, I don't know anything. I found his rifle, but I did'n find him." He didn't want to tell her about the blood on the grass and the Indian ponies.

She nodded decisively. "He's dead. I'm gonna be alone now." She bowed her head, and started to cry.

He put his arms around her shoulders. "He'll prob'ly show up. You know Lucky; he prob'ly took a notion to ride down to Mexico, and see what kind o' deer they have. I'll look in on you 'til he does. You'll be okay."

She wiped her nose with the hem of her skirt, and nodded. Looking up at him with a tear-streaked face she asked. "You hungry? You want somethin' to eat?"

She was just a girl back then, barely nineteen, but already the mother of two-year-old twins and already a widow.

CHAPTER 3

The Forsythe Acting Company is taking their fourth curtain call after their performance of Taming of the Shrew. The tour has been a rousing success in Pittsburgh, Cincinnati and now Louisville. Julius Principe, now billed as Jacob Prinzikov and Petruccio in the play, is anxious to be finished. Gloria Holbine, the shrew, has invited him up to her private suite to celebrate another successful performance. This is their fifteenth performance in five weeks and their fifteenth celebration. Gloria has proved to be no shrew in real life, and her flair for drama extends into her boudoire. It has been an exciting tour with the boudoire celebrations as imaginative and as satisfying as the performances.

Julius, now Jake to his friends, has been an actor for as long as he can remember. That is he has donned costumes and acted out fantasies for as long as he can remember. He hadn't discovered his love of theatre, however, until his freshman year at the Citidel, when he joined the drama club and won the leading role in Hamlet. Oh, he had learned many other useful things at the Citidel; things like Military science, fencing, equitation, the use of firearms and, another of his favorites, London Prize Ring rules of self defence; he not only made the boxing team, but had become the featherweight champion of his class. Then in his Junior year, he had broken his mother's heart by dropping out of school to serve the Confedercy as a spy. The very things that made him an exemplery student had also made him one of the most successful spys in the Confederate espianoge service.

It was when he was asked if he could infiltrate the Washington social scene that he discovered just how good an actor he was. He had created his most famous character, Julia Principal. Not only had Julia infiltrated the social scene, she had been sought after and courted by no less than four high ranking army officers and two members of Mr. Lincoln's congress. General Barnard was only two buttons away from discovering that Julia's ample bossom was nothing more than cotton stuffed leather pouches and not the warm, soft flesh that he was expecting to grasp.

The false bosom was a rather ingenious device. He had gotten the idea while visiting his uncle's sheep farm.

Sheep are notorious for not accepting another ewes' orphaned lambs. They will kick them, butt them away and may even stomp them to death if they try to suckle with her own lambs.

Julius' uncle had cut the udder from a dead ewe and made a soft leather bag, teat intact, which he could fill with warm milk and hand feed his orphaned lambs.

It was a simple matter to have his aunt fashion the udders onto a halter and pad them with cotton. It was quite convincing, especially when viewed through a tight fitting ball gown.

One of the things that helped him as a spy was an acute sense of obversation. He could scan a room and later tell you the names of every person in there, including their ranks or stations in life. He could tell you how many women, and whether any of them might pose a threat to Julia in cornering an influential officer or senator. Within minutes, he knew every path of escape in case a fast escape was necessary. He also knew every pantry or closet where he could stash a change of costume in case he needed to cease being Julia and become Major Jason Prichard.

Because of this ability, on his third bow, he spots a familiar face in the fifth row. Instantly his mind flashes *danger, danger.* It takes him only a minute to place the face and the word *Pinkerton* comes to mind. Yes, he remembers now, the man was always in the background whenever Secretary Seward was present. He was National Security Service.

Pug is sitting in the fifth row of the Louisville Metropolitan Theatre. He's never been one for plays and such, but he has actually enjoyed the performance. His quarry isn't that hard to pick out, up on the stage, now that he knows who Julia Principal actually was. If he'd thought about it at the time, he would have seen a strong family resemblance between Mrs. Julia Principal and Major Jason Prichard.

He remembers the striking young woman at the parties in Washington and Baltimore. Most of the unattached men there couldn't keep their eyes or hands off of her. She'd been tall for a woman, around five feet eight or nine, maybe a hundred and forty pounds, nice full figure, nice face, if a bit angular. It was the soft brown eyes, flirting eyes, that caught men's attention, and held them; that and the outline of what lie beneath, pushing at her bodice.

He shakes his head as he looks at this well built, handsome young man. *How did he put his act over on me, a trained detective? I, of all people, should have seen through it.* Grudgingly he thinks, *this man is good.*

When the curtain closes for the final time Julius turns to Gloria, and plants a big kiss on her mouth. "I can't come up tonight, sweetheart. In fact, I've got to leave town right away. I'll get word to you as soon as I can, and you can come to me."

She gives him a startled, incredulous look. "Oh, Jake, are those people still looking for you?" She has known since the beginning of their relationship that he was involved in something with the Confederacy but she was never told the extent of it.

He gives her a cocky smile. "Nope, they've found me."

She grabs his hand, and pulls him at a trot toward her dressing room. "Come on, I'll help you get away."

As soon as the curtain closes for the last time, Pug jumps from his seat, and runs behind the stage. Different actors are entering the various dressing rooms. Two men are going into one room, and he glimpses the tail of a woman's gown disappearing behind a door just before it closes. He rushes up to the door where the two men had gone, pulls his little Kerr .44 caliber pocket pistol from his waistband, and throws the door open. The two men are sitting at their dressing tables, taking off their makeup. One has taken off his curled wig, and is bald. The other has short grey hair. Neither is Principe. He slams the door before either can say anything. He opens the next door, and the man sitting at the dressing table is the squat little fat man who had played the part of the father. He curses, and slams that door. The next door he throws open catches two women in various stages of undress. A buxom blond with nothing on but a pair of bloomers throws her hands across her bosom, and screams. He closes the door, and then remembers, *am I chasing a man or a woman.* He throws the door open again to further screams, and cursing from the women.

While the blond ducks behind a dressing screen, the one sitting at the dressing table looks at his reflection through the mirror. Her pale eyes are flashing fire. "What do you want here? Can't you see we're dressing?"

Brandishing his pistol he yells, "Where is he? Where is Principe?"

"We know no Principe, sir. There is no Principe here."

"Prinzikov," he corrects, "where is Prinzikov?" Just then something cracks his skull, and he goes to his knees. He isn't knocked unconscious, but the room is spinning, and all he sees is a red blur. He is aware of something, or someone, rushing past him, and then someone is taking his Kerr from his hand. Grogily he stands up, and shakes his head. The two women are still in the room, and there is a fat policeman putting handcuffs on him. As he is being escorted out of the theatre he looks over his shoulder at the two women. One is definitely the pretty brunette with the pale eyes who spoke to him through the mirror, but the other, the other is a small blond, not the buxom woman he saw naked from the waist up. He shakes his head again to try to dislodge the cobwebs. Surley it couldn't be. He distinctly saw the woman's bare bosom. Or did he?

******

Jeremiah Peabody steps down from the St. Louis to Kansas City train. He's a rather nondescript little man, not the kind of person you would take notice of, bespecktacled, a little rotund, a little stoop shouldered, his thinning hair is slicked down with a curl on his forehead, his mustache resembles one of the brushes in his sample case. He gathers his sample case under one arm, and his valise under the other, and heads off toward a boarding house, six blocks away. When the bell boy shows him to his room he tips the young man two bits, generous, but not extravagant.

Inside the small room, his pot belly disappears when he takes off his jacket and vest. His shoulders rise a half inch when he removes the tight galluses hunching them forward. He runs his hand through his hair, ruffling it, making it fuller. He removes the mustache, and lays it on the dresser, and then removes each bushy eyebrow, and places them next to the mustache. He lifts his valise to the bed, and begins to unpack. First he takes out a dull grey dress with a high collar and long sleeves; the type of dress a school teacher or librarian might wear, next comes a ministers dark suit with white collar, and then the rough homespun of a farmer.

With little pieces of Jeremiah Peabody lying about the room, Julius Principe lies down on the bed, his hands behind his head, and stares at a flickering candle standing on his night stand. *Okay, now what?* He thinks. *Am I safe out here on the edge of the frontier? Should I send for Gloria, get a new identy, new profession, and settle right here in Kansas City, or should I continue west, maybe Denver, or on out to San Francisco. How far will I have to go to lose this Pinkerton man? Australia?*

******

Bernice Goldblatt has worked as a secretary in the Chicago office of Pinkerton Detective Agency for seven years now, but she knows, and more importantly, Allan Pinkerton knows that she is far more than a secretary. She has a list of operatives throughout the United States which she can contact in a matter of hours. Some of her contacts are Federal Marshalls, small town Sheriffs and in more than one case a tavern owner or hotel clerk. One of her more valuable talents, however, is her ability as a sketch artist. She has sketched more wanted posters for her boss and, or, his detectives than she has written business letters for them.

"Hey Bernie," Pug Mahone slaps a theatre handbill on her desk, "see what you can do with this for me."

She picks it up, and looks at it. It is a full length picture of an actor in full Shaksperian costume. "Okay, what do you want me to do with it?"

"Mmm, maybe take off the mustache and the curley wig for starters."

Quickly she sketches the basic shape of the head and shoulders with average eyes, nose and ears, and a conventional haircut, then looks up at Pug. Her heart flutters when she glances into his face. There's something about his rugged, battered features that has always appealed to her. He looks pretty much like what he is, a Hell's Kitchen street fighter born to a potatoe-famine Irish immigrant family, son of a New York police officer, someone who learned to make his way in life with his fists before he ever started school at PS99 on forty-second street, and yet, whenever he looks at her it is with a tenderness that makes her knees weak. Yes, she supposes she's a little taken with him despite his roughness.

"Make his face a little softer. No beard shadow"

She rubs out the angular face and makes it rounder.

"Good, now you've got to work on the eyes. He's got very expressive eyes, like he's flirting with every woman he glances at, and his mouth, make his mouth more sensual."

"Sounds like he'd make a pretty girl." She quips.

He stares down at her. "What are you, a mind reader? That's your next job. Turn him into a woman, a pretty woman." He lays the Julius Principe folder on her desk. "Study this, and see what you can come up with. You can reach me at the River City Hotel in Natchez Mississippi."

******

On their visit up the canyon to the Garza place, Jack Leary formed an immediate friendship with Carlos Garza. At seventeen Carlos is only a year and a half older than Jacky, but Jacky is a good two inches taller. Jacky's one quarter Negro blood is evident, but then, so is his quarter Creek blood, and his Father's Scotch-Irish blood. He's a good mixture, a handsome young man with curley brown hair, hazle eyes and toffee brown skin. He has a quick smile and ready wit, but an age beyond his years shows in his eyes during unguarded moments. The war was hard on his entire family, but for Jacky it was especially hard. He was the one who had to cut Nancy down when she was hung in the old live oak tree in front of their home, and it was him who blew his sister's murderer, Tibodaux's, head off to save Andy's life. He had done it with calm deliberation, but still it left a scar on his subconscious.

Now at fifteen he is beginning a new life in Texas, and it suits him just fine. For the most part he has been able to forget his sister's body swinging above the dead mule; and he has created a mental block against his own act of murder. At night sometimes, after the lamp has been blown out, he will remember sighting through the scope of the sniper rifle, bringing the cross hairs to rest right at the base of the Cajun's skull, but then he doesn't remember anything until he and Andy are riding through the woods back to Leary Point. Of course he doesn't try to remember, the visions just come to him in the dark. Sometimes he will wake up shaking and sweating, but can't remember the dream that caused it.

He's happy though, in the daylight hours, meeting Carlos at Rincon Canyon, and riding up onto the mesa, swimming naked in the Frio River, exploring the cave near Andy's old cabin, where the two rock cairns are, the one built by the Comanche, how many eons ago, and the one built by the Spanish conquistador, Capitán Ramirez, to honor his friend Father Bonafacio, a mere two-hundred years ago.

Andy has told them that they can explore all they want as long as they

45

don't disturb the two monuments. The wooden crosses and old Spanish scroll, explaining how the Spaniards had taken refuge in the cave during an Indian attack, are still on the Spanish alter, and the Comanche lances and bows and arrows are still on the Comanche alter.

They have tried to read the scroll, and examined the obsidian points on the lances, but they honor Andy's request and treat the alters with reverance.

Last night was a good night. He remembers his dreams and they were nice ones. He remembers one of them vivedly, it involved a dark haired girl in buckskins. He doesn't know if she was Indian or Mexican, but she was beautiful and now, in the light of day, he is embarrassed by what took place in his dream. He'd like to talk to Andy about it because he's dreaming dreams like that more and more lately. Well, maybe another time.

He picks up his boot and bangs the heel on the floor, then turns it upside down to dislodge any scorpians that might have decided to spend the night in there.

Andy is sitting at the small table on the far side of the room sipping a cup of coffee. "Mornin,' you goin' down for breakfast?"

He shakes his head. "Naw, Carlos wants me to help him break that new horse Chico brought in."

Andy looks up with a knowing smile. "You sleep okay? You giggled half the night."

Jacky can feel the heat rise in his face. "Uh, yeah, but I had some funny dreams."

"Girl dreams? I remember those. I used to dream about Nancy like that, after I left for sea. Don't do that much anymore. I wish I did. I miss 'em."

Jacky sits down across from Andy, pours a cup for himself. He looks deep into the cup as he speaks. "Dreams about, uh, you know, kissin' an' huggin' an' all that other stuff?"

"Yeah, all that kind of stuff. Why? You think Nancy was too pure for all that other stuff?"

Jacky looks up startled. He's never heard Andy talk about what went on between him and Nancy. He knows there was a deep love between them and he certainly doesn't think Nancy was above that kind of love, after all, they got Annie. He just never thought about it.

"What are you now, fourteen, fifteen? It's nothing to be ashamed of. Dreams like that are a natural part of growin' up."

Jacky grabs his sombrero. "Gotta go, Carlos'll be waitin'." He hesitates at the door. "Thanks, see ya this afternoon."

When Jacky is gone and Andy is alone he heaves a deep sigh; yes, he misses the intimacy with Nancy, her caresses, his caresses. How can he go on without her? What would she have him do? He will love her for the rest of his life. He can't change that. The question is will he ever be able to love anyone else? Would Nancy want him to love again?

He steps to the window and looks across the river. Ilsa, Annie and the boys are playing some sort of game in the front yard. Ilsa throws her head back and laughs, Annie runs up to her with her arms out and Ilsa scoops her up and rains kisses on her little face.

She's a good woman, he thinks, *she's a good mother to her boys and she'd make a good mother for Annie.*

As he watches the scene across the river, he remembers a time when they had become very close. Had they actually fallen for each other, and neither of them would admit it because technically she was a married woman?

******

Andy rose early and threw a few sticks on his fire to warm up the cabin. The cold of the early morning seeped through the cracks in his walls. He ate a breakfast of jerky, prickly pear fruit and spring water, and then went out to locate Blue. She felt the chill and half-heartedly tried to shy away from the saddle. He finally saddled her and rode down the slope towards Ilsa's.

He tied Blue to the rail fence and called from the porch, "Ilsa? Ilsa are you here?" He stuck his head inside. "Ilsa?" The house was empty.

Suddenly panic gripped him. It had been several months since he had found Lucky's rifle and the Comanche sign, almost a year, still, a cold fist grabbed his heart.

He ran out onto the porch and snatched the reins loose. Blue was running before his foot reached the stirrup. He was in a full gallop and didn't even know where he was going. He turned and started up the trail to the escarpment. When he reached the stand of mesquite trees he heard her laughter. When he galloped through the trees and skidded Blue to a stop she turned with a start. "Oh, I didn't even hear you coming up. You nearly scared me to death."

"I know." He said a little too sharply. "You're going to have to be more careful. What are you doing so far from the house?"

Ilsa looked like she had been whipped. "We're just looking for turkey eggs. I was going to make you an omelet for supper."

He felt a twinge of regret for being so stern with her. "I know, but you shouldn't be so far from home without an escort. Anyway, I like looking for turkey eggs too."

She gave him an incredulous smile. "No you don't. Men don't like that kinda thing."

He lifted her up on Blue and threw the boys up behind her. When he started walking down the trail to the valley Blue followed like an obedient dog. As they approached her cabin, Hawk came splashing across the shallow ford at a gallop. "Ilsa, ride for my place." He reached an arm down and swung Andy up behind him. "Comanche," he yelled, "hit the Macgregor place about an hour ago, got Brian pretty bad. Colin was fightin' 'em off from the barn when me an' Chico rode in on 'em. They pulled back toward your place. That's when I seen you come waltzin' down the trail an' decided to warn ya. The Macgregors are holed up at my place." As they approached the steep walls of Rincon Canyon around Hawk's place they could hear the Indians screaming from behind. Andy jumped clear of the buckskin and grabbed each little towhead boy by the belt and ran for the house. Hawk dismounted on the run and yanked Ilsa off Blue as she galloped up. The Comanche hit right behind them. Lances and arrows struck the closing door.

"Whew, that was close!" Hawk breathed a sigh of relief. "How's Brian?"

Brian raised his head from the cot. The lance head protruded from his shoulder. "He's okay." He grinned.

Becky Macgregor was worried. "He ain't okay neither, an' he's gonna be worst if he don't lie down."

Hawk leaned over and looked at the wound. "He ain't gonna be okay if we don't get that thing out of 'im."

The firing from the sleeping loft stopped.

"Besides Becky, we gotta get it out of 'im. You can't very well tailor his clothes to fit around it."

She began to cry and swore, something she almost never did. "Damn you Hawk Hawkins, this boy's lying here diein' and you make fun of him."

He put his arm around her shoulder. "He ain't diein,' Becky. Alls we gotta do is get this thing out and stop the bleeding. He'll be good as new."

"Will it hurt, Hawk? I mean pullin' it out?" Brian asked, wide eyed.

"Did it hurt goin' in?" Hawk asked.

"Yes sir, it sure did." Brian confirmed.

"Then I reckon it'll hurt just about as bad comin' out." Hawk said.

"Dawgone! I's afraid you's gonna say that."

"Andy heat that runnin' iron up so's we can brand this critter." He took a firm grip on the broken lance. It was slippery with blood.

He rummaged around in his ferrier tools and pulled out a pair of horseshoe pullers. "You ready Andy?" He got a grip on the lance head with the pullers.

"Hey Brian." Colin called from the loft where the other men were watching. Brian turned his head to see what his brother wanted and Hawk yanked at the lance head. Andy rammed the red-hot running iron into the hole. Brian screamed and fell back unconscious.

The Comanche gathered for a pow-wow in full view of the cabin but out of rifle range. They smoked to the four points of the compass, sang their death songs, and then attacked again, but the men inside took a heavy toll of their attackers. The Comanche then tried to burn them out, but the mostly sod hut didn't burn well, and the loss they took riding in to shoot their fire arrows, or throw torches made further attempts less than profitable.

At dusk they retreated back to their pow-wow sight, and settled down for the night.

Hawk opened the shutter a crack, and peeked out. "They won't hit us again tonight. They'll probably dance all night; call on their spirits for guidance, and try again first light. We better try to get some rest before they come."

The party in the house stationed two watches, and the rest scattered themselves about the house to try to get a little sleep. The sleeping loft was covered with sleeping bodies. Ilsa lay down next to Colin and Becky with her two boys, one cradled on each arm. It was not particularly comfortable for her, but the boys were resting peacefully.

Andy had taken a first watch. When he was relieved he stepped gingerly between the bodies looking for a place big enough for him to lie down.

Colin pulled up closer to Becky. "Here," he whispered, making a small space between his back and Ilsa.

Andy lay on his back, and pulled his hat down over his eyes. The space was so small one shoulder touched Colin's back; the other touched little Fritz, resting on Ilsa's arm.

Sometime during the night the baby whimpered, and Andy reached over to touch him and quiet him. When he did this, his hand fell across Ilsa, coming to rest right above her heart, and he could feel it fluttering like a captured bird. He started to pull it away, and then didn't. He could tell that she was awake, and wondered what she was thinking. He lay that way for a long time. Finally he turned on his side, facing her, and looked directly into her open eyes. There was a little smile on her lips. After a moment she freed her off arm, and turned towards him. They were so close he could feel her warm breath on his cheek. Suddenly their lips were touching, softly at first, and then more urgently. *Why not,* he thought, *I know she's a widow, and she knows she's a widow. Why not?* And this is the way they feel asleep, their breath mingling, her cheek pressed against his.

When morning came, the Comanche had indeed danced all night, and conferred with their spirits, and the answer they received was the best possible, for their next action was to race their horses to just short of effective firing range, make obscene gestures, shout insults, and then ride off, driving a small herd of Chico's horses, up the escarpment trail without firing another shot.

******

Supper is finished, the women are cleaning up the dishes, and Andy has retired to the rocking chair in front of the massive living room fireplace. In the six months since their return from Mississippi, he has taken to rocking Annie to sleep before he goes back to the cabin across the river. It's difficult to tell who enjoys the ritual the most, him, Annie or Collie, the black and white bitch, who lies at his feet, and listens while he hums, or tells Annie some little story. When Annie is put to bed, Collie follows him across the river, and when he goes inside, she returns to her four pups in the smoke house.

"She asleep?" Lula whispers.

Andy nods, and lifts the baby into Lula's arms. As she settles her platinum curls into Lula's shoulder she whispers in a sleepy voice, "Tell Dai night."

Lula leans her down for a kiss on the forehead. "Goodnight my precious girl."

"Night Dai," She whispers.

Ilsa gets her boys up from where they're playing marbles on the cow skin rug, and herds them off towards their wing of the house. "Night Andy." Then louder, "night Mama Lula."

"Ilsa, sit with me a couple of minutes. I'm not ready to go up to the cabin just yet."

She ruffles her boy's heads, and closes the door behind them. "Get to bed now. No foolin' around."

She sits on the wide stone hearth in front of the fireplace, pulls her skirts around her ankles, and faces Andy with a soft smile.

"Remember the day the Comanches struck Hawks place? I was remembering that this mornin.'"

She thinks about that night, and instinctively knows what he's talking about, not the Indian attack itself. "Yeah, I remember." She pauses just a minute, then continues, "I been doin' some rememberin' of my own."

"Yeah, what were you rememberin'?"

"Oh, I got to thinkin' about that night the wolves came. You remember that?"

He nods. He's contemplative for a long few minutes. "Whata ya reckon kept us apart, Ilsa? Was it my zealous sense of loyalty to Lucky, thinkin' that he might come back?"

She shrugs, "Partly I reckon, but I reckon it was just bad timin.' We dit'n know about Lucky an' then you 'n' Hawk decided to take your herd to Mississippi." She stares into his face a long time, nibbling her lower lip. "You left me, Andy. I was all alone an' you left me. When Chico came back with Blue an' that ugly ol' steer, an' said you was goin' to see an old girlfriend, I was devastated. I cried, Andy. I cried like a baby. I prayed every night that you'd find her married, or fat or somethin,' an' come home to me—but you dit'n."

His voice is soft, consoling. "I'm back now, Ilsa."

She stands, shakes her head, her chin trembling. She's obviously wanted to get this off of her chest for a long time.

"Yes, you came back, but not to me, an' not alone. Nancy came back with you, Andy. When you walk through the pecan grove she walks beside you. When you ride up onto the mesa, she's ridin' with you. I can't compete with her, Andy; she's not flesh an' bone. She's just a memory."

He opens his mouth, but no words come out. How can he explain to her that he belonged to Nancy even before he came to Texas, before he met her; that Nancy was his destiny, and nothing could have ever changed that?

She stands, and stares at the closed door long after he and Collie are gone, and then the sobs begin.

Lula hadn't meant to listen, but since she heard it all she feels compelled to go out, and speak to Ilsa. She wraps a shawl around her shoulders.

Ilsa senses Lula's presence more than sees her. She turns away, and dabs her eyes with the hem of her skirt.

"Come 'eah, Baby. Mama Lula ain't had no daughtah to hold, and comfort in a long, long time."

Ilsa turns, and lets Lula engulf her in her long arms.

"Baby, I know you ain't asked, but let me tell you a story about a young slave girl what fell in love with her mistress's husband.

"When my mistress, Ann, married John Leary, she brought me up to Leary Point wid 'er. She was twenty-two an' I was eighteen. First time I evah seen John Leary I thought he was the mos' handsomest man I evah laid eyes on, but he was Mz. Ann's husband, an' I was her slave girl. She was so in love wid him, an' he worship her.

"Well, aftah Nancy was born Mz. Ann nevah did get healthy agin, an' jus' befo' Nancy turned eight, Mz. Ann died. Well, I could see dat John was grievin' hisself into a early grave. Aftah almost a yeah, he ain't eatin' or sleepin' or nothin'.

"One night I went to him. I jus' know he gonna trow me out, and sell me down de rivah, but I guess he could see how much I love him an' how much he need to be loved by somebody, an' he took me in his arms. I did'n expect nothin' but to ease his pain, but den one night he said what we was doin' was a sin an' he said we needed to marry. I could'n believe a rich plantation owner want to marry a slave girl. We could'n get married nohow 'cause o' de law, but we exchange vows to each othah one night, down by de rivah, with nobody to witness but God hisself.

"Fo' nigh on to twelve yeahs, befo' he got killed in de war, dat man loved me an' I loved him an' dey be de happiest days o' my life.

"Why I'm tellin' you dis is 'cause I know you an' Andy can make a good life togethah. You need each othah and yo' chil'en needs a momma an' daddy.

"I nevah expected to replace Mz. Ann in John's heart, an' I don' guess I evah did, but like I said, I became a lovin' wife an' he became a lovin' husband an' I was mama to Nancy.

"I know, I know, Nancy bein' my baby 'n' all, maybe I should be tryin' to keep you away from 'im, but dat don't serve no purpose atall. You love him 'n' he loves you. He don' know it yet, but he does."

Ilsa dries her eyes, and gives Lula a beatific smile. "Thank you Mama Lula. I do love 'im, I have for a long time, but I cain't just go crawl into his bed. Even if he dit'n run me off it wut'n make him love me."

Lula holds Ilsa out at arms length, and looks deep into her eyes. "When he sees I've made you my new daughter, he'll realize he can make you his wife.

"Honey, cain't nothin' evah remove Nancy from my heart or his, but mos' hearts is a big place. Deah's room fo' more den one love in deah.

"I done come to love you 'n' he loves you too. He jus' needs some proddin is all."

Ilsa's eyes are glowing now. "No wonder Nancy loved you so. You're so wise. I'm mighty proud to be your new daughter."

Andy has brought in a fresh heifer and an orphaned calf to join her own.

Longhorn heifers are generally pretty good about accepting another's calf, but still he wants to watch, and make sure there isn't a problem.

He drank a cup of coffee in his cabin this morning, and then skipped breakfast. He told himself that he had too much to do to eat breakfast this morning, but down deep he knows that he didn't go to the main house simply because he didn't want to confront Ilsa after last night.

Life has become a conundrum, a problem without solutions. He can sense the old feelings for Ilsa returning, in fact, last night he wanted to take her in his arms, and smother her with kisses, but his sense of loyalty to Nancy is still too strong.

He's so engrossed in thought he doesn't hear Lula come up behind him.

"Mornin' Andy."

He spins around. "Lula, you startled me."

She leans her long brown arms on the top rail of the corral. "She gonna take dat calf?"

"Yeah, I think so. She acted like she wouldn't for a while, but now she's lettin' 'im suck."

"Cows is pretty smart I guess. Dey can sense when it's time to let go of what's past and move on to de new."

Andy gives her a knowing glance. "You didn't walk all the way out here to talk about cows did you Mama Lula?"

"No honey, no I did'n. You know dat girl loves you."

He's silent for a long moment. "We used to be real fond of each other. It's just that when I let the feelins have their sway, I feel like I'm cheatin' on Nancy."

"Nancy loved you; no question 'bout dat, but you know what, she loved you so much she was willin' to forgive you if you'd been dallyin' wid dat Spanish woman."

His first thought is Dolores, but Nancy didn't even know Dolores, then he remembers Lupe, whom he met aboard the Basque smuggler, Torbellino. Nancy must have read in his ship's log telling of his friendship with her. "Spanish woman? You mean Lupe, why, I never—."

55

"I know you did'n 'n' dat's what I tol' 'er, but you know what she said? She said, 'Mama, I could forgive him if he took up another woman. I could bear that; but Mama, I couldn't bear it if he stopped lovin' me.'"

He gives Lula a sheepish grin. "Well, she needn't have worried. I never even thought about any other woman, an' I'll never stop lovin' her."

"She knows dat, but I think she'd tell you it's okay to open your heart an' let Ilsa in. You can love the memory of Nancy, and still give Ilsa yo' right now love. You do love her; any fool can see dat, besides, you got a hankerin' fo' 'er dat you ain't gonna be able to ignore much longer."

Andy's eyes twinkle. He places his hands on her cheeks, and kisses her on the forehead. "You're a wonderment Mama Lula. What would we do without our Jjajja?"

Lula waves a dismissive hand. "Oh, hush up an' go tell dat sweet girl what you know you need to tell 'er."

Andy finds Ilsa in the chicken house, gathering eggs. She has them in her apron, holding it gathered at the corners, creating a shallow sack. He strides up to her, takes the eggs out one at a time, and lays them back in the straw. Then he lifts her under the arms until her eyes are level with his.

She gives him a shy smile. "What?"

"Come go for a walk with me. Let's walk in the pecan grove, just you an' me."

"Honest, just you an' me?"

"I promise. From now on it's just gonna be you an' me."

He pulls her up against his body, and meets her lips with his. "Me an' you, Ilsa. Will you marry me?"

"Yes," she whispers, "but it ain't just me an' you Andy. We already got us a family. We got us two sons, a daughter and a grandmother, a very special grandmother."

As they are sitting beneath a giant cypress tree on the bank of the river, a tree whose trunk is seven or eight feet in diameter and whose crown punctures the sky, Andy says, "See over there where the rapids are? I think I'll put up a rock dam there, and make a lake here. Would you like that?"

She snuggles into the crook of his arm. "Umhum, I think that would be nice. It'd give the kids a good place to swim."

He turns, and kisses her for the umpteenth time. "I'm happy Ilsa. I did'n think I'd ever be happy again."

"Me too," she murmurs, "I'm happy 'cause I love you, an' I believe that someday you'll love me too."

He holds her tight against his chest, cradling her like a child. "I love you now, Ilsa, please believe that. I wasn't sure that I could love again, but I do love you. I know that now."

"You know what Mama Lula tol' me? She tol' me I would be her daughter now."

He nods. "She's a smart ol' bird. She seems to be able to see into a person's soul. I think it might be her African blood. An ol' African man I once knew and loved had the same ability."

CHAPTER 4

Brian Macgregor eases back from the canyon rim to where his partner Juan "Rip" Ford is waiting.

"How many you count, Mac?" Rip asks.

"I count six, how 'bout you?"

"I counted six around the fire, but I counted seven saddled horses. One's missin.'"

Brian nods. It's just like Rip to notice things like that, that's what makes him a good Ranger. At seventeen Rip is five years younger than Brian. Brian has been a Texas Ranger for five years.

When Texas entered the Confederacy, his brother Colin decided that he would take his family, and move back to Covington, Kentucky. Brian decided to stay. When Colin left the Frio valley, the two brothers made a pact that neither of them would join either of the opposing armies. That way there would never be a chance that they would face each other in battle.

As the able bodied men of Texas left in mass for the war "back east" the frontier became a boiling cauldron of mischief. Kiowa war parties raid the farms and ranches of the Red River Valley. Mexican bandits raid the borderlands, and the Comanche raid all the way from the Llano Estacado to the Rio Grande valley. For only a couple of hundred old men and boys, it's a formidable task to keep the peace in a place the size of Texas.

Rip has been in the Texas Rangers all of his life. Abandoned on the doorstep of the famous Ranger, Captain John "Rip" Ford, Juan grew up following his adopted father on nearly every campaign the old man went on.

"How many captives you count?" Brian whispers.

"If you can go by the blanket rolls, there's four."

Brian nods. "Yeah, that's about what I figure. Reckon they're all women?"

Rip nods. "Sure, there's no trade for men."

"Yeah, but you reckon there's any kids?"

Rip just shrugs.

Perfecto Diaz is in no sense of the word, perfect. It was a slander against mankind when his mother named him that. He was an ugly baby with a head as big as a muskmelon, a cleft palate and tiny pig like eyes. He has an aversion to water, whether for use on the outside of his body or inside. The closest thing to a bath he's had recently is when he got caught in a rain shower about a year ago, and if it's not mescal, pulque, tizwin or cheap whisky, he doesn't drink it. He is the lowest form of humanity. He is a dealer in human captives, a Comanchero. He trades in both Mexico and Comancheria, but isn't welcome in either place. He will not trade in male flesh because there's no profit in it, and he doesn't like to be bothered with children. On this very expedition he took a three-year-old boy from his mother, and bashed his brains out with a rock.

This has turned out to be a disappointing expedition. He was able to trade some tobacco, tizwin and a busted musket for four adult white women and an Apache, but then the little boy's mother went out of her mind when he killed the joven (brat), and he had to cut her throat to stop her wailing.

Then Moises took the Apache into the bushes, and spoiled her value so he put a bullet in Moises' head, now he's down by two captives and one of his men. Of course, the tobacco and tizwin he took from a cibolero up on the Canadian, and the musket wasn't any good anyway, so it would be all profit. It's just that it hardly pays to make the trip to Chihuahua for three captives. Well, perhaps he can pick up a few more before he reaches Chihuahua.

"How d'ya want to hit 'em?" Rip asks.

"Just like always, you come in from one side, me from the other, guns ablazin'. Any luck 'n' we won't shoot each other."

"What about the missing one?"

Brian shrugs. "He ain't likely to volunteer to walk into a gun fight. Once he hears the ruckus he'll likely start high tailin' it as fast and as far as his legs'll carry 'im."

Rip nods his agreement.

"Give me about a half hour to get to the bottom of the canyon, give me a chupacabra call, wait for my answer, and go in." He doesn't need to go over the details; he and Rip have been working together so long now they both know the drill, and both are experts at making the nighthawk sound.

Perfecto sits back from the fire, and watches the Apache preparing for bed. She has already tried to wash her face with saliva on the hem of her tunic, brush her teeth with a willow twig, and comb her waist length hair with her fingers.

His already small eyes narrow to slits. She is a handsome mozuela (wench) with that glossy black hair and smoke grey eyes. Since Moises has already defiled her there is nothing more in value to lose now. He gets up, and speaks to one of his men. "I'll be back in a few minutes. Watch the other captives until I get back, and if you let any of them escape you know what happened to Moises."

Cara-de-rata grunts, and moves closer to where the three women are stretched out on the ground. He is a cutthroat himself, but he is afraid of Perfecto.

Pilar Mendez looks up at the horrible man standing above her. She trembles involuntarily as she realizes what is about to happen to her again. He grabs her by the hair, and drags her into an arroyo. She is transfixed on the hole in his face that is supposed to be his mouth. She clenches her eyes shut when he bends over her, but instead of his rough hands groping at her, he lurches back, makes a gurgling sound, and falls, his legs kicking spasmodically, to the ground.

Brian claps a hand over her mouth, and makes a motion with the other hand for her to be silent. She nods her understanding. A nighthawk makes its low, mournful call from the other side of the clearing. The young man above her whistles his own nighthawk call, draws both pistols, and steps into the circle of light, firing with both hands.

She clasps her hands over her ears. The gunfire is deafening. She knows she is being rescued, but she is still terrified. The firing only lasts a minute, but it seems like an hour. She cringes into the sandy wall of the arroyo when she sees the silhouette of a man coming towards her.

"Are you okay? Did he hurt you?" Brian asks in Spanish.

She shakes her head. "Not this one, but another one, yesterday," she whimpers.

He nods, understanding. There's no need making her explain.

"Brian Macgregor, I'm a Texas Ranger." He shows her his star. "Most folks just call me Mac."

"Did you kill them all?" Her eyes are huge, and the color of a rainy sky.

He nods. "Me and my companero did. Couldn't save one of the captives though, she tried to run, and one of the Comancheros shot her. Did you know either of the others?"

The girl shakes her head. Her thick black hair, headband and deerskin clothing say she's an Indian, but her features, blue-grey eyes and speech proclaim her to be pure Castilian.

61

"Where are you from?" Brian asks.

"The Jicarilla reservation. My father has a trading post there."

"Jicarilla, isn't that Apache? Somewhere up in New Mexico?"

She nods her head.

"You're a long ways from home? How'd you get messed up with this bunch?"

"My father was sending me and my brother to the Indian school at Trinidad Colorado. Our coach was attacked. My brother and all of the outriders were killed. They took me captive. I don't know why they didn't kill me as well. I wish they had."

"Your pa Spanish?"

She gives him a quizzical look. "Sí, how did you know that?"

"Your speech mostly. We don't hear Mex spoke like that down here in Texas."

"Can I go home?" Her eyes are floating in tears.

"Well, we'll try to figure out a way, but it's likely to be a real chore. As you can see, travelin' across the Llano can be real dangerous. I'll take you to our ranch for now. There's a real nice woman there with a couple o' boys, and not too far away there's a Mex family." He gives her a sympathetic glance. He knows it's highly unlikely that she'll ever go back to northern New Mexico.

When it is discovered that the other captive is from the Red River Valley Rip agrees to escort her home while Brian starts southeast towards the Frio River. They will meet up again at the Ranger headquarters in San Antonio.

Jack Leary slams through the front door the way he always does, sails his sombrero across the room at the horns hanging over the mantle, and stops in mid stride to the supper table. His jaw drops, and he stares awkwardly at the young woman standing by the sideboard next to his mother. His cheeks burn as he realizes that this is the same young woman from his dreams. He catches Andy's grin. Andy knows. Ilsa's eyes dart from Jack to Andy, darn that Andy, he's told her. If his skin wasn't already burned to terracotta orange, he's sure his face would be flaming red. He stumbles over, and picks his sombrero out of the ashes in the fireplace; he's never actually hit the horns, much less hung his hat on one of them.

He feels like he's walking on stilts, as awkward as a day old colt. He begins batting at a small smoldering spot in the crown of his hat, and he can feel her eyes on him. Why didn't he just stay out at the camp tonight?

"Johnny," his mother says, "this is senorita Mendez. She will be staying with us for a while."

"Pilar." She smiles shyly.

"Pilar?" He mumbles. Her blue-gray eyes are a counterpoint to her dark skin and thick black hair, hair as black and shiny as the teardrop shaped obsidian he found in the Comanche cave.

"Sí, ése es mi nombre, mi nombre Christiano."

"Her name is Pilar, Pilar Mendez." He hadn't even noticed the man sitting at the table with Andy. "She don't habla English. She don't much talk Mex like we know it either, more like pure Spanish mixed with 'Pachy."

Pilar looks up at Lula with a dumbfounded look. The English has left her confused. Lula hands her a stack of plates, and motions toward the table. "It's alright, honey, we gonna get along jus' fine, alls we gotta do is fin' Johnny's brain an' put it back in fo' 'im."

Pilar begins to set the table, but her eyes keep darting up to look at the handsome young man who can't seem to keep his eyes off of her, even though he is talking with the men at the table.

"Could o' knocked me over with a feather," Brian is saying, "when I saw you was back Andy. Then you could o' picked me up with the same feather when Ilsa tol' me you two was married." He shakes his head anew at the news. He has tactfully avoided any mention of what Andy went through during the war, or that he had married Nancy Leary while he was away. He had made over Annie though, and told her and Andy what a beautiful child she was.

63

"Yeah," Andy says, giving Ilsa a loving glance, "we rode over to Encina couple o' months back an' tied the knot." He hesitates a minute, glancing at Lula. "We saw right off that we needed each other. More important, that we loved each other."

Pilar leans across to set a plate in front of Jack; she smiles at him when he looks up at her, and her scent envelopes him like fog. It is the smell of mesquite smoke, buckskins rubbed with sage, and something else, something feminine, something like the smell right after a rain, when all of the dust has settled, and the air is filled with the aroma of wet cedar and wild flowers. All of a sudden the conversation seems to be coming from another room. The others in the room fade into vague shadows, and all he is aware of is her leaning over him. Her lips are Indian-full and purple-red like the fruit on the prickly pear cactus.

"Jack! Jack!" Andy is shaking his shoulder. "You okay little brother? I thought for a minute you might fall out of your chair. You sick or somethin'?"

Jack rouses himself. "No, no. Just thinkin' about some stuff is all." His mind searches for whatever it might have been that he was thinking about. "Just thinkin' about, uh, about that paint colt, what a nice horse he's gonna make one o' these days."

Andy gives him a questioning look. "Paint colt?"

"Yeah, I thought maybe Mac might like to go down an' see 'im after supper. He's a real nice lookin' colt."

Brian laughs. "I helped Ilsa bring that colt into this world. I know what he looks like."

Ilsa lifts a steak the size of both of her hands onto Jack's plate, and gives him a knowing smile. "He is a fine lookin' colt, though, maybe Pilar would like to go down an' see 'im after supper."

Jack shrugs as if it is of no consequence to him one way or the other. "Well, I s'pose if she wants to I could take 'er."

"Yeah," Ilsa encourages, "I'm sure she would enjoy it."

In Spanish she addresses Pilar, "Jack wants to know if you'd like to take a walk with him after supper. He'd like to show you one of our new colts. Do you think you'd like that?"

Pilar's eyes flash at Jack. As shy as he has seemed around her, she can't believe he's invited her to take a walk. She nods enthusiastically.

As they walk along she pauses on the stone bridge across the creek. "Es tan hermoso." She exclaims. (It's so beautiful.)

Jack shrugs. He knows she's making a comment about the creek, and probably the giant Cypress trees along it, but he hasn't mastered Spanish yet.

She points to him. "Jack o Johnny?" She pronounces it Shack and Shonny

"Me? Oh, you mean 'cause Mama calls me Johnny 'n' everybody else calls me Jack?" He taps his chest and points to her. "Johnny. Let everybody else call me Jack but you call me Johnny."

She smiles, understanding the gesture if not the words, but shakes her head. "Juanito." She points to herself and then to him. "Pilar, Juanito."

"Como mucho años you—uh—usted?" (How much years you?)

She giggles behind her fingers. "Cuántos años son yo? Diecisiete, y usted?" (How old am I? Seventeen, and you)?"

He fumbles in his mind for diecisiete. She holds up ten fingers and then seven. She points to him with a questioning look.

He holds up ten fingers and then six. What the heck, he'll be sixteen in a few weeks.

They continue their walk and their sign language conversation. He shows her the colt, and she makes over him, but it's obvious that they are more interested in getting to know each other than see a horse. By the time they get back to the house there is a definite bond between them.

Andy is waiting in the cabin when Jack walks in. "How was your walk?"

Jack slaps the heel of his boot into the piece of deer antler that serves as a bootjack, and slides his foot out, enjoying the freedom by wriggling his toes. "It was good. I'm gonna have to brush up my Spanish though. We had to get by mostly on sign language tonight."

"Wal, I guess Injuns'r pretty good at sign language. She's Apache you know."

Jack shakes his head. "Did'n no Apache give her them eyes. Did you see the color of 'em?"

Andy doesn't answer the question. The color of her eyes isn't something a person would miss. "How'd she seem? I mean she seemed okay goin' for a walk with you, but—."

"Why would'n she seem okay? I would'n bother 'er."

"Mac thinks she was raped by one of her captors. At least she said one of 'em hurt 'er. I just thought it might make 'er a little skittish alone with a man, somebody she did'n really know."

The knowledge that she might have been treated roughly shows in the pain in Jack's eyes. "I did'n know," he mumbles. Then his eyes flash up at Andy. "I'm glad Mac killed 'em. I wish I'd been there to help."

Andy just nods. "Wal, now you know, you might want to go a little slow, not do anything that might frighten her. She's been through a lot."

As he lays there in the dark, Jack wonders if he will dream about her again tonight, now that he knows she's a real flesh and bone girl. In a way he wants to, but at the same time he doesn't. He drifts off to a dreamless sleep thinking about her walking towards him with her small brown hands stretched out to him, a big smile on her face, and her shiny black hair falling around her shoulders.

Just before he drops off, he prays, "Lord, she's the most beautiful thing I ever saw. Did you send her to me? Is that why you put her in my dreams, so I'd know 'er when she came? So I'd know you'd sent 'er?"

Pilar feels comfort in Annie's little body snuggled next to her in the bed. She stares into the dark, and thinks about all that has happened to her in the last several months. At one point, she wished that she had been killed along with her brother, now she's glad she's alive. The Texas Ranger has said that somehow they'll find a way to get her home. She wants to go home and see her parents, but these are nice people, and they have gone out of their way to make her feel comfortable and welcome. She wraps her arms around Annie, and thinks of the boy she has just met. *I'll be all right here until I can go home,* she tells herself.

Jack wheels the mustang out of the corral; he spins a couple of times, and then prances toward the ford. Jack likes to ride him because he's spirited. It's almost like his blood is just too hot for him, or like Jack himself, he's young and wants to do everything with a flourish.

Jack searches the yard as he rides past the house, trying to look like he's not searching the yard, but she's not there.

When he reaches the river he sees her up to her knees in the shallows, playing with Annie. She's wearing one of Ilsa's dresses, and has a white ribbon tying her hair back. He feels the heat in his face and ears when his blood rushes from his heart into his veins.

Pilar looks up when she hears the man on horseback approach. A smile etches her lips, and then widens into a grin, showing her even white teeth, when he lifts his sombrero, and makes a bow from the waist. It's an awkward bow from horseback but she gets the gist.

"Hola Pilar. Buenos dias."

She raises her hand in a shy wave. "Buenos dias, Juanito."

******

Pug Mahone leans against the rail of the riverboat, takes a drag on his thin black cigar, and sips at the whisky in his glass. It's been a pleasant ride down from St. Louis. He's had a chance to do a little drinking, a little gambling, and just relax.

He could probably have made better time taking the train but he decided to treat himself to a river cruise.

The woman at his elbow has been a pleasant distraction when he has tired of gambling. She's not what you'd call beautiful but she's not ugly either. She's young, at least young to him, probably in her mid twenties, maybe pushing thirty. She says she's the matron at an all-girl's school in Paducah, Kentucky on her way to visit her family south of Memphis.

It wasn't hard to pick her up. She had lost heavily at black-jack a couple nights ago, and he had staked her to another hand, they had shared a few drinks, and before the evening was over he was taking her hair down in her cabin.

He's not particularly fond of southerners, especially delta people; maybe it's the swamp fever that most of them seem to carry in their blood. They seem slow, lethargic, in some cases, like Miss Sally Borden, dim witted.

He's used to New Yorkers, brusque, rude, looking for a way to cheat you out of your suspenders or anything else they can get. Come to think of it he doesn't much like New Yorkers either.

"You wanna go back in an' play some more cards?" She asks softly.

He takes another sip of his whisky, and flips the stub of his cigar out into the dark. "This is your last night aboard isn't it?"

"Umhum." She confirms.

"Do you really want to spend it playing cards?"

She shrugs; actually she doesn't want to go back to her cabin with him tonight. She was somewhat tipsy the other night, and when she woke up the next morning, and realized what she'd done, she was almost overcome with shame and guilt. The next evening she let him come to her because—well, she doesn't know why. Tonight she'll go with him simply because she doesn't have the strength of will to say no. She's always been one to blindly obey those who exercise authority. "If you want to," she says meekly, meaning play cards.

He takes her by the elbow, and guides her down the companionway to the passenger's cabins. When he takes the pins out of her hair, and lets it fall around her shoulders; he nuzzles her neck and whispers, "Now isn't this a better way to spend our last evening together?"

A tear breaks over the rim of her eye, and rolls down her cheek. "Yeah, I s'pose." She mumbles.

When she sees her family waiting for her on the dock her heart throbs in her breast.

Her mother waves. Her father lifts a farm-hardened hand to his lips, and blows her a kiss. The young man who was her "fella" before she took the job in Paducah wrings an old flop-hat in nervous hands.

She thinks of a book in her library at school, *The Scarlet Letter*, and wonders if they can see the big letter H painted in red on her bodice, and then she feels his hand on her arm.

"How 'bout a goodbye kiss before ya leave?"

She half turns, and gives him a weak smile, "Not in front of my family, they still believe that I'm a good girl," and unsteadily, she moves down the gangway.

Pug finds the US Marshall's office near the waterfront in Natchez Under the Bluff. The US Marshall is his kind of lawman, lean and tough, but with calm brown eyes; the kind of man who can handle himself in a bad situation, and do it with calm deliberation.

The Marshall rifles through some papers in his file cabinet. "Yeah, here it is, the Land Commissioner, Rene Labeaux. I remember it, strange circumstances. Eye witnesses say it was an accident, that Labeaux and this fella yer lookin' fer, Butler, got into a scuffle an' Labeaux fell over the rail of his boat, and hung himself like a side of beef on a bailin' hook."

"D'ja follow up on it?" Pug questions.

The Marshall bristles a little. "I did, but I did'n go chasing him out to the Great American Desert jest to question 'im about somethin' that was obviously an accident. I went out to the Leary plantation, but the overseer out there said that the place had been taken over by the Commissioner, Labeaux, an' there weren't no Butler out there. Some o' th' darkies out there said they thought he took a couple o' the former slaves an' struck out fer Texas. I wired the Marshall in Galveston, but he said he'd never heard of a Butler in his area, likewise the Marshall in El Paso. Texas is a big place, 'n' like I said, it was a accident."

"D'ya know who Butler was? He was already a wanted man, an enemy of the state."

"Look," the Marshall says, "I remember a long time ago seein' a flyer out on 'im fer piracy on the high seas or some' other such nonsense.

"I'm a southerner. I did'n take part in the late war, but I ain't got no truck with them that did. If I tried to track down every Confederate that killed a Yankee, it'd be a lifetime career.

"What he did durin' the war ain't no concern of mine. You got recent paper on 'im my office'll give you all the assistance we can, otherwise I done tol' ya all I know."

Pug nods. He could probably wire the Secretary of War's office, and put pressure on the Federal Marshall's office but what would be the point, after all, he is really only a bounty hunter doing unofficial business with an unofficial organization in Washington.

"Thanks for your help. If anything new turns up will you pass it on to the Pinkerton Detective Agency in Chicago?"

The Marshall puts out an almost dainty right hand. *He can probably draw and fire faster'n greased lightening,* Pug thinks.

"That I'll do," the Marshall says.

Pug nods again and shakes the delicate but strong hand. The Federal Marshall Service certainly isn't required to share any information with a private detective agency, no matter that's it's the biggest, most successful one in the nation.

Back in his room at the River City Pug tosses both folders onto his bed, Butler/Donavan—Principe/Principal/Prince/ Prinzikov. *Where do I go from here? I'm at the end of two cold trails. Do I go back to Louisville, and try to pick up a man who's like a ghost, or do I go out to the Great American Desert, an area of over a million square miles, and hunt for a needle in a haystack.* He picks up

Butler's file, and shuffles through it. *If he owns land in Texas there must be a record of his title in Austin.* He glances at Principe's folder. He shouldn't have divided his attention. He's never done that before, once he started on the trail of a subject he always stayed with it until he had his man, and he'd always gotten his man in the past. The Pinkerton Agency has a reputation for always getting its man.

I need a drink, maybe a drink and a little female company, maybe a couple of drinks, some female company, and bust a head or two. Nothin'll clear a man's head like a little saloon brouhaha. But first I need to wire Bernie, and see if she's been able to turn up anything on Principe.

He drains his beer mug, his third, and slams it down on the table. At a table across the room several men have started an arm wrestling contest, the continuous winner, a big riverboat man, has just defeated a young man wearing bib overalls, fastened with one strap. "I can whip any man in this saloon." He shouts. "In fact, I can whip any man in this state."

Pug takes a little lead cylinder from his pocket, folds into his fist, and ambles over to the boatman's table. He leans the loaded fist on the table, and pushes back his bowler with the thumb of the other hand. "From the sound of you, you're Ohio River-trash-Pollack an' I say ya can't whip a New York Irishman."

The riverboat man rears back in his chair, and starts to rise. Pug's right hand comes up from the table, and nails him a solid blow under the chin with the loaded fist, and the brouhaha begins. The riverboat man sags in his chair, but two of his companions advance toward Pug. The young arm wrestler backs up to Pug's back. "Laissez le bon temps roulez," he says.

Pug is about to say thanks when a fist catches him hard in the ribs. His left hand jabs at his assailant's face, and is followed by a roundhouse with the loaded right fist to the man's jaw. The assailant's eyes roll back, and he crumbles as if every bone and muscle in him just melted.

The third man looks at Pug, at his friend lying inert in the sawdust, and then at the door. Even if he has never heard the adage *he who fights and runs away, lives to fight another day,* the wisdom of it is not lost on him, and he disappears through the swinging door.

Pug lifts the riverboat man by his belt, and unceremoniously tosses him head first out the door. The young arm wrestler does the same for the man lying inert in the sawdust.

"Thanks for the help." Pug says.

"Wal, looks like you handled 'em pretty easy without my help."

Pug feels his tender ribs, and flinches. "Maybe, but knowin' my back was covered helped." He extends his hand to the young man. "Pug Mahone."

"Gator Hebert." He pronounces it "Gaitah E-beyah."

Pug eyes the strapping young man, and wonders if there's any way he can use him. He flashes his PI badge. "You ever hear of a guy named Labeaux?"

Hebert gives Pug a dubious look. "Yeah, I heerd of 'im." He's always been suspicious of a man with a badge. "You de law?"

"Well, I ain't actually the law, but I'm huntin' the man that killed Labeaux."

The bayou man chuckles. "Dit'n nobody kill 'im, not o' purpose anyhow. Man name o' Butlah flung 'im off the upper deck of a riverboat, his throat was ripped out on a bailin' hook hangin' in a net. Man, dat was a sight, blood sqouitin' evah wheah."

"You saw it then?"

"Oh yeah, I seen it. I be woikin' on Labeaux boat. I heerd a commotion up on de uppah deck; when I look up I seen ol' Labeaux body come sailin' ovah de rail. Next ting I know, de bailin' hook be stickin' under his chin and blood be sprayin' like a waterfall, covah de whole lowah deck."

"Did you know Butler?"

Gator shakes his head. "Knew of 'im. What I heerd is Butlah married Labeaux sweetheart. Real bad blood between 'em. Not only did Butlah take his girl away from 'im he also stole his boat, the Marie Labeaux."

"The woman, missus Butler, you know her?"

Hebert hangs his head in shame. "Yeah, I knew 'er. Dat be a bad business." He looks up, and his eyes show a deep pain. "Labeaux take a bunch o' us up to de Leary plantation to look fo' Butlah." He shakes his head as if he's trying to rid himself of a bad memory. "I did'n take no part in de hangin,' dat was all Labeaux an' Thibodaux." He pauses as if he doesn't want to go on.

"Who'd they hang? Not Butler, he's still a fugitive."

"Miss Leary, dat is, missus Butlah. Dat Thibodaux put a noose aroun' her neck an' somebody shot her mule right out from under 'er. Must o' broke 'er neck quick like 'cause she did'n kick 'r gag 'r nothing. Her pretty head jes' roll to de side, and 'er eyes close."

Pug notices the tears brimming in his eyes. "How come Thibodaux didn't have to stand trial for it?"

Finally Hebert gets a gleeful look, and he wipes his eyes with the back of his hand. "Dat little niggah boy o' hers, some say he was her half brothah, he blowed Thibodaux head off wid a shot gun 'r sumpin; nothin' left but a ragged neck pumpin' blood like a fountain." He looks Pug right in the eye. "Dat was one bloody day. I nevah seen so much blood in one place."

"How come the law didn't go after the boy?"

"Oh, dey went up to de plantation, but Labeaux had stole it by dat time. Nobody was left but some darkies that woiked de land fo' 'im."

"So, sounds like the whole affair has been dropped as far as the law is concerned."

Hebert gives him a sly look. "Not if yall's still lookin' fo' Butlah."

Pug grins. "Like I said, I'm not the law. I work for an organization in Washington."

Hebert gets a grim look about his mouth. "De way I sees it he ain't guilty o' nothin.' How come de gument be so interested in 'im?"

Pug shakes his head. "I ain't paid to figure out the right or wrong of it, just to bring 'im in."

CHAPTER 5

At three weeks and five days short of being six years old Annie is a miniature of the beautiful woman that she will someday become. Long, shapely legs support a very cute, very feminine body. Her face is what might be called a kitten-face with enormous deep blue eyes, framed by platinum curls.

Unlike Nancy, her mother, she knows she's beautiful, and worse, at six years old, she knows that she holds a strange power over the male of the species, and at five she had already learned how to use that power to her advantage. Independent and strong willed, she doesn't say, *may I do so-and-so*; she says *I will do so-and-so.*

When she strides out of her bedroom she is decked out in a pair of Mexican riding pants with small conchos running down the outside seam of each leg, a checkered shirt with a deep blue scarf around her throat, a rawhide vest, a pair of slope-heeled boots and, hanging by a chin strap, her flat crowned, brush-popper hat rides on her back. Her hair is pulled back in what's being called a pony's tail.

Lula turns from the washbasin, and gives her the once over. "Well, ain't you de Miss Priss dis mornin'?" Annie has been dressing herself now since their arrival in Texas.

Andy looks up from his plate of scrambled eggs and potatoes, and his eyes show surprise and pride. "Mornin' Princess. You do look mighty pretty this mornin.'"

Annie flashes him the smile that is reserved for only him. It's one of adoration and admiration. "Mornin' Dai." She rises to her tiptoes, and kisses him on the lips. "You purdy too."

He nods to her. "Well, thank you princess." He gestures at her costume. "What's the occasion?"

She looks down at herself as if to say, *what, this old thing?* "I gonna go see 'Suela today."

He picks her up, and places her on his lap where she takes a big spoonful of his eggs, and then a sip of his coffee. "I'm sorry Baby, I can't take you up there today. I've got to ride up to the escarpment camp today, maybe when I get back."

She shrugs. "Machts nichts, I can go by my own self."

"Oh, ho ho, I don't think so. You're a might small to ride up there on your own. Do you even know the way by yourself?"

"'Dogo knows de way." Kidogo is her silverdust mustang with four black legs, and black mane and tail. At just under fourteen hands high, he's not really a pony, but he's small for a horse. When Andy got him, he named him Bwana Kidogo, which was the name Monk, the old African, gave him aboard the *Queen of Scots.* The literal translation from the Swahili language is Small Master. In 'Dogo's case it means something more akin to Little Man.

Andy shakes his head in despair. "Well, even if Kidogo does know the way I can't let you go alone. What if you got thrown, and broke a leg or something?"

She gives her father an incredulous look. "'Dogo not ever trow me."

Andy knows that the horse would never intentionally throw her. "Maybe not, but what if he slipped crossing the river, and fell, or a rattlesnake made him jump; you might fall off."

"Dai, me 'n' 'Dogo ain't scared o' no rattlesnake. 'Dogo'd stomp on his head 'n' kill 'im."

"Where do you get such a hard head, little girl?" he answers, mussing her bangs.

She takes her tiny knuckles, and raps him gently on the forehead. "My Dai give it to me."

When she scrambles down, and goes off to play, Andy assumes that's the end of it. Annie, however, makes a beeline to the corral.

She's too little to throw her saddle onto Kidogo's back, or reach up to his ears to bridle him, but she's as resourceful as she is hard headed. She takes her bridle over to the corral, and climbs up to the top rail; when Kidogo comes over to see if she has a treat for him, and get his ears scratched, she slips the bit between his teeth, and slides the halter over his ears. He follows her around like a puppy as she goes to the tack room, pulls her saddle down from the saddle rack, and takes it over to the feed box, where she struggles it up into the box. Once in the box, it's no chore at all to transfer it to his back. All that's left to do now is pull the cinch down tight enough to keep the saddle from slipping. To do this, she climbs out of the feed box, threads the cinch strap through the cinch ring, flips the cinch strap over the saddle, grabs it under his chest and, using all of her weight, swings on it until it tightens to the desired hole. From that point, it's a simple matter to wrap the loose strap in the fore-in-hand knot that will keep it from trailing. She's never been taught to do all of this except by watching when the men saddle their horses.

She doesn't cross the bridge, and ride past the house, which is the shortest way to the ford. Instead she skirts along the base of the limestone cliffs, crosses the creek near the cave, through the scrub-oak and mesquite thicket, and then behind the poultry house. When she sees the poultry house she remembers the 22.20/410 over-and-under that Ilsa keeps there to keep snakes and varmints away. She dismounts while still in the thicket, and drops her reins on the ground under Kidogo's nose. He's ground broke, and will stand right there as though he is tied to a stump.

She breaks open the breach, and checks to see if there are shells in it. She pulls each shell out, checks them over. They look good so she puts them back in, and snaps the barrel back into place.

She likes the gun. She's always thought that it is just her size. Her daddy has let her shoot the 22.20, and she's a pretty good shot, but she's never fired the 410. It doesn't have much of a kick, but her daddy has always thought it was too much for her. Since she doesn't have a saddle scabbard on her small saddle, she just ties it under the fender skirt with the latigo strings. She smiles to herself. She likes the feel of the rifle under her leg. She strokes the smooth stock with her fingers. *And Dai thinks I ain't big enough to ride up to 'Suela's house by my own self.*

Kidogo's ears pivot back and forth, and he rumbles deep in his throat. She senses his nervousness, and unconsciously her left hand grips the saddle horn. She reaches under her leg with her right hand, and unties the latigos holding the over-and-under in place. "It's okay," she croons. "I feel it too. Be my good boy, and just stay steady."

When they reach the river, they are well above the shallow ford. The river is narrower here, deeper, and faster as it courses through the canyon.

She doesn't know what has made Kidogo nervous. She wonders if an Indian is trailing her, although she has never seen an Indian, except for Pilar, of course. She has heard stories of the Comanche raid many years ago, but the Comanche have not raided around here since then. Whoever it is, they are not going to catch her unaware.

As Kidogo splashes through the river, she deliberately rides him around several boulders. When she thinks she is hidden by the big rocks, she slips from the saddle into the water, and lets Kidogo splash on out behind her. Warily, she selects the shotgun trigger, places the stock against her shoulder, and peeks around the boulder. She studies the terrain on the other side, scanning the scrub, but sees nothing. She doesn't want to shoot blind, or even make a snap shot at any movement. After all, it might be her Dai following her. No, she must wait and identify her target.

She lets out a long sigh, and has about decided that she has been spooked by phantoms that aren't really there when she catches a movement just on the other side of the boulder from her, and slightly above. She looks above her on the rock, and looks directly into the yellow eyes and tawny face of a small cougar. It's not a dozen feet from her. She's not even aware that she has aimed and fired until she feels the jolt against her shoulder, and hears the scream. The kick from the 410 has knocked her over into the river, and she comes up sputtering, wiping water from her eyes, and searching frantically for the trigger that will fire the 22.20.

The first thing that she notices is that the cougar is no longer on the boulder above her, then she sees the stream of blood running down the rock face. She edges around the boulder, and there at the river's edge is the dead cat. The back of its head is blown out.

"Maldito!" She swears softly in Spanish.

The minute Andy opens the door to the tack room he notices that Annie's tack is missing. A quick inspection of the corral reveals that Kidogo is not with the other horses. He lets out a frustrated sigh. *What am I going to do with her? She's getting a little too independent for her own good.*

He whistles softly, and Blue trots up to him. He's glad it's her, and not one of the other horses. Barak is a big strong horse, but he's not the brush-bred mustang that she is. He slips the hackamore over her nose, and then swings up bareback. Collie has followed him out to the corral, as usual. He points to the ground. "Collie, find Annie!" She sniffs the ground, and takes off, belly to the ground, in the direction of his old cabin. He finds the trail without any difficulty, and follows it at a steady trot.

When they are about a half a mile from the river he hears the shotgun blast. With only the tightening of his knees, and feeling his fist knot into her mane, Blue jumps into a flat run, striding over cactus and mesquite scrub like the brush-popping pony she used to be.

He draws his Walker Colt, and hits the ground running even before Blue hunkers to a squatting stop.

Annie looks up startled when he comes splashing through the river. "Hi Dai," her voice quavering. "Look 'at I shot."

His eyes look like gray storm clouds, and the muscles are working in his jaw.

" 'm I in trouble?" She mumbles.

He ignores her question. "Are you alright? Are you hurt?"

She shakes her head. "You gonna tell Jjajja?"

He wraps her in his trembling arms. "Now, you don't really think you're gonna be able to keep this from your Jjajja do you?"

Her little mouth turns down at the corners. "I'm 'n trouble!"

******

Bernie Goldblatt shuffles through the pile of telegrams on her desk. They are all from her operatives around the country. Her contact in Louisville could only tell her that Jacob Prinzikov had disappeared after his contact with Pug. Most of the others came back negative. She actually has two that look promising, one in Seattle and one in Kansas City. The one in Seattle says that there is a new actor in town who does on-stage performances of Francis Scott Keys reading the Star Spangled Banner from a stage prop in the form of a ship, and Lincoln reading the Gettysburg address from the back of a train. The one from Kansas City is from a young woman who moonlights as a cleaning woman at the Muhlbach Boarding House. Her telegram tells of a single man in the boarding house who has dresses, a minister's outfit, farmers clothing and a soldiers uniform, in his closet. Also, she has seen, in one of his dresser drawers, a false mustache, side burns and eye brows.

Bernie taps the telegram in front of her, and a smile plays across her lips. "Mr. Principe, I believe we have you."

Immediately, she sends her young runner to the telegraph office with a wire for Pug in Natchez. She hopes he is still there. If not, however, he will probably be en route back home, and she will tell him in person. She likes this idea best. He may give her one of his crooked smiles of satisfaction.

She picks up another wire. This one has been here for a few days. She taps it thoughtfully. She hasn't mentioned this one to Pug yet. He can only pursue one fugitive at a time, and she thinks Principe should be his first priority. Still, she should probably tell him about it, and let him make up his own mind. This one is from Austin, Texas. It tells her that an Andrew J. Butler does, in fact, hold titles to land in Uvalde, Bandera and Edwards counties. She lays it aside. She will tell him about it after he gets to Kansas City.

Pug probes a sore rib as he limps through the River City lobby towards his room. *I'm getting too old for this kind of foolishness,* he thinks. Then he smiles, and winces at his split lip. *But I do need it occasionally.*

"Mr. Mahone, Mr. Mahone!" The voice is that of a small black boy in a red uniform with a little red monkey-hat on his head. "Sir, you has a telegram at the desk. I been up to yo room, and been pagin' an' pagin' ya."

Pug smiles, and flips him a dime, then turns and, without a limp now, hurries to the front desk. "You got a wire for Mahone?"

The desk clerk smiles his best customer-service smile, and proffers the wire. "Yes sir, came in a couple hours ago."

Pug snatches it without even a glance at the desk clerk, and retires to one of the lounge chairs in the lobby. *Found Principe-stop-Muhlbach Boarding House KC-stop-loose the derby-stop.*

Pug smiles, ignoring his painful lip. What a girl. It's just like her to remind him that his green bowler is a dead giveaway, and would certainly be recognized by Principe. Not that he can effectively disguise himself the way Principe can. He is a big lumbering man with a battered face. No, he can't disguise himself very well, but there's no need advertising himself with an Irish green bowler. He returns to the front desk. The desk clerk is a little less conciliatory, but nods genially.

"How's the fastest way to Kansas City? Is there a train or fast coach?"

The clerk takes a schedule from under his counter and studies it. "Well, there's an overnight mail coach from here to Memphis."

"What time does it leave?"

"They leave the town post office at midnight, make a stop at Jackson, and straight through to Memphis.

"I doubt they'll take passengers, though." He shouts at Pug's retreating back.

At the post office Pug watches two men loading the mail coach. As the desk clerk said, it has no inside seats for passengers. One side door opens into a cargo bin filled with crates and boxes. He strides up to the older of the two men. "You the driver?"

The man looks him over before answering, and then after expelling a stream of brown tobacco juice, answers, "Yep."

Pug holds up a satchel with the eagle emblem of the United States government on the side. At the same time he flashes his old National Security Service badge. "Government courier. I need to escort this to Memphis."

The driver notices that the satchel is handcuffed to Pug's wrist. He turns to the younger man. "Lije, you ride on the boot this trip. The Fedman'll ride shotgun to Memphis. The young man, boy really, nods; he doesn't really care. If he rides on the boot, he can curl up amongst the mail sacks, and go to sleep.

To Pug's satisfaction the driver is not a talker. He doesn't ask about the contents of the satchel or Pug's business in Memphis. Also, the road from Natchez to Jackson is the old Natchez Trace, and they make excellent time. The eastern horizon is just beginning to show hazy gray as they pull into the Jackson main post office. Here the team is changed, and the driver and shotgun rider have breakfast, and rest for an hour.

Pug follows them into the café, and sits at a table by himself. He makes a show of unfastening the handcuffs from his wrist, and attaching them to his ankle to free up his hands for eating. He smiles to himself as he wonders what they would say if they knew that the contents of the satchel was nothing more than a spare shirt and his green bowler derby.

He finishes his meal, takes the napkin from his shirt collar, and walks to the hat rack standing by the door. He looks over the hats hanging there, and without a sideways glance chooses a brown slouch hat with a wide brim big enough to partially hide his face.

The stage driver looks up as Pug comes into the post office yard. "Ah, right on time. I didn't want to have to leave ya." He says, not unkindly. "Nice hat. I thought you might be needin' a hat out here in the hot sun."

A two-day coach ride, on top of the saloon brawl, has taken its toll, and the steady rocking of the train car, and clickity-clack on the rails lulls him into drowsiness. He feels the comforting bulge of his Kerr .44 in his coat pocket, and pulls his floppy brim down over his eyes. *With any luck, in a few of days, I'll be heading to Washington City with my prisoner—unless, of course, I have to shoot him.*

"Next stop Kansas City!"

Pug's head snaps up. He stretches, and rubs his face vigorously, as though that will rub away the weariness of the long journey. Except for getting up to eat his meals, and go to the bathroom he has slept most of the trip. He rises, and goes back to the lavatory. Inside he removes his shirt, senses his own body odor, and gingerly fingers the purple bruise on his rib. *Hope I broke that boyo's jaw,* he thinks vindictively. He removes the spare shirt from his satchel; he's glad that Bernie had the foresight to send fresh clothes. He takes a damp towel, washes his upper body, and then brushes the flop hat with the same towel. It's a pretty nice hat, probably some Mississippi planter's hat.

He doesn't go to the Muhlbach Boarding House. Instead he takes a small room above a general store and barbershop on the outskirts of town. He can scout out the boarding house from there without arousing suspicion.

His first stop, though, is the barbershop. Barbershops are the best rumor mills in any small town.

"Yeah," says the shoeshine boy, "I seed a guy like dat. Was livin' ovah to de Muhlbach. Ain't deah no mo dough. Miz Emma say he gotted hisself a job ovah to Overland Park. Ain't nevah been to Overland Park. Mights jes' takes myself a trip "cross de riveah some day."

The barber gives the shoeshine boy a scathing look. "Whachu wanna go cross the river fer? Ain't nothing over there but rough mountain men, hide traders an' Injuns. They scalp a little black rascal like you fer sho."

******

Some folks will tell you that herd animals, including those of the Bovine persuasion, come under the heading of fright-to-flight. The fright-to-flight theory is that the animal will bolt and run at the first sign of danger, and then, in most cases, herd up to protect themselves, but as soon as the immediate danger is over they spread out again to graze, forgetting that there was ever a danger. This would imply that animals such as this, including animals of the Bovine persuasion, have no long-term memory.

Be that as it may, certain Longhorned cattle have been known to travel thousands of miles to return to their home range, and return to an area within a mile or two of where they were born. And, of course, we know that dogs, cats and horses will remember a beloved master, or an abusive owner for years after they're gone. This was the case with the scarred, one eyed, old steer called Beast.

He remembers the day, when he was just a young bull, when a Black Bear attacked him in a Resaca. It was a battle to the death. One that left the bear with Beast's right-side horn broken off in its body, trampled in the mud of the Resaca, and Beast dragging himself into the brush to either die, or by some miracle, recover. He did recover, of course, but he would carry the scars of that battle for the rest of his life. His broken horn had grown into a blunt club that twisted down past his jaw; his right eye was mostly covered by scar tissue, and deep scars marked his right shoulder and ribcage.

This year, as he comes down off of the Staked Plains, he lifts his nose in the air, and catches a familiar scent. One he hasn't detected for many years, but one that jogs a memory of a very long trail drive, swimming a very wide river, and a human he had come to accept as a trail-companion, if not a friend. He raises his head high, and tests the air again. It is unmistakable; the human from his past is near, somewhere.

Andy reins up on the caprock, pushes his hat back, and watches, with great satisfaction, the large herd of Longhorns making their way down the steep trail from the escarpment. He chuckles to himself when he sees that the lead steer is none other than Beast.

Annie rides up next to him on Kidogo, crooks a leg over her saddle horn, and rests there. Since her episode with the cougar, rather than subduing her in any way, it has made her even more independent. She had helped Andy skin and tan the hide, and now uses it as a covering for her bed. Lula, of course, scolded her severely, but Ilsa only held her tightly, and wept, which hurt her worse than the scolding.

"Lots o' calves this year." She smiles up at her father. "I like that."

He smiles back at this girl who it seems, just a few short of months ago, was only a baby. Now she seems years older. He shakes his head. It has been a couple of years. She has learned so much about the ranching business. She knows now that if a cow misses a year without having a calf she might as well become table meat. She points. "Is that ol' Beast?"

Andy runs a hand through his silver hair. "That's him. Best swimmin' steer I ever saw. Once swam the Mississippi River."

Annie flashes him her special "Dai" smile. "I know. You and Tio Chico have only told that story about a gajillion times."

"Well, it's true."

She knows it's true. She also knows that it was this same cattle-drive that took the life of Consuela's father, and the same drive that brought Andy and Nancy together. Without that cattle-drive there wouldn't be an Annie.

Andy turns to Jack and Yoni, who have since ridden up. "I think before they head back up to the high plains next spring, we need to drive some of 'em to market. I got a flyer from a Mr. McCoy in Abilene, Kansas the other day, inviting Texas cattlemen to bring their herds to the rail head there. He claims to pay the highest prices for Texas beef. Maybe we can make this place pay a little. I understand that Snyder, Pierce and Slaughter will all start herds up the trail this spring. I figure we can do a spring round up, and put together a herd of a couple of thousand."

Annie looks over at Yoni, and then up at her father, and grins. "Yeah, Dai, come spring, they'll be restless, and ready to start moving north on their own. Won't be nothing to jus' keep 'em movin' till they reach Kansas." It never enters her mind that she won't be taken along.

******

Brian Macgregor hands the letter across the table to Andy. "Don't know what this is all about, but thought you might be interested."

It's not really a letter, just a note from a clerk, an old girlfriend of Mac's, in the land office in Austin. It reads:

> *Dear Mac,*
>
> *Thought you might be interested to know that I have recently received inquiries about your pardner at the ranch. Seems that the Pinkerton Detective Agency in Chicago is interested in his titles to that land. I don't know what it's all about but they wanted to know the exact location of his holdings. I was obliged to give them plot numbers etc.*
>
> *Are y'all in some kind of trouble?*
>
> *When are you goin to come to Austin again? I think you owe me a nice dinner for this.*
>
> *Luv ya,*
> *Linda*

Since the reconstruction government has taken over in Texas many strange things have taken place. Many Texans returned from the war to find their land condemned and confiscated. Shootouts are commonplace, blood feuds have been declared, and not a few lynchings have occurred. Texas has always been a place where the law of the six-gun sometimes prevails and justice is dispensed by self-appointed vigilante mobs.

Andy directs his question more to Ilsa than Mac. "We don't owe back taxes do we? I mean, I don't s'pose you paid any U.S. government taxes while we were part of the Confederacy."

"No, but we paid our taxes to Texas. I don't think it has anything to do with taxes." She says.

"I rode into Austin to see Linda before I came here. It don't seem to be tax related. Besides, if it was taxes, the state would've just sent the sheriff out to collect it. I know the Bandera sheriff; he's a good ol' boy, an' a ol' Confederate soldier, served under Colonel Ford in south Texas. It must be sunthin' else to get the Pinkertons involved. You ain't a outlaw are you Andy?"

Andy cringes. "Yeah, matter of fact I am. For several offenses, not the least of which is piracy on the high seas, that an' I busted out o' Federal prison an' stole a Yankee horse."

Mac's face goes hard, and he shakes his head. "Yeah, that'd do it I reckon. The guv'ment must've hired the Pinkertons to run you down, and bring you in."

Andy shakes his head. "I should o' known they wouldn't just let it drop. I heard they arrested Semmes and Lee for treason. I should o' known Welles wouldn't just forget about me and the other Commerce Raiders. We put a powerful hurt on their shipping during the war." He looks Mac in the eyes, holds out his wrists. "You need to take me in?"

Mac snorts a chuckle. "They ain't about to involve what's left of the Rangers. Matter of fact the Reconstructionists are tryin' to disband us. Say we're nothin' but a remnant o' the rebel army."

Ilsa kneels down in front of Andy, and takes his hands in hers. "Maybe you oughta stay up to the escarpment until this blows over. If any body comes here lookin' for you I can lead 'em astray."

He lifts her and kisses her gently on the lips. "It's been a couple o' years since the end o' the war. If a Pinkerton shows up here before we start the drive, I'll deal with it. If they show up after the drive, then you can lead 'em astray, tell 'em we drove the cattle to Mexico City instead o' Kansas."

"Yeah," Mac interjects, "as me Scottish grandfatherr would've said, 'dinna' get yerr knickerrs in a twist, lad.' If they haven't looked for you, or found you in two and a half years, they ain't likely to show up tomorrow. If they come to Ranger headquarters askin' a bunch o' questions, they won't get straight answers. They might get sent to Quanah's camp to look for ya. "

******

The one thing you'd have to say about Julius Salvador Principe is that he is versatile, versatile and adaptive. Whether he is an actor, a female spy or, now, a bull whacker, he throws himself into his roll with abandon, and he becomes the character.

Actually it isn't hard for him to *become* a bull whacker. The roll suites him; he enjoys the rough life on the trail. He enjoys the physical aspect of it, walking alongside the gigantic freight wagons, swinging the long ox whip, and cracking it over the backs of the lumbering oxen, sleeping in a bedroll under his wagon, gambling around a campfire with the other teamsters, the occasional brush with Indians; and it gives him a certain amount of anonymity. Indeed, half of the men out on the plains, whether they are freight drivers, buffalo hunters or just drifters, are fugitives of one sort or another. Out here, people don't ask a bunch of questions about a man's past.

When he had presented himself to Bull McKenzie, of McKenzie's Overland Park Freight Lines, McKenzie had looked askance at his slight build, and had doubts, but when he shook hands with the man, and felt his firm handshake, he had decided to give him the job anyway.

"Mr. McKenzie, Pug Mahone, Pinkerton Detective Agency."

McKenzie looks up at the man speaking, and nods. "Mr. Mahone, what can I do for you?"

"I'm looking for a man that I'm told works for you, name of Julius Principe."

McKenzie shakes his head. "Don't have anybody in my employ by that name. Got a lot of Smiths and Joneses, but no Principe." His grin gives away his meaning.

Pug takes out Bernie's flyer, spreads it out on McKenzie's desk. "Looks somethin' like this."

McKenzie studies the artist's rendition. His facial expression doesn't give away whether he recognizes the man or not. "What's he done?"

Pug's been at this detective business long enough to know when he's being shaded. "Law firm of Meyer, Meyer & Rosen hired us to find 'im. Something about an inheritance I believe." He lies glibly.

McKenzie thinks long and hard before answering. He doesn't want to give up one of his employees to the law, but if the boy has, in fact, inherited something, he doesn't want to be the one to stand in the way of him getting it. "Looks a little like one of my employees. Could be him I guess." Actually the flyer is a dead ringer for the employee the men call Shakespeare. "If you want to just leave the papers with me I'll see that he gets them when he comes back in."

Pug shakes his head. "Can't do that. Not legal. I gotta make sure it's him, and then hand them to him personally, and get a signature." He shrugs. "Otherwise Mr. Pinkerton don't get paid, an' if he don't get paid I don't get paid.

"You said, 'when he comes back in,' when'll he be back in?"

"Hard to say," McKenzie scratches a bushy, gray, mutton-chop, "sent 'im with a string of wagons down to Indian Territory; new fort they're building down there. Gonna round up all the hostiles, and try to keep 'em on reservations. They'll deliver the freight to Camp Medicine Bluffs, then pick up a load o' buffalo hides, an' bring 'em back up here. They could be gone two or three months, maybe half a year."

Pug takes a long breath, and lets it out slow. "I hate to make a trip all the way to Indian Territory just to find out this ain't the right guy. You say he didn't use the name of Principe when he hired on, what name did he give you?"

"Wal, we don't stand on ceremony around here with formal names. Like I said, we got a lot of people that goes by the name of Smith or Jones. We got one guy that signed on simply as Kennesaw Mountain, an' this'n," he taps the picture of Julius, "the men just call 'im Shakespeare. He's all the time spoutin' lines from some play or other. He's quite an entertainer. Shoulda been a actor I guess."

Pug can barely contain his glee, but just nods. "Well, thank you Mr. McKenzie. You've been a great help."

McKenzie puts out a thick hand. "Hope he's your man. He's a good boy. I'd like to see 'im get his inheritance."

"Oh, he'll get what's comin' to him," Pug smiles, "I can assure you of that."

******

The winter of 68/69 starts off easy enough, the weather stays warm until Christmas eve, but Christmas morning dawns crisp and cold with a light smattering of snow on the ground, and then on January first a blue-norther blows down out of Canada with nothing to stop it but a rail fence with the top two rails down. The wind howls down the front range of the Rockies dumping tons of snow in the Great Plains, across the panhandle of Texas, and down into the Staked Plains.

Buffalo and cattle by the millions turn their tails to the wind, and drift south. Those who don't wander into an arroyo, and suffocate in ten-foot snowdrifts make it to the Edwards Plateau and the protected river valleys of the Texas hill country.

Annie now saddles up every morning, and rides out to the herds with her father and the boys without pretense. She prides herself on being as good a cowboy as Jacky or the twins. She can't physically handle the larger cattle, but then neither can Fritz or Yoni. She can rope the calves though, and drag them into the holding yard for the men to castrate and brand. She has become useful, and Andy and Ilsa agree that if she is with hi he can keep an eye on her.

The cowboys spend days of frozen riding, preparing the herds for the trail drive, and nights sleeping on the frozen ground to begin again at daybreak the next morning.

Annie dismounts, and tosses her reins to Yoni. "You mind cuate (twin)? Just toss 'im some hay. I'll rub 'im down in a little bit."

Then to one of the Mexican cowboys, "maldición, it's colder'n a well-digger's cul—." She darts an apprehensive glance at her father. "Ooops."

Andy shakes his head in dismay. "Little girl, where do you get such a mouth?" He gives her a look that tells her to walk soft. "I want you to come home with me tonight, and sleep in your bed. It ain't proper for a little girl to spend so much time in a line camp with a bunch of hardened cowboys."

She looks over at Yoni, who is dutifully rubbing the mud off Kidogo's chest. *Yeah*, she thinks, *some bunch of hardened cowboys*. But she just hangs her head and says, "Yes sir."

She knows who he's talking about, and it's not Fritz and Yoni. He's not even talking about her uncle Jacky or Chico or Carlos. He's talking about the five men that Chico brought back from Villa Acuna, all good cowboys, but not sweet, clean cut boys like Fritz and Yoni.

The worst of the group is a swaggering, swearing, braggart of fifteen named Paco Hinajosa, but the best cowboy Andy has ever seen, and a hard worker.

Jack, Carlos and the twins think he's someone to look up to because of his rough cowboy skills.

Annie thinks he's the cutest thing since bows on a bonnet, and flirts unabashedly. Having grown up around Dolores, Consuela and Pilar she knows Spanish, and has no trouble conversing with the men from Villa Acuna, and she seems to delight, to the consternation of her father, in swapping crude comments with them, especially Paco.

Ever since his imprisonment at the Point Lookout detention camp in Maryland, during the war, Andy has hated cold weather. He doesn't like sleeping on the hard frozen ground. He sometimes wakes up in the middle of the night remembering the deprivation, and at those times he wants only to snuggle closer to his wife, and find comfort in her strong, loving arms.

It is primarily for this reason that he has decided to return home tonight, and sleep in his own warm bed, that, and the need to get Annie away from the camp for a while.

He has come to depend on her for a good many things around camp; things that she can handle that would take a cowboy away from more important work; plus the fact that he just likes having her around.

Jack has decided to come in for the night as well. He claims that he needs to talk to Lula about something, but Andy has to smile because he knows that Jack's reason for wanting to come in isn't that much different than his own; he misses Pilar. They haven't come right out and said that they are in love with each other, but it's all too obvious.

They part company at Mac's cabin, which is now Jack's cabin, with no more than a lifted hand.

Pilar busies herself around the house until Andy and Ilsa slip off to their room, and Lula and Annie are in bed. Then she wraps a blanket around her shoulders, takes a plate of food, and slips out the kitchen door. She makes her way across the ford and up the path to the cabin. The door latch is out, but she knocks anyway.

"Come," Jack calls, thinking it's Andy or his mother.

She opens the door, and slips inside. There is a fire going, but it hasn't been going long enough to take the chill out of the room. "I brought you some supper. Are you hungry?"

He's hungry alright, but not just for food. He's hungry for the sight of her. "I'm starvin'," he answers. "Whacha got?"

"Just some steak and eggs and frijoles."

He takes the plate and starts making short work of the food.

She sits watching him with a little smile on her lips. Then after a while she says, "Juanito, why have you never tried to kiss me?"

He's in mid swallow, and he nearly chokes before he can get it down. "What?"

"Well, I've been here for nearly a year now, and you must know how I feel about you. I was just wondering why you have never tried to kiss me. Is it because of what happened to me on the Llano Estacado? What the Comancheros did to me? Do you feel that I'm defiled because of it?"

He jumps up, and kneels by her chair. "No Pilar. No! Well, maybe because of what happened, but not because I think you're defiled. I just wasn't sure how you'd react if I just uped, and kissed you. I thought that what they did might make you afraid of—you know."

She takes his hand in hers. "Oh Juanito. I could never be afraid of you. You are not like them. You are kind and gentle. Yes, what they did was awful, a terrible experience, but it didn't make me afraid *you*, or of love. With the man that I love, I believe it will be a sweet and wonderful thing."

He just stares, unblinking. "Pilar, are you saying that you love me?"

"Yes Juanito. That's what I'm saying."

"And that you want to have—love with me."

Her smile widens. "Someday, yes."

As Ilsa undresses, and gets ready for bed, Andy sits by the fire, letting the heat permeate his body. How many times, when he was laying in the wet, frozen sand of Point Lookout prison camp, that boggy peninsula sticking out into Chesapeake Bay, with nothing more to cover him than a holey fisherman's sweater and a pair of ragged canvas pants, would he have committed murder to be warm.

He tries not to remember the bone numbing cold; how his bare feet turned blue, and he thought he would probably lose some of his toes to frostbite. He tries not to remember the cruelty of the guards, and the near starvation, but still, these thoughts come unbidden to his mind sometimes.

Ilsa knows instinctively when the depressing memories come on him, and she knows that only she possesses the means to rid him of these thoughts. She slips up behind him, puts her arms around his shoulders, and whispers in his ear, "Come to bed now, and let me warm you."

Sometime later, in the dark, she knows he's still awake. "How's the work going with the cattle?"

"Okay I guess. That bunch that Chico brought has helped."

"How long before you'll be ready for the drive?"

"We could go any time I reckon, but I'm not going to start out until it warms up." He chuckles. "I may wait until I see the first Blue Bonnet." Then more seriously he says, "I'll probably wait until the spring calving is done."

She is quiet for a long while, and then, "When you leave I want to go with you."

He sits up in bed. "You want to go on the drive?"

"Not the whole drive. I just want to go as far as Fredericksburg. I need to see my muti n' vati." She has always used the German for mommy and daddy. "I haven't seen them in a long time."

He waits a moment to answer, and then says, "That'd be okay I s'pose. You could ride in the chuck wagon with ol' Chepito. You could even help 'im with the cookin'—if he'll let you."

"I thought it would also give Annie a chance to meet her new opa n' oma. We might even stay there until you came back home."

"Yeah," He says, "maybe that would take some of the edge off telling Annie she can't go on the drive."

CHAPTER 6

Pug has some decisions to make now. He's already decided that he made a mistake dividing his efforts, trying to work both cases at once. He had made the decision in Natchez, after receiving the wire from Bernie, to find Principe, bring him to justice, and then go after Butler.

He rereads the other telegram from Bernie. The one he received after he arrived in Kansas City: *Found Butler-stop-Ranch headquarters on Frio River in Bandera county-stop-Informant says starting spring trail-drive up Chisholm Trail to Kansas-stop-Good hunting-stop.*

He knows Bernie got him back on track sending him to Kansas City, and then sending him the telegram about Butler. Now she is telling him that Butler may be on his way up the Chisholm Trail with a herd of cattle.

If Principe is, in fact, at Camp Medicine Bluffs in Indian Territory, he can deal with him, and then continue down the Chisholm Trail, and find Butler. With any luck at all, he will find him somewhere on the trail in Indian Territory. It would be nice to kill two birds with one stone. He chuckles at the irony of his thought.

******

Trail Log:
Escarpment camp
Cave Creek Ranch
Monday, February 16, 1869

Old habits die hard. After I made the decision to drive a herd up the trail to Kansas, I decided that I should keep a record of events, as I did on the various ships I served on through out my maritime career.

As suddenly as cold weather came in January, warm weather followed it in February. The warm Pacific winds blew across the Baja peninsula, across Mexico, and up into southwestern Texas. What little snow had accumulated on the Edwards Plateau is now gone.

By the second week of February it is nearly shirtsleeve weather, and after a hard days work, a man has to mop the sweat from his hatband.

The cattle have become restive, and a certain excitement and sense of urgency pervades everything. Certainly, there will still be a couple more cold fronts move through, but winter is over; I know it, the cowboys know it, and the cattle know it.

When Andy and Jack arrive at Chico's place, he and Carlos are at the corral.

"Que tal, amigo!" Jack shouts as he dismounts.

Chico is in the round-pen, riding out a bronc he has just broken. Occasionally the animal will begin to crow hop, and then settle down to his training.

"You about ready to start up the trail?" Andy asks from his perch on the top rail.

"Ciertamente. When do you want to leave?"

"I figgered we could start by the end of the month. There's still some loose stock over by Hondo Springs. We need to bring them in." He hesitates, and then says, "By the way, Ilsa and Annie are gonna go along as far as Fredericksburg."

Chico doesn't say anything, just purses his lips, and nods.

"Lula and Pilar are gonna stay here. They can keep a looksee on Dolores, and her on them. In fact, if she wants to move down to the house, I'm sure they'd be happy to have her there."

Again Chico just nods. He rides to the gate, and drops the rail. The green-broke horse shies when the rail hits the ground, and Chico has to grab the saddle horn to keep from being dumped.

"You goin' to ride him?" Carlos asks. "Maybe you better change to Mouse."

Chico is pulling the horse's head down, and tight against his shoulder. "No, he's okay. He needs to learn who's the jefe around here."

He has only been away from the others for a short time, trying to flush a ravine that has become choked with Mesquite, Canyon Hackberry and cactus. He is riding along the ridge, throwing rocks into the brush, when he jumps a pair of young steers. As they crash through the brush, his horse spooks, rears, and spins. Before Chico can bring him under control, the edge crumbles, and horse and rider tumble into the tight ravine.

Chico is stunned, barely holding on to consciousness. A throbbing pain is radiating up his shin, into his thigh. He is aware that the horse is on top of him. With his free leg, he tries to free himself from the screaming, thrashing animal, but the more he struggles, the more the horse struggles. He lies still, hoping that the horse will do the same, but the terrified horse is trying to roll, and gain his feet. Chico hears the sickening snap as the bone in his leg breaks. Even in the fog of semi-consciousness Chico knows that if he doesn't act quickly, before he passes out, the trashing horse will crush him. His pistol leaps into his hand as though it is a living thing, and without even thinking about it, he fires point blank into the base of the horse's skull. Blood and brains splatter across his chest and face, but he doesn't know it. He has succumbed to the pain and darkness.

Andy's head jerks up at the sound of the shot. He waits. If it is a signal, there will be another shot.

"Whatta ya reckon it is Dai?" Annie asks.

Andy just shakes his head. He knows it could be anything. One of the boys may have shot a rattlesnake.

"Woooo!" He calls out the traditional cowboy yell to establish location.

"Woooo!" Comes back to him from several locations.

Within a couple of minutes cowboys are riding into the clearing by twos and threes.

He draws his own Colt, and fires into the air.

"What is it?" Carlos and Jack ask simultaneously.

Andy looks around. Everyone is there except Chico. His only answer is, "Spread out, and search the thickets. Chico may be in trouble."

They find him just before dusk. His leg seems to be broken in at least two places. One is a compound fracture, with the bone sticking through the tear in his flesh. The other is just a bump on his shin.

Four days later Andy and Chico sit on the mesa, and watch as the herd below starts out on the long road to Abilene, Kansas.

Chico's right leg is sticking straight out in its splint and bandages. He refused to stay behind, and likewise refused to ride in the chuck wagon with Chepito and Ilsa. Dolores had thrown one of her well known Latin fits, and cried, until Chico told her that if she didn't shut up he would send her to sleep in the chicken house, and not even tell her goodbye when he left.

"You okay?" Andy asks.

"Ajuste como violin," Chico grins, and then shrugs. "It loses something in the translation, huh? Of course, what does 'fit as a fiddle' mean anyway?"

Somehow there is a thrilling pride as the two men watch the herd of a couple thousand longhorns leave the bosque along the river, and stretch out into the juniper and cedar covered hills. The Mesquite, cypress and oak trees, except for the live oaks, are still bare, and so there isn't any thick foliage to block their view.

The chuck wagon is ahead, and to the right of the herd, a position it will maintain throughout the whole trip. Jack Leary and Annie are riding point, and at a distance of about fifty feet back, the old lead steer, Beast, plods along, swinging one magnificently curved horn and one blunted, club of a horn. This is not his first trail drive, and he takes his job seriously, bawling back instruction and encouragement to his four or five lieutenants, spread out behind him.

The swing riders and flank riders on either side of the herd are busy trying to keep any herd quitters from breaking for the brush, and the two drag riders push the herd from the rear.

Chico looks over at Andy when one of the vaqueros from Villa Acuna spurs after a young steer that has left the herd, grabs it by the tail, twists it around his saddle horn, and deftly slams the steer to its back. The steer gets up, shakes himself, and then meekly returns to his place in the herd. "That Paco, he's one fine cowboy." He grins.

The first day is all thrill and excitement, even for the veteran vaqueros, none of who have ever been on a long trail drive. So, when they cross the Guadalupe River, and make camp on the north side there is a spirit of joyful exuberance.

Annie, her plate of frijoles in her hand, walks up behind Paco, and pushes his sombrero down over his eyebrows. "Hola vaquero. Mind if I sit next to you?"

He moves over on the Cypress log to make room for her. Yoni, who is propped in the fork of his saddle, watches silently, but with hooded eyes.

"Teach me how to bust a steer by the tail, like you did today," Annie says.

Paco gives her an incredulous look. "You can't bust a steer like that. You're just a chiquita, a nene. (a small girl, a babe). I don't even know why you're on this drive. You should be traveling in the wagon with your mother."

Annie bristles. "I'm not such a nene. I'm almost a mujer. It's clear that you don't know much about women; they mature much faster than boys. You're the chiquito, the nene. How old are you anyhow, twelve?" She knows perfectly well that he's seven years older than her.

"Even if I am only twelve that still makes me many years older than you." But, he has noticed her leggy, firm-bodied appearance, and responds with a good-natured laugh. "Okay, even if you are a mujer, you are probably too small to tail one down, but you can also bust him with la reata. Catch the cuernos, the horns, flip the rope under the flanco, and ride hard to his off side. The result is the same. Even a mujer can do that."

She gives him a swat on the back of the head that knocks his sombrero off, and then bursts into squealing giggles as he jumps up to chase her around the fire.

When dark comes, the coffee has been drunk, the cigarettes smoked, and the days stories told, each man gets his bedroll from the chuck wagon, and spreads them around the camp clearing. Annie takes hers, and places it near the fire, between Paco's and Yoni's.

Andy, who is taking a turn around camp, stops, and stands above where she is lying, scoops up bedroll, Annie and all, and deposits her at the back of the wagon. "Under there will be your bedroom until we reach Fredericksburg." He says with a smile.

Her cheeks burn, and tears come to her eyes when she hears Paco's and Yoni's soft laughter.

******

Otto Schloedier, pronounced Shlydeer, looks up from his work in the barnyard. "Wehr ist das?" (Who is that?) He mutters to himself.

His son Ernst, who is working in the field, takes off his hat, wipes his brow, and squints at the wagon approaching on the road. It's not a buckboard or buggy. It's bigger than a buckboard, but not as big as a Conestoga.

Otto looks like he has just been plucked out of the Bavarian Alps. He is wearing a pair of knee length leather pants, called lederhosen, and a green Tyrolean hat with a boars tail decoration sewn on the side. His waist length jacket is what is called a jaegermeister coat.

Ernst, on the other hand looks like any other Texas farmer, with canvas bib-overalls, and a wide brimmed straw sombrero.

"It's Ilsa!" He shouts. "Ilsa has come home."

"Ilsa?" Otto also shouts. "Mit meine gross kinder?" (With my grand children.)

Marta Schloedier straightens up from weeding her vegetable garden when she hears the commotion. She repeats the name she has just heard shouted. "Ilsa? Mit Yoni und Fritz?" She hurries out the garden gate to run to the big chuck wagon that has stopped in the yard.

Yoni and Fritz, riding behind the wagon, dismount on the run, and dash to their grandfather. "Opa, Opa!" They yell in unison as they jump into Otto's arms.

Annie dismounts slowly, and walks hesitantly up to the big German man. He has a very merry face, with sparkling blue eyes and rosy cheeks. She thinks she'll like him, but suddenly she feels shy.

He notices her standing there, fidgeting. "Und wehr ist das?"

"That's our new sister, Annie," Fritz says.

"Your new sister." Otto repeats. "Du bist sehr schöne, new sister." (You are very beautiful, new sister.)

Not only is Annie fluent in Spanish, she has learned quite a bit of German from Ilsa. "Danke schöne, Opa," she says with a short curtsy.

He looks at her a moment longer, as if studying her. "Ja, Du bist sehr schöne. Do you think you could give a new grandpa a hug?"

Marta has helped Ilsa down from the wagon, and is holding her at arms length. Her eyes are glowing. "Oh, meine Ilsa!" She hugs Ilsa to her bosom, and then holds her out at arms length again, looking deep into her eyes. Her smile can only be called blossoming. "How far along are you?"

Ilsa ducks her head, and then glances shyly up at Andy. "Only about seven weeks." She mutters.

Andy looks first at Marta, and then at Ilsa. His frozen smile can only be called dumfounded.

"Muti," Ilsa says quickly, "this is my husband, Andy."

By now Otto has come up with Annie and the twins. He looks at the blue coat Andy is wearing. Even though the coat has been lined with an old Indian blanket, and has bone buttons instead of brass army buttons, the cut and color are definitely U.S. military. "You served in the Union army?" He asks.

Andy knows that, like many of the German settlers around Fredericksburg, the Schloediers were Unionists during the recent war.

"Sorry to disappoint you, sir, but I was Confederate."

The old man's eyes narrow, and he chews his lower lip, but he only nods.

Ilsa tries a bright, but trembling smile. She knew that introducing Andy to her father would be tense, but now she also has the extra tension of Andy just now finding out that she's pregnant. "Vati, I see you've already met my new daughter."

He opens his arms to his daughter. "Oh, ja. And a beautiful one she is too."

Andy is standing in front of the hearth, watching the crackling fire. Ilsa is at her vanity. She rises, and walks over to him. "Please don't be mad at me." She begs.

He just shrugs. "When were you going to tell me about the baby?"

There is a long silence. Then, "I dunno."

He turns, and looks into her eyes. "You don't know?"

"I was gonna tell you as soon as I found out, but you were busy with the round up, an' I just kept putting it off. Then, the more I put it off the harder it was to tell you." She turns away from him, and dabs at her eyes with her nightgown. "Andy, when you left before I would have done anything to keep you from leaving. But now, well, I's afraid if you knew I's in a family way you'd think I did it on purpose just to keep you home."

"So, you were just gonna let me ride off, and not let me find out about it until I came back?"

"I'd o' told you before you left, I reckon."

He is quiet for a long time. "Well, you were right. Now that I do know I'm not sure I should leave. I could send the herd with Chico 'n' Jack and the vaqueros. I don't have to go."

She spins around. "See, you do think I did it just to keep you home. I dit'n Andy, honest I dit'n. That's why I wanted to come here, so you'd know that I's with my muti, an' you could go." She gives him a tremulous smile. "If you stayed all you could do is watch me get fat, an' waddle around like a goose, an' watch the horizon, wishing you was with you're herd. 'Sides, you'll be home 'fore he gets here."

He takes her in his arms. "He? You're carrying a son?"

She shrugs. "You already have a beautiful daughter."

He lifts her chin, and places a gentle kiss on her lips. "I already have two sons too."

"Would you care if it's another girl?"

He grins an ironic grin. "I wouldn't care, but I'd be willin' to bet Annie wouldn't like it. She's been little-miss-princess too long to share that distinction."

"Don't sell Annie short. My bet is she'd handle it just fine," she says gently.

When everyone is around the breakfast table Andy says, "Otto, I's wondering if Ilsa and Annie could stay here at the farm for a few months, until I get back off the drive in fact. He glances over to Marta. "I think she needs to be with her mother until—well, until I get back."

Marta nods knowingly.

"Of course." Otto answers. "I would love to have my Ilsa and my beautiful grand daughter here for the summer."

Annie's eyes flash up at her father, and she can feel the heat rising in her neck and cheeks. *Ilsa and Annie stay here until after the drive. No! I must have heard him wrong. He can't be thinking of leaving me behind.* She feels the tears burning her eyes as she rises from the table, and bangs the screen door behind her.

Andy shoots Ilsa a grim look, lays his fork beside his plate, and rises to follow his daughter out.

"Uhoh." Jack mutters.

Otto starts to rise, but Ilsa gently puts a restraining hand on his arm. "They need to do this alone, Vati."

Annie hears her father coming into the stable where she has run to hide. There's no way out, so she just turns her back on him.

"Annie, I'm sorry. I should have talked to you before I blurted it out."

"How can you even think of leaving me behind?" She screams. "Don't I do as much as any of the other vaqueros?"

"Yes," he admits, "you're as good o' cowboy as any of them. It's not a matter of how much you do——."

"So, it's just because I'm a girl!" she cuts him off. "I wish I *was* a boy? I can do anything a boy can do. It's not fair."

He wants to take her in his arms, and comfort her, but he senses that that would be the wrong thing to do under the circumstances. She feels vulnerable enough being female without him treating her like one.

"A very wise man once told me that sometimes what's fair ain't always what's right, and when right is stronger than fair, you go with right. You're right, it's not the fair thing, but it's the right thing."

She doesn't have an answer for this, so she just shakes her head stubbornly. "If I was your son instead of your daughter you wut'n leave me."

"Well, it doesn't matter because you *are* my daughter, but yes, I would leave you even if you were a boy, because of your age. You're only eight, Annie. If you were an eight year old boy I still wouldn't take you."

She spins around, pure blue fire coming from her eyes. "I'm almost nine. Yoni and Fritz're goin,' an' they're only twelve."

"I haven't decided if Yoni and Fritz are goin' or not, and they're closer to thirteen than you are nine.

"Whether you like it or not you are an eight-year-old girl. A cattle drive is no place for an eight-year-old girl."

"If I was thirteen would it matter?"

He hesitates, opens his mouth to speak, but she cuts him off again. "Of course it wut'n. I cut'n go if I's twenty." She strikes an over exaggerated female pose, and her voice is dripping with sarcasm. "I'm just a girl."

For a moment he wishes Jjajja Lula were here to talk some sense to her. He certainly doesn't know what to say to her. "Annie, you heard that Ilsa is going to have a baby. She needs you here to help her through that. She's counting on your help."

She gives him an exasperated look. "Oh please, Dai. Ilsa don't need my help. She came here so that Oma can help her. Besides, I know a lot more about bustin' steers than nursing a pregnant lady."

Her blunt, course speech has always been a point of contention, and now her use of the word pregnant almost stuns him. Ilsa wouldn't even say she was pregnant. She said she was in a family way.

"Well, whether you help Ilsa or not is your business, but you're not going on the drive, and if you hate me for that, too bad."

She bites her lip to fight back the tears. He must be a mind reader. She had almost shouted, *I hate you*. "I don't hate you, Dai," she mumbles.

He puts his arm around her shoulders. "You just don't like me much right now is all, huh."

She blinks back the tears. "I don't like not going with you, an' I don't much like being a girl. I'd rather be a cowboy."

"Ain't being a cowgirl good enough?"

She shakes her head. "Nope."

"Well, I wouldn't want you to be a boy. I'm quite happy with you being my daughter."

******

"Hey-yup!!" CRACK!! Julius cracks his ox-whip just to the right of his off, lead ox. He has learned the bull-whackers trade quickly, and has become fairly skilled with the whip.

He doesn't particularly like the term bull-whacker. The whip is seldom used to strike an animal. It is used mainly for direction control, telling the ox to either pull more to the right or left, depending on where it is cracked, and a talented skinner can flick a tick off an ox's ear without inflicting any pain to his animal.

Sometimes the whip, a devise with a twelve-foot cracker chained to a six-foot handle, is used to tap an ox on the neck, shoulder or flank, but a good skinner almost never has to resort to whipping his beast.

Wherever the saying, "dumb as an ox," came from I can only venture a guess. Probably from the same ignorant individual who came up with, "sweats like a pig," or "makes good horse sense." The truth is a pig doesn't have sweat glands, and a horse doesn't have good horse sense.

An ox will follow a road or trail, and even on the open range cattle will follow a path to a water tank. Without a bit in his mouth a horse is as likely to go tearing out across broken ground, or go rip-roaring through a mesquite thicket, as not. An ox will plod on at his own comfortable pace while a horse, even one pulling a wagon, will run until his heart bursts. If an ox comes to an obstacle in the road he will wait patiently until it is removed, or seek a way around it. A horse, even one pulling a wagon, will try to jump it.

Perhaps the problem is that the man is too much like the horse. The horse compliments the reckless streak in man, and both are prone to leap before they look.

The wagon train has been on the road now for a week, and has made camp on the Marais des Cygnes River.

"Friends, Romans, Countrymen, lend me your ears. I come to bury Caesar, not to praise him."

Dressed in a tunic made from an old sheet Julius postures before the men laying around the campfire, in the circle of wagons.

He is unquestionably popular with most of the men. As rough as they are, they enjoy his performances. The man who calls himself Kennesaw Mountain is spellbound. To him Julius is the smartest, most talented man he has ever known.

"The evil that men do lives after them. The good is oft interred with their bones. So let it be with Caesar."

He moves over to where Kennesaw Mountain is sprawled on a buffalo robe, and waves a dramatic hand in his direction. "The noble Brutus hath told you that Caesar was ambitious. If it were so, it were a grievous fault, and grievously hath Caesar answered it." He nods his head grimly, and then in a loud voice. "Thrice times we offered him a kingly crown. Thrice times he did refuse. Was this ambition? When that the poor hath cried, Caesar hath wept. Ambition should be made of sterner stuff. Yet Brutus says he was ambitious, and sure, Brutus is an honorable man."

When he finishes Mark Antony's funeral speech he drops his head, waves an indiscriminate hand at Kennesaw Mountain, and in a stage whisper, says, "And this, this was the unkindest cut of all."

Some of the men sit silent, with eyes glowing in the firelight, not knowing or caring that Julius had left out parts of the speech. Some rub a calloused knuckle across their eyes. Kennesaw Mountain stands, and begins to clap.

"Shakespeare, how'd you come to know all them fancy words?"

Julius trusts his new companions, but no one talks about the life they led before the plains. It's just an unspoken rule. If anyone even knows that he is from South Carolina, it's only because they recognize the unique pattern of speech.

"Oh, I dunno Mountain, I just learned 'em I guess."

"Wal, yore a caution, that's fo' shore. You ain't no fancy pants like most o' them theatre boys."

Julius grins. "Who says I'm a theatre boy?"

Smith nods to himself. *Oh, he's a theatre boy alright. Mountain is right; he ain't no fancy pants, but he's sure 'nuff a theatre boy.*

"You ever ban to the teatre, Mountain?" No one has ever been told that Oley the Swede is from Minnesota, but like Julius, his speech gives away his background.

Mountain thinks hard, like maybe it's something buried deep in his memory, then shakes his head. "No, no I ain't."

"Dan how you know dem teatre boys is fancy pantses?"

"I seen Booth onct." The man called Squint speaks up. "Before he kilt Lincoln. I don't think he was no fancy pants."

Julius smiles to himself. What would these rough drovers think if they knew that he had masqueraded as a woman, and pulled it off with astounding credibility?

"Do 'to be or not to be,'" Old Sykes says. Of the teamsters he's the only one on this trek who uses his real name. He's the wagon-master, and has known Bull McKenzie most of his life.

"Not tonight boss, I need to go kiss my boys goodnight." By now all of the men know that it has become a ritual with Julius to go check on his string of nine oxen before he turns in for the night.

"Wait up Shakespeare. I'll go with you." Kennesaw Mountain falls in beside him. At six feet nine inches, and three hundred twelve pounds he dwarfs Julius' five foot eight, one hundred thirty-eight pounds. The only other person on this trek that even comes close to his size is Oley the Swede at six-four, two hundred sixty pounds.

As they move out of the firelight they both chuckle when Pork Bottom's voice reaches them. "T' be 'r not t' be. 'At's what we be askin' ye." He's the only person on the trek who is shorter than Julius, but he is nearly as wide as he is tall.

Julius steps up to his picket line. Each drover has their own line, stretched beside or behind their wagon, and each one is responsible for their own stock.

"Hullo boys." The oxen know his voice, and low softly as he approaches. He reaches out, and scratches the curly hair between Big Jake's horns. Big Jake is a huge red Durham, who loops a long black tongue out to try and lick Julius' hand.

Julius checks each picket rope, and removes a rock where they will have to sleep. "G'night boys. See ya in the mornin'"

******

To say that the days following the Butler's arrival in Fredericksburg are strained would be an understatement. Andy and Ilsa have made peace of sorts, but there is still an uneasiness between them. She feels guilty about him finding out about her condition the way he did, and even if he isn't resentful about not knowing, he feels guilty about leaving her at a time like this. It is a subject that is carefully avoided by both of them.

As for the relationship between Andy and Annie, well, again, there is a fragile truce. Surprisingly Annie hasn't brought up the subject again, and Andy sure isn't going to open that can of worms if he doesn't have to.

Then, there is an unexplained undercurrent of tension between Otto and Ernst. When they speak about the farm they are cordial and businesslike, but there is never any affection shown between the two of them. Otto plays with the children, and Ernst plays with the children, but never together. They take their meals at the same table, but their conversation beyond "pass the potatoes" is almost nonexistent.

"Andy, can I talk to you a minute?" Andy turns abruptly at the sound of Ernst's voice.

"Sure. What's on your mind?"

"When you start up the trail I'd like to throw in with you."

Andy just nods. The request surprises him, but he is open to hear what Ernst has to say.

"I've got a few head of cattle up in Willow Creek canyon. Not many. Not enough to warrant a trail drive on my own, but if I could throw them in with your herd it might pay."

Andy is thoughtful for a few minutes. Ernst is a farmer. It is obvious that his love is the farm, growing corn and hay, and his orchards of peach and apples and pears.

"How many steers you got?" Andy asks.

"Oh, I don't have any steers, but I've got about fifty cows with half grown calves."

"Dairy cows?"

"Most of 'em 're Holstein and Friesian. Good beef cows as well as milk."

"You sure you want to do this Ernst? Don't Otto need you here on the farm? How would he feel about you leaving him just before spring planting?"

Ernst shakes his head sadly. "He'd just as soon I left. Truth be known he'd just as soon I hadn't come back from the war."

Andy searches the other man's eyes. "Because you joined the Confederate army? That the reason for the friction between you?"

Ernst shrugs. "It goes deeper than that. It seems like he blames me for my brother's death."

"Why? Because you fought for the Confederacy and your brother fought for the Union?"

"It's worse than that I'm afraid. I was with Hood at Gettysburg, and Rudy was with Hancock."

Ernst shakes his head, and the old guilt and pain flood over him as if it had happened only yesterday. As he tells Andy his story, Andy can see that he is reliving it in his soul.

"My country? My country? What is my country, Vati? What is my country? By birth I'm German, but when our family came here this country was part of Mexico, and we were supposed to be loyal Mexican citizens. Then Texas won its independence from Mexico, and we were loyal to the Republic of Texas. Then Texas became a part of the United States, and we were loyal to the U.S. Now Texas has joined the Confederacy. I am being loyal to my country, Vati. The Confederate States of America is now my country."

Otto's open hand struck like lightening, leaving a livid red mark across Ernst's cheek. "How dare you speak treason in my house? Go! Go to your traitorous Confederacy. You are no longer my son, and this is no longer your home."

When Otto left the barn in a rage Ernst dropped to his knees, and the sobs wracked his body. He didn't want to leave with a rift between him and his father. He couldn't even go to the house now, and say goodbye to his mother. He rose, and like a man in a slow dream, he pulled his saddle down, and placed it across his horse's withers.

"I hope you're happy now. You've broke the old man's heart." Ernst turned to find Rudy standing in the barn doorway. "Leave me alone, Rudy. I'm leaving. I'm leaving tonight."

"Yeah, you'll leave tonight. I'll see to that, but don't think about stopping by the Nimitz Hotel to see Sarah."

"She's my best friend, why wouldn't I see her before I go. I can't tell my own mother goodbye. Maybe Sarah will carry my love to Muti for me."

Rudy's eyes hardened, and his chest seemed to expand. "She's not your best friend. She's my fiancé, and you stay away from her."

"What's the matter Rudy? You think you can't trust Sarah?"

"Oh, it's not Sarah I'm worried about. It's you I'm not sure I can trust. I mean, after all, you are a traitor."

Without thinking, Ernst swung at Rudy. Rudy easily ducked the awkward swing, and punched Ernst in the solar plexus. Ernst went to the floor with a grunt, hugging his middle. Rudy stood over him glowering, and then something came over him, something akin to evil, and he began to hit Ernst against the ear, pounding him to the ground. His boot caught Ernst in the ribs, and then in the head. He picked up a shovel, and swung it above his head.

"Rudy!"

Rudy turned to see Marta standing in the doorway. His eyes had an eerie red glow, as if they were filled with blood. He turned back, dropped the shovel across Ernst's back. "I'm going to the Nimitz. If you try to see Sarah, I'll kill you."

Marta watched helplessly as Rudy strode past her. "Ernie, Ernie, what has happened to you? Why must you go this way?"

Ernst was still gagging for breath. "Even if I didn't join the Confederacy I couldn't stay now, Muti," he whimpered. "Vati says I am no longer his son, and this is no longer my home."

"This will be your home for as long as I live. Promise me that when this awful war is over you will come home. Things will change. Hard feelings will be forgotten."

Ernst shook his head.

"Ernie, promise me."

He looked at her, and smiled. His father was a robust man, with the strong arms and hands of a farmer, but the true strength had always been in his mother.

"Okay, I promise. I promise that I'll come back here, even if it's on my way to California or someplace. I will come back here first."

"You will come back here to stay. This is your farm."

"No, It's Rudy's. He's the eldest son. It'll be his and Sarah's."

She gave him a knowing look. "What about the place up on Willow Creek. The one you and Sarah used to go to when you were kids. The one where the little waterfall spills over the cliff when it rains?"

"How did you know about that?"

"A mother knows these things."

"Well, that was a long time ago. She's his fiancé now."

"Yes, she's his fiancé, but she's still your friend, your best friend I think you said."

He swallowed hard, shook his head to clear the confusing thoughts. He loved Sarah. He had always loved her, but *she* had always loved them both, two brothers, so much alike, but so different. He had hesitated, loving her from a distance, but Rudy had been bold, courting her, and winning her hand, while he had relegated himself to best friend status.

Well, I probably won't survive the war anyhow, he thought, *so it'll be a moot point.*

"Will you tell her I've gone, Muti?"

She stared at him for a minute, and then nodded. "Yes, I'll tell her."

He rode up to Willow Creek that evening, and made camp at the cedar-bough lean-to he and Sarah had built together.

How many years had it been? A time before she became Rudy's fiancée, before he became her brother-in-law to be.

How young they were, just a couple of kids playing house, her the mother, him the father. She had given him his first kiss here. What had happened? Why had he stepped back when Ernst stepped forward? Was it because he loved her too much, or was it that, even then, he held his older brother in awe and fear?

"Were you going to leave without telling me goodbye?"

He jumped nearly out of his skin at the sound of the voice. "Where's your horse? I didn't hear you ride up."

Sarah motioned toward a clump of mesquite a little ways away.

"How did you know I was here?"

"Where else would you be?"

"I mean—did Muti tell you I had left?"

"No, actually Rudy rode into town, got drunk, and bragged about how he had given you a lickin,' and sent you packin.'"

"Yeah, well, I guess he did that alright."

She stepped over, and looked at the purple bruise on the side of his head. She leaned forward and kissed it. "Hurts a lot I guess."

"Not so much now, thanks."

She kissed it again. "Sometimes his temper gets the best of him," she sighed.

There was an awkward moment, and then he took her shoulders, and turned her to face him. "I love you Sarah. I have no right, but I do."

She gazed into his eyes. "I know you do, Ernie."

For a long while they just stood, and stared into each other's eyes. Both at a loss for what to say, and then, without thought, and certainly not planned, their lips touched, their arms embraced each other, and like frightened birds their hands fluttered over each other, unbuttoning buttons, and yanking at loose clothing, and as the kisses rained, and the hands fluttered, love had had its way, and overtaken them before either could mount a defense.

They spent the night in the lean-to they had made together, so many years ago, and when the sun peeked over the cliff to the east, they sat by the fire, silent, almost dumbfounded at what had taken place.

Finally she stood, and fluffed her tangled hair. "I need to get back."

"What happens now?" He asked.

She shrugged. "Well, you'll ride off to the war, and I'll ride back to Fredericksburg."

"I mean after you ride back to Fredericksburg? Will you tell Rudy what happened?"

She leaned forward, and kissed him. "I've got some decisions to make first."

This pleased him. "Will you marry me when I come back?"

She gave him a sly smile. "That's one of the decisions I have to make."

When she was mounted, and ready to leave she looked around at the Willow Creek canyon, snuggled between towering limestone walls. "I've always loved this place."

"Yeah, me too. After a battle," he said, "when I return to camp, wounded and weary, I'll think about this night, and this place. It's what will get me through the war."

"You will get through the war, Ernie. You will come home. You must come home."

"Yes, I'll come home. I'll come home to see if you still love me," he said. "You do love me don't you?"

"I've always loved you Ernie." She removed the bandana from around her neck, leaned down, and tied it around his. "Here, bring this back to me."

He was silent for a minute, watching her intently. "But you still love Rudy, too," he finally said.

She bowed her head slightly, and the answer was not much more than a whisper. "Yes."

When she was gone he went back to the lean-to. He untied the bandana, and pressed it to his lips, and the emotion welled up inside of him until it made him ache. "I will come home to her," he said. "She will be mine, if I have to kill Rudy to make it so."

Andy watches enthralled as Ernst unburdens his soul. "And you came home, but Rudy didn't."

"Yeah, I rode out of Willow Creek, joined up with Hood, fought, and was wounded at Gaines' Mill, Manassas, Sharpsburg, and finally Gettysburg."

"Did you ever see Rudy again?"

Andy can tell he has struck a nerve by the haunted look in Ernst's eyes. "Yeah, we charged up Cemetery Ridge, lost thousands of men on that charge, got to the top, and held it for 'bout half an hour before we was pushed off. Bodies was everywhere, and gore. You couldn't even tell the color of some of the uniforms for the blood. I got hit in the shoulder and thigh, and a saber had skittered across my ribs. I was layin' there, bleedin' 'n' cryin,' and suddenly there was a Yank standin' above me with his bayonet raised above me. He would've skewered me too, but a mini-ball took his head off. I looked through the smoke to the top of the ridge, and a Yank soldier was lowerin' his musket. It was Rudy. He just smiled at me,

114

and then continued to chase my regiment back down the hill. Can you believe out of all those thousands of men in that battle I'd see my own brother?"

Andy nods. "Yeah, I can believe it. I believe in that kind of stuff."

I never saw him again after that. I was taken to a Yank field hospital, and eventually paroled. I asked around, and found out that he never made it back to the top of the ridge."

"He saved your life." Andy states the obvious.

Ernst just nods solemnly. He looks up at Andy with that haunted look. "I've often wondered what would have happened if the situation had been reversed. Would I have saved him?" He shakes himself as if to shake off the notion. "Well," he continues, "I was shipped back home, convalesced for a year or so, and then just stayed on. Vati and I made a peace of sorts, but I don't think he's ever really forgiven me."

"What about Sarah? Did you 'n' her ever get together?" Andy feels like he is intruding on private ground, but has to know.

For the first time a look of contentment comes over Ernst's features. "Oh yeah, she's still around, she and her son, Ernst Rudolf. We call 'im Rolf." He studies Andy's expression for any sign of shock. "He's about the same age as Annie. What is she nine or ten?"

Andy doesn't really have to struggle with the math. The boy would have been conceived about the time Ernst and Rudy left for the war.

Ernst sees the unasked question in Andy's eyes. "I used to wonder which one of us was his father, but then I decided it don't make any difference." He smiles up at Andy. "Once I settled that in my mind, I's able to ask her if she'd still marry me."

Andy returns the smile. "And she said yes, of course."

"That's one reason I need to make the drive with you. When I've sold my cattle, I'll have enough to buy the land up on Willow Creek. She'll go up there with me, but she doesn't want to come out here to live."

"How do your folks feel about the boy? I guess they know he's their grandson."

Ernst just shrugs. "Muti may suspect that he might be mine, but I'm sure Vati believes him to be Rudy's. He calls 'em Opa and Oma."

Andy stands, and puts out his hand in a handshake. "We can swing by Willow Creek, and pick up your herd on the way to the Llano."

CHAPTER 7

Pug has elected to take a passenger train from Kansas City down through western Missouri to Joplin, and then the Butterfield Stage on to Ft. Smith, Arkansas. From Ft. Smith there is a fairly good wagon road through the Nations to McAlester's trading post, but from there it's pretty much open country across the Indian Territory. Still, it will be faster than trying to angle across Kansas into Indian Territory, and it'll for sure be more comfortable. It is still only the middle of March, and the wind out on the prairie cuts right through a man.

With the wagon train making only six or eight miles a day on the trail he should get to Camp Medicine Bluffs, on the Cache River, at the foot of the Wichita Mountains, well before they do.

******

Julius pulls his buffalo coat tighter around his shoulders, and ties the wool scarf tighter around his ears. The Neosho River is in full flow, but still ice crystals float past, and he has to break the skim-ice along the shore for his team to drink.

"Hey, Mountain, I thought it was supposed to be spring." Kennesaw Mountain's team has pulled up beside Julius' to drink.

"Spring back east, maybe, but not out here." He looks at the sky. It is foreboding and black. "Looks like we might get a few snow flurries this evening."

Pork Bottom has ambled up. "Too cold fer snow, more likely a ice storm. I seen ice storms so bad, thick ice covers everything. Almost lost my team once't out here. Ice started to form on their muzzles an' they 'most smothered to death afore I could break it off. Had to tie gunnysacks over their noses to keep the ice from formin.' The weight of the ice took down trees big as Mountain's waist. Couldn't even get the wheels to turn on the wagons. Froze up tighter'n ol' Dick's hatband. The wagons looked like some kind of ice castles, solid ice from top to bottom. Woke up in the mornin,' and icicles big as my arm hangin' from the sides of the wagon; had me pinned in like prison bars. Why it was plumb scarey."

Julius chuckles. "How tight is ol' Dick's hatband anyhow, Pork?"

Pork Bottom grins. He's enjoying the attention. Usually it's Shakespeare who gets all the attention. He digs at a flea in his armpit. "Wal, they say ol' Dick had a size nine head, an' all he could buy at the haberdasher's was a size eight an' seven eights, That'd make it purty tight I reckon."

"Guess we better make camp an' try to cross tomorrow." Sykes has come up from where he has left his own team back up the trail. "I'll need to scout the river an' see can I find us a good place to cross. Be nice if'n it'd just freeze all the way over, then we could outspan 'em, and skate the wagons across."

"Ain't likely," Squint says.

"Still, it'd be nice," Sykes answers.

Julius is skeptical. "Can you really skate a wagon across a frozen river?"

Sykes gives him an incredulous look. "Wal, shore you kin. Me an' ol' Bull was haulin' a load up to Ioway once't. Cedar River froze plum to the bottom. Why we jest outspanned them oxes, locked the wheels, give 'em a big shove, an' across they went. O'course they switched ends about five times afore they got across, but they skated over slick as a whistle." He takes off his fur cap, and scratches his head, then squints at Julius to see just how far he can take this story. "Did the same thing with the oxes. They stepped out on that ice, an' their feet splayed, couldn't take one step, so we got behind 'em an' jes' started shovin' 'em. Looked like a bunch of fat ballerinas skatin' across there, sashayin' and waltzin' around."

"I'd a shore liked to seen that." Mountain says.

******

Annie looks up at the soft tap at her door. "Quien?" She's sitting cross-legged on her bunk in her bloomers and chemise. Her riding skirt, shirt and rawhide jacket are lying across the chair on the other side of the room.

Ilsa opens the door a crack, and pokes her head around. "Hi Darlin,' you already in bed?"

"No, not yet."

The herd had left at daybreak, and even though Annie had said her goodbyes with a minimum of emotion, Ilsa is worried about her. In fact Ilsa's worried about her because she showed so little sorrow or emotion. She expected her to throw a hissy-fit, as any eight-year old girl might. "May I brush your hair for you before you go to bed."

Annie flashes her a loving smile. "Sure."

As Ilsa strokes Annie's hair with the brush she says softly, "Well, I reckon they're camping somewhere up on Willow Creek tonight."

"Yeah, I reckon."

"I want you to know I understand how disappointed you are, but Annie, I agree with your father's decision whole heartedly."

Annie shrugs. "Well, if I wasn't a girl maybe I'd be campin' up on Willow Creek tonight too." She turns toward Ilsa, and her eyes are brimming with tears. "It ain't fair. I hate bein' a girl. It just ain't fair."

Ilsa takes her in her arms. "Oh Annie, honey. Don't ever hate bein' a girl. Girls are God's special creation." She holds the mirror up so that Annie can see her own reflection. "Look at my beautiful daughter. God made you the way you are. He made you a girl, an' He made you beautiful."

"He also made me a cowboy," Annie says. "He made me to love the outdoors an' campin,' an' ropin,' an' bustin' steers."

Ilsa laughs in spite of herself. "No Darlin,' your daddy made you all those things. God only made you a pretty little girl, and someday you'll thank Him because He did."

Annie smiles at her reflection. "Sometimes I like bein' a girl. I like the way I feel when boys smile at me. I like ribbons on my bloomers, 'n' I guess I like bein' purty."

Ilsa shakes her head, remembering when she was a gawky little girl, not nearly as pretty as Annie, but also remembering how she felt when boys smiled at her, or held her close at a dance, and yes, pretty, delicate things, like bows and lace on her undies.

"Anyway, your daddy told you it wud'n because you're a girl that you dit'n get to go. Rolf dit'n get to go an' he's a boy. He dit'n get to go because he's only nine."

Annie gives her a skeptical look. "Yeah, but Rolf dit'n really want to go. Did he?"

"Well, he asked Ernie if he could go with him, an' Ernie told him maybe next time, that he was too young this time."

Annie raises her eyebrows at this new information. "Yeah, but the cuates went."

Ilsa begins the process of braiding Annie's hair into a thick French braid for bed. "Well, the twins are almost teens." She turns Annie around on the vanity stool to face her. "This is just between you an' me, okay?"

"Okay."

"I dit'n want the twins to go. Your dad an' me had words over it. He almost dit'n let 'em go because of it, but they begged me, an' I relented. That might become a decision I'll regret."

Annie places her hands on Ilsa's face, and kisses her on the lips. "They'll be okay, Mom. Dai won't let anything bad happen to 'em."

TO GLORY AND BEYOND

Ilsa holds up two ribbons, a pink one, and a baby blue one. "Which one do you want in your hair tonight?"

Defiantly Annie reaches into her ribbon drawer, and pulls out a leather latigo string. "This one."

Ilsa laughs. "Not ready to give up bein' a rowdy tomboy, an' be a pretty little girl just yet?"

Annie glances over to where her too obvious clothes are laid out on her chair, ready to be slipped on again. "Guess not."

"You're not gonna sleep in your undies are you? Where's your gown?"

Annie pulls it out from under her pillow. She shoots another glance at her clothes. "No, but I's gonna go out to the privy before bed 'n' I dit'n want to wear my gown out in the yard."

Ilsa scowls at her. "Oh honey, I wish you'd use the chamber pot. I don't like you goin' out there in the dark."

"Okay, maybe I will. G'night."

"G'night baby. Don't forget your prayers."

"No'm I won't."

Ilsa turns, and starts for the door. Annie rushes over to her, and throws her arms around Ilsa's waist. Almost frantically she says, "I love you Mom. Please don't worry about—," she hesitates only a second, "the cuates."

At daybreak Ilsa is up and helping Marta with the breakfast. "You seen Annie yet Muti?" Marta shakes her head. "I guess I better go get her up. It ain't like her to sleep in like this."

As soon as she opens the door she knows something isn't quite right. Annie isn't in bed. In fact the bed is made up neatly, and on the pillow there is a note. With trembling fingers Ilsa opens the paper, and begins to read the childish, block letters.

> *Dear Mom,*
> *Please dont be mad at me. I had to go. Dont worry about me. I'll be O.K*
> *Dont send Opa after me. If you bring me home ill just run off again.*

I love you.
Annie

Ilsa folds the note, collapses onto Annie's bed. "That child!" And then she begins to sob, "My poor baby girl. Out there all alone. What's she gonna do when dark comes?"

She drops to her knees beside the bed. "Oh Lord, please watch over her, 'n' keep her safe. I know she's a headstrong little girl who thinks she's more grown up than she is, but she's just a baby. Please watch over her as one of your precious lambs."

Otto is pacing the living room with long strides, clenching and unclenching his fists. "I'll saddle up, and ride after her. If I leave right now, I can probably catch her by the time she reaches Willow Creek."

"And then what Vati?" Ilsa speaks up, "Lock her in her room until the drive's over? She says she'll just run off again, an' I know she will. Besides, she'll prob'ly catch the herd by the time you could catch her. If she left right after I tucked her in she prob'ly caught up to 'em at Willow Creek. They'll 've camped there for the night."

Otto sits heavily in his overstuffed chair, and looks up when the old grandfather clock bongs seven o'clock. "Reckon Andy'll whip 'er an' bring 'er back?"

"I never seen him whip 'er. He might bring 'er back, but not if she threatens to run away again. What would be the point?"

Otto sighs deeply, gets up, and walks out into the yard. In a few minutes Marta follows him out. "You admire her for this don't you?"

Otto spins around at the sound of the voice. "She's got spunk. Still I'm worried about 'er."

"Of course you are. We all are, but if there's a child anywhere in the world who's capable, she is."

The herd is easy to follow, even in the dark. They have left a churned up road fifty feet across. Annie rides slow, and on several occasions she rides off the trail to ride back, and cut her back-trail to see if anyone is following her. She has already made up her mind that if they come after her, or if her father takes her back, she'll run off again, and again, and again. Sure they could lock her in her room, or even chain her to her bed, but she'll find a way to get away again. The only thing she dreads is her Dai's anger when she finally shows herself.

She stops well before she gets to Willow Creek. The cattle are down for the night; in fact they'll be rising soon to begin the next days drive.

She makes a cold camp in a dry creek, and spreads her blanket out to grab a couple of hours sleep before she starts out again. She has decided that she won't ride into their camp until after they've crossed the Llano. That way they'll be two nights out, and therefore less likely to try to take her back.

She wakes when she hears the cowboy camp stirring, and decides she'd better find a good place to hide until they're well up the trail. It'd be too easy for a drag rider to drop back, and discover her. She finds a small gruta in the cliff face, or place where the roof of an overhang has shelved off, and left a wall of debris obscuring the entrance. She buckles a feedbag of oats over Kidogo's head. This'll keep him quiet for a little while. Then she finds a game trail leading to the top of the cliff.

From up here, she can see the whole valley. She sees Ol' Beast as he takes his place as lead steer, and her Dai as he rides out in front. She has a moment of panic when Fritz looks her way, and lifts his hand as if in a wave, then she realizes that he's just pushing his hat back to wipe his forehead.

This vantage point gives her a sense of grandeur. She can see the drive from point rider to drag rider. She sees Paco leave his position at drag, and ride back, almost to where she spent the night, to bring in a wandering calf, and at the same time, see Esteban, at the swing position, on the far side of the herd.

Is this what it's like for you God, watchin' the world from heaven? Are you watchin' me like I'm watchin' the herd? Can you see everything like I can? Do you know everything everybody's doin'?

She hangs her head, and feels a rush of guilt. *Are you mad at me for bein' so stubborn 'n' all? I'm sorry if you're mad at me. Please don't let Dai be too mad at me either.*

She watches for over two hours as the herd moves up the valley, and then disappears into a pass between two mountains. She looks down to where she left Kidogo, but can't see him for the brush and debris in front of the little cavern.

It's funny, here she is, a little girl in a wilderness of deep canyons, boulders and mesquite, a place where rattlesnakes, wildcats, wolves, feral hogs, and who knows what other dangers lurk, and yet she has no fear. In fact all she feels is a sense of wonder at the beauty around her.

She picks her way down the game trail, finds Kidogo just as she left him, and begins her lonely trek behind the herd. She tries to stay at least a couple of miles behind them, but several times she rides over a hill to find them just below her.

The drive has made good time today. By picking up the old military road, which stretches from Ft. Clark to Ft. Croghan, they have made it twenty miles to the point of land where the Llano joins the Colorado. There is a cantina here and a small fishing camp called Dos Rios.

Ernst rides forward from his position at point to where Andy is riding out in front of the herd. "Andy," he shouts, as he approaches. Andy turns, and waits for him. "We're only about a mile from the Slab. That's a good crossin'." He looks at the western horizon, where the sun is turning the sky orange and gold. We could cross it tonight, and camp in a meadow just the other side. That'll put us a ways up the Colorado before tomorrow evening."

Since Ernst has spent his entire life in and around these hills and mountains, Andy has come to depend on his knowledge of the country. He nods. "Whatta ya think we should do, follow the Colorado straight north 'til it turns west at the horseshoe bend, and then cross it?"

"Yeah, that's as good a plan as any. There's lots of rough country along the Colorado, especially near Eagle Canyon, but if we stay on the army road to Ft. Croghan it's just as rugged."

"I know, me an' Hawk went through Ft. Croghan back in 62, when we was takin' a herd to Ft. Worth, to the Confederate army, or thought we was takin' it to the army at Ft. Worth. We got there just to find out they'd already gone to Virginia. Had to take 'em all the way to Vicksburg."

"That when you swum across the Mississippi?"

Andy gives him a sharp glance. "You know about that?"

Ernst nods his head. Yeah, he knew about it. That's when Andy had left the Frio ranch, with Ilsa a fresh widow, to go to Mississippi, and marry Nancy. He had gone to sea then, and become a commerce raider, only to come back after four years to find his Nancy dead.

"I heard." Is all he answers.

Chepito has made a pot of son-of-a-gun stew with beef, venison, quail, yucca root, and chili peppers for supper. He is a good cocinero, and keeps a pot of frijoles and tortillas handy to go with the stew.

Andy has finally come in after making a circuit of the herd, and checked on his nightriders. He has just relaxed on his bedroll with his supper on his knees when Esteban rides into camp.

He strolls up to Andy, glancing around surreptitiously, as though he has something to hide. "Señor, a quiet word, por favor."

Andy lays his plate on the bedroll, and strolls around the end of the chuck wagon, out of hearing of the rest of the men. "Qué pasa?"

"Señor, I felt that you should know that the herd is being followed."

"What makes you think they're following us? This is a pretty well traveled road."

"No señor. Ciertamente, she follows us. I rode around her, and found where she camped last night, only a mile from the herd, and tonight she is camped on the other side of the river in a pecan grove."

Andy is incredulous. "She? You mean a lone woman is following us, and camping almost within sight of us at night."

"Not a lone woman, señor. It is your hija."

"My—!! You mean Annie? Annie is camped on the other side of the river?"

"Si señor."

Her camp is not hard to find. She hasn't tried to conceal it tonight. She has a small campfire going under a large pecan tree. She is sitting there, her saddle blanket thrown over her shoulders, and a cup of steaming liquid in her hand.

She doesn't start when she hears her father's voice come out of the darkness. She has more or less expected it.

"Annie? What are you doin' out here? Is everything alright at home?"

When she looks up at him, he can see the tears brimming in her eyes. She nods an answer to his questions, but only says, "You want some pecan tea?"

"Pecan tea?"

"Yes sir, I cracked some pecan shells 'n boiled 'em with the leaves. It's a little bitter, but it's pretty good."

He shakes his head, and smiles in spite of himself. Only his Annie would run away from home, and then offer some pecan tea when caught.

She tries to speak, but the tears flow freely now, and her voice breaks as she tries to speak around the sobs. "If you send me back I won't stay. I'll just run away again."

Andy's voice is calm. "I'm not going to send you back, Annie."

She throws her arms around his neck. "I'm sorry Dai, please don't be too mad at me."

"You're sorry? If you're sorry why'd you do it?"

Her eyes flash up at him, and then she looks down. "I ain't sorry I did it. I'm sorry you're so mad at me." She gives him a long look, chewing on her lower lip. "You can whip me if you want to."

He hugs her to his chest, and now it's hard for him to speak. He holds her away from him. "What would you suggest? That I lash you to the chuck wagon wheel, and whip you with the buggy whip?"

Her eyes are huge blue orbs, but she nods seriously. "Not you. Somebody else. One of the vaqueros."

Arriving in camp, Andy grabs her by the scruff of the neck, and marches her into the circle of light from the campfire, barely letting her feet touch the ground. "My daughter has disobeyed me. I told her she couldn't come on the drive, but she ran away from home, and followed us anyway. She has decided that her punishment should be a whipping. She wants one of you to do the punishment." He holds out a length of trace line, inviting. He doubles it over, snapping it loudly.

There is a nervous shuffling of feet as each vaquero looks around at his compadre. They're not sure if he is serious, or just joking. Several shake their heads, and walk away.

Paco looks around with a smirk. What a bunch of cobardes (cowards). If they think I'm afraid to whip her they'd better think again. If the Jefe wants someone to whip her I can certainly do the job.

He is about to step forward when he sees a movement out of the corner of his eye. The old cocinero raises the tailgate of the chuck wagon with a bang, and then, when he's sure he has everyone's attention, he makes a great show of sharpening his butcher knife on the whetstone.

Paco swallows dryly. Who knows if the old coot would actually cut your throat while you sleep? Also, he has heard that the old man carries a vile of rattlesnake venom around his neck. He could pour venom into your coffee, and no one would even know he had poisoned you.

"Señor," Chepito speaks up. "Give her to me to help in the cocina. I will work her like a Lipan squaw." He walks over, and takes the strip of leather from Andy's hand. "And if she slacks off in her duties I will lay on the strap myself."

Andy nods. "Bueno, I will leave her discipline to your discretion then."

After everyone has gone to their blankets Chico walks over to where Andy is reading his old coverless bible. "Would you really have allowed one of them to whip her?"

Andy looks at him with a sly grin. "Spare the rod, and spoil the child."

He points to where he has been reading. "Actually what it says is, 'He who spares the rod hates his son, but he who loves his son chastises him at the right time."

Chico does not share in the humorous tone. "She's not your son, she's your daughter, your very young daughter." He takes out his revolver, and twirls it on his index finger before sliding it back into his holster. "I will tell you now, the old man saved someone's life tonight. If anyone had touched the strap I'd have dropped him with a bullet to the heart."

Andy lays his hand on Chico's shoulder. "Amigo, have you ever seen me strike Annie?"

Chico shakes his head.

"And you won't. Nor will I ever allow anyone else to, but it was important for her to think I would, and it was more important for *them* to think I would."

Chico thinks for a long spell, and then says, "No amigo, this time you're wrong. I don't want to ever tell you how to raise your daughter, or sons," he adds, "but what is important is that she knows that you would never let anyone, or anything, harm her. If it is important to show the men a strong hand, so be it, but not at the expense of your daughter."

Andy just stares at him, and then slowly nods. "Gracias amigo."

Chico slaps Andy's cheek lightly. "Por nada. What do you have me around for except to keep you out of trouble."

As Annie prepares for bed under the wagon she hears a tap on the wood side. "Quien?" She asks softly.

"Chiquita, it is me, Chepito, the cocinero."

Annie sticks her head out from under the possum belly. "Yes sir?"

"Excuse me for bothering you. Did they say you were on the trail for two days?"

Annie ducks her head. "Yes sir. I was a very bad girl."

Chepito shrugs. "No importa. Have you had anything to eat?"

"Umhum, I had a bisquit and' some jerky the first day. I ate some pecans this evening, and made some pecan tea."

"Pecan Tea?" He questions.

"Uh-huh. I boiled the shells an' leaves. It was kinda bitter, but it wat'n too bad."

He raises his eyebrows. "Next time throw in some ground mesquite beans. They'll sweeten it a little."

"Thank you," She says softly, "for not letting 'em whip me, but you should have. I deserved it."

He gives her a severe glare. "Just remember, if you don't obey me, and obey immediately, I will whip you in front of everyone."

She knows he is lying; at least she thinks he is. "I won't be no trouble. I'll mind you"

He pats her head. "I know you will. Are you hungry? I found some quail eggs, and boiled them. I have two left. Would you like them?"

She feels her stomach growl at the thought of boiled eggs. "You sure?"

"Mmm, I've had all I want. If you don't eat them I'll just throw them out."

"Okay," she smiles, "I'll eat 'em."

Annie's eyes pop open when she feels something rooting at her side. It's still pitch black. At first she wonders if it's a feral hog under the wagon, then she hears a voice.

"Chiquita, get up! It's time to start the desayuno for the men."

"Desayuno?" She protests. "What time is it? I just went to sleep."

"It's nearly three o'clock. The vaqueros will be rising hungry shortly. They need full panzas to start the day. Get up, or I will lay the strap to your lazy hide."

"Ohhh," she groans. It's never really occurred to her that someone has to get up well before the men to have their breakfast ready in order for them to start the day at daybreak.

After she has ground the coffee beans, peeled the potatoes, chopped the onions, brought in more wood, and helped Chepito carve slices from last nights roast, he tells her, "Eat quickly, so that you can clean the pots before we start on the trail."

When she has finished all of her assigned chores she takes her rope, and heads in the direction of the remuda.

"Where are you going?" Chepito shouts.

She turns sharply. "To catch up Dogo, n' take my place on the herd."

He slaps his leg with the trace line. "Your place will be walking behind the chuck wagon, filling the possum belly with wood, yucca roots, and whatever you can find for food. Do you think these things magically appear in the camp at night? No, someone must gather them daily."

She looks longingly at the men catching their mounts for the day, drops her head, and mutters, "Si señor."

******

Trail Log:
Logan's Gap
2 days north of the Colorado Crossing
Saturday, March 7, 1869
When we crossed the Colorado, at the horseshoe bend, the land began to level out and dry out. The live oak and pecan groves all but disappeared, and the scattered mesquites, hackberry and scrub oak are stunted and almost bare of leaves. A tall man on a long legged horse can see right over the tops of them. There are no deep canyons here, no bluffs, no giant boulders, or acres of cap rock, looking like the crust of the earth has poked through the topsoil, as it was in the hills between our camp at The Slab and the Colorado.

Annie has been diligent in her duties as cocinera, trudging behind the chuck wagon, picking up firewood, digging up edible roots etc. Old Chepito has been true to his word, working her hard, and keeping her busy. She's been at it for a week now, and I've decided it's time for her punishment to end. I miss her, and I need her.

Anyone who thinks that a trail drive is nothing but excitement and adventure is sadly mistaken. Countless hours are spent plodding along behind slow moving cattle, who are more interested in eating the succulent new grass shoots than eating up the trail. On the other hand, anyone who thinks that a trail drive is nothing but plodding along behind slow moving cattle is also sadly mistaken. There's some new danger out there every time we saddle up. Fortunately we haven't encountered any Apaches or Comanches yet, but we're in their country now, so I've doubled the nighthawk riders. That's another reason I need Annie to start riding herd again.

Crossing the Colorado we almost lost Mateo. His horse went down in a deep pool, and he can't swim. He grabbed one of the steers by the tail to be pulled across. It worked this time, but I couldn't help but remember how Hawk had tried to ride a steer across the Mississippi, and was gored to death. I think next river we cross we may have some swimming lessons.

He lays down his journal, and walks over to where Annie is scouring the pots with sand. "Annie, I want you to saddle up, and ride point with me tomorrow."

She throws an apprehensive glance at Chepito, who grins, and nods.

"Chepito, sorry to take away your help, but I miss my daughter. I need to have her with me for a while."

The day has turned out warm, and the sun is bright. Most of the men plod along with heads bowed, and hat brims pulled low over their eyes.

Andy looks up, and shades his eyes. He squints but can only see that a rider is coming toward them. In the shimmering dust, he seems to be floating a foot above the ground, his horse's hooves pounding, but clearly visible above the brown mist below him.

"Looks like Paco," Annie shouts. "An' he's ridin' like the devil is after 'im."

When he gets nearer they can see that he's waving his sombrero, and shouting at the top of his lungs. "Cuidado, Fuego!! Es el extremo del mundo!! Even though both Andy and Annie are fluent in Spanish he switches to English. "The whole land is on fire. I think it's the end of the world!"

Two hundred yards from the herd his horse stumbles, and goes to his knees, throwing Paco over his head; but being the horseman that he is, Paco summersaults, scrambles to his feet, and begins running.

Chico, who is riding swing, spurs his horse into a gallop, but Annie has already spurred forward, and is lifting Paco up behind her saddle by the time Chico gets there. He continues on to the fallen horse.

Both Annie and Paco spin around at the report of Chico's pistol. The horse is no longer thrashing, and Chico is removing Paco's saddle and bridle.

When Andy rides forward Paco swings down to the ground, and trots up to him. "Señor, it is the fires of hell I believe, more higher than— than—." With his limited experience with the outside world he can't think of anything high enough to compare it to.

Andy realizes that he is talking about a prairie fire, which can sometimes burn with an inferno as high as fifteen to twenty feet, and travel at 60 miles an hour. "How far?"

"I don' know Señor, maybe five, maybe ten miles. As soon as I saw the smoke, I rode over the hill until I could see the flames, and then, as you can see, I ran my horse until he blew out his heart."

Andy turns to Annie. "Jita, I'm going to start a backfire. You ride to the chuck wagon, and tell Chepito to drive into the middle of the blackened area. Chico, turn the herd, and get them into the area that has already burned. We have to keep them in a tight pack, and milling, otherwise they will smell the fire, panic, and bolt right into it. If we keep our heads, the fire will burn around us, and we'll be safe."

Immediately he wheels Barak around, and races to the leeward side of the herd, swings down, and on the run begins new fires, which quickly flare, and rage to the south and west, away from the herd.

By the time Annie reaches the chuck wagon the advancing wall of flames is visible on the horizon, and the towering pillar of black smoke rises into the heavens, turning the mid-day brightness into the darkness of Hades.

Chepito, being forward, and to the east of the herd, has already turned the wagon away from the flames, and is bouncing across the rough ground, back toward the herd.

Paco, still behind Annie's saddle, shouts in her ear, "Get in the wagon. Take down the canvas, soak it with water from the water barrel, and get under it! Don't come out for any reason until the fire has passed. He reaches around her, and grabs the reins, swinging Kidogo right behind the wagon. "Jump!" He screams. She kicks her left foot free of the stirrup, and leaps across onto the wagon bed. She doesn't try to unfasten the canvas covering; she just pulls her Bowie knife, and hacks the latigos loose. Paco has kicked the top off of the water barrel, and is sloshing bucket after bucket of water on her and the canvas. "Estancia debajo allí, Annie. Lo significo." (Stay under there, Annie. I mean it!)

Turning the herd isn't too hard; they have smelled the smoke, and seen the fire in front of them, and have turned on their own. Getting them to go into the still smoldering, hot-under-foot, smoke-smelling burn is more difficult. They reach the charred ground, and try to turn away from it, and go to the yet unburned grass on either side. The cowboys have created a corral of sorts by tying their lariats to each other's saddle horns, riding forward, and literally pushing the herd into the burned over area. Andy rides forward, drops a loop over Beast's horns, and drags him, bawling and slobbering into the safe area. The rest of the herd reluctantly follows their leader.

Annie can hear, and feel, the fire burning right behind them now. She peeks out from under her covering of wet canvas, and sees the flames towering above the tailgate like some gigantic red, orange and black tidal wave, fixing to break right over their heads, and then it just disappears, and the ground around them is already black. She looks out, and can see the cattle milling. She sees the cowboys holding them with their rope corral, and the fire raging on all sides of their little charred island of safety. Within minutes the fire has passed them, and is racing away to the west.

Andy subconsciously counts heads. "Where is Annie?" He shouts.

Her little soot-smudged face comes out from under the canvas, and peeks over the wagon side. "I'm here, Dai. I'm alright."

"Is everybody okay? Did we lose any stock?"

Chico rides up to him. "We lost a couple of horses from the remuda, and four calves were trampled. Old Eloy has some minor burns, and Mateo took a horn in the calf, but it's not bad. Other than that all is bueno."

Andy takes off his hat, and kneels in the soot. The rest of the cowboys begin to dismount, and kneel around him. The last to do so is Paco. He doesn't kneel, but he does remove his sombrero, and stands quietly.

When he is finished praying silently, Andy goes over to Paco. "You know amigo, when you came in you were screaming that you thought this might be the fires of hell. In a way you weren't too far off the mark. The fires of hell are raging all around us, but Jesus has already started a backfire for us when He took our sins on himself at the cross. Alls we have to do is believe that he did this for us, and move into the area he has already burned for us. We just have to trust him, that if we move ourselves, and our loved ones, and our herds into the island of safety that he has created, well then, the fire will burn all around us but not be able to touch us."

Chepito steps forward. "Señor Jefe, I would come into this island of safety you speak of, but I fear that I am a very bad man. I have done all of the things the priests of my youth have said that I should not do."

Andy walks over to Barak, and takes a beat up old, coverless bible out of his saddlebag.

"You know of San Pablo, Chepito?" He says as he finds the passage he is looking for.

"Oh si señor. He is un hombre del biblia."

"Well, let me read you what San Pablo had to say about that." As he reads he tries to translate it into simple everyday Spanish that Chepito will have no trouble understanding.

"He is writing to his friends in Rome because they felt, as you do, that they had to be right with God before they could receive forgiveness, and he says: '*But God showed His great love for us by sending Christ to die for us while we were still sinners. And since we have been made right in God's sight by the blood of*

Jesus, he will certainly save us from the judgment. For since we were restored to friendship with God by the death of His Son while we were still His enemies, we will certainly be delivered from eternal punishment by His life.' Do you understand what all of that means Chepito?"

Chepito thinks about it for a while, and then says. "I believe, señor, that he is saying that I am still his friend, even though I have not kept the priests commandments, that I need not fear the judgment."

Andy smiles. "Well, they're not the priest's commandments; they're God's commandments. The priests just remind you of them."

Paco has been silently listening, and now speaks up. "So, what you are saying is that I can continue to be a sinner, and receive this forgiveness?"

"Let me read you something else San Pablo says to the Romans: *'So, since God's grace has set us free from the law, does this mean we can go on sinning? Of course not.'* When you come into the island of safety that Jesus has made with his blood you must leave the flames of hell outside. If the fires can still burn there, what good is it?"

"So," Paco persists, "if I enjoy doing my sins, and don't want to give them up, then I can't receive the forgiveness?"

"If you will believe, and come into the island of safety, Paco, you won't enjoy your sins anymore. You will still sin sometimes, but the shame of doing them will keep you from enjoying them. When San Pablo says, *'we will certainly be delivered from eternal punishment by His life'* he is saying that his life, the life of Jesus, comes into your body as your own life, and if Jesus was unable to sin, you will be unable to sin." And then he adds, "and enjoy it."

"Señor Jefe," Chepito asks, "what must I do to have this life of Jesus in me so that I will no longer enjoy my sins?"

"Just ask him, Chepito. That's all, just ask him."

Chepito shakes his head. "I'm afraid I've never been much of a praying man, Señor Jefe. I haven't been in the church since I was a child."

"No la hase, Viejo. (It doesn't matter, old-timer.) Shall I help you pray?"

The look in Chepito's eyes can only be described as gratitude and affection. "Would you do that señor?"

Andy lays his hand on the old cocinero's shoulder. "Father, this here's Chepito. He hasn't followed your Son in his life. In fact, he has sinned most of his life. He knows he's a sinner, and he wants to ask Jesus to forgive his sins. He knows that he will probably sin again, but he asks that his life will become that of Jesus, and that from now on his sins will make him cry from shame." He looks up to see that Chepito's eyes have never left his, and are glowing. "Is that correct, Chepito? Is that what you want to pray?"

"Señor, that is exactly what I wish to pray. Thank you for helping me. Will you pray with me again, and teach me to speak with God the way you do?"

"Any time, Viejo. Any time."

When Andy puts his hat back on, and starts to walk away, he sees that Paco has already mounted, and is riding away. He shakes his head in sorrow. Some will come, and some will not, but his job ends with the telling; the rest is up to God.

He turns to find Barak, and nearly walks into Annie. She is standing with her arms up, the way she did when she was only two or three. He lifts her up, and she throws her arms around his neck. "I love you so much Dai."

CHAPTER 8

Camp Medicine Bluffs is a raw community of Sibley tents, two-man shelter halves, and a few wickiups hastily erected on the open prairie. There is no hotel or restaurant, but there is a sutler's tent where a man can buy weapons, ammunition, tobacco and whiskey, and there is a soddy, with no windows, dug into a clay bank, which is used as the military jail. The only other residences are the Kiowa and Southern Cheyenne villages stretched along Cache and Wolf creeks.

Pug has purchased a wigwam from a Shawnee brave for a stainless steel mirror, a twist of tobacco, and a colorful saddle blanket. The brave says that for his Irish-green derby, he will throw in an iron cooking pot, and one of his squaws; Pug declines, maybe for another saddle blanket, but not his green derby.

He is sitting at one of the plank tables outside the sutler's store when a black sergeant rides up, flips his reins over the hitching rail, and strides into the sutler's. "Hey Marlow, the wagon train with all the building material is camped on Big Beaver, should be coming in 'bout noon tomorrow I 'spect."

"Bout time," Marlow answers. "Now maybe I can build a real store."

"Wouldn't count on it," the sergeant says. "Most o' them supplies is for building the fort stockade and barracks. You'll be lucky if ya kin buy enough lumber to put a deck under yore tables out front."

Daylight finds Pug sitting his horse on a small rise overlooking the trail from McAlester's trading post. Below him an impressive sight stretches out for at least three miles. The freight wagons in this train are ten feet high from the axels to the bows, and the wheels are nearly six feet in diameter with six inch wide, hard rubber, tires; each is pulled by nine oxen, yoked three abreast. Pug watches as the first wagon passes. The skinner is a fairly nondescript man, a wide brimmed flop hat is pulled low across his forehead, and a scraggly gray beard covers his face. Pug figures he is the wagon master because he's at the lead wagon, and the only one mounted. Not his man. He watches as it passes, and scans the next in line, also not his man. This man is short, but sports wide shoulders and a huge beer belly. Pug unconsciously smiles. *I'd like to see him pass himself off as a woman, even a big fat, ugly woman.*

As the wagons pass, Pug begins to get discouraged. Except for two giants, most of the men look pretty much the same. Same dusty trail-worn clothes, same beard covered faces, same shambling walk, and then the last wagon in line comes in sight. There's nothing in particular that would set this man apart from the others. He has shabby trail clothes, heavy winter coat, slouch hat and beard the same as they, but even shuffling along beside the oxen he carries himself with a certain grace.

Pug watches as Julius grasps the whip handle in both hands, swings the twelve-foot leather popper around his head once, and with a backlash cracks it above the heads of his oxen with a report that sounds like a rifle shot. "Haw Rube, haw a little," he calls.

A strange feeling of admiration comes over Pug, and it's not the first time since he started tracking Julius. *He's like a chameleon the way he adapts to his surroundings, and his movements are like a graceful dancer.*

Sykes leaves his oxen to plod down the trail on their own, and rides back down the line of the train, stopping to speak to each man as he passes.

"Hey Mountain," he shouts in a too loud voice. "Everything goin' okay?" When he gets within soft voice range he says, "You got yore gun handy? It may be nothing, but there's a guy sittin' a horse up on the ridge to the left. Just keep yore eyes peeled, and stay alert."

The man known as Kennesaw Mountain walks back to the water barrel on the side of his wagon, takes off his hat, and pours water over his head.

In his peripheral vision Pug sees the giant go to his water barrel, but his attention is on Julius, so he misses it when the man takes a revolver out of the toolbox on the side, and tucks it into his waistband.

Sykes moves on down the train, stopping to speak to each man, as though this were a routine supervision.

"Hey Shakespeare, don't look up but there's a man up on that bluff watching us. He may have a gang hiding down the road to bushwhack us, or he may just be a curious farmer. Just the same, keep yore weapon handy an' yore eyes open."

Julius doesn't have to look up to know who the man is. He knows it's the Pinkerton man whose been chasing him. What he doesn't know is whether to tell the rest of the crew. If they were going to camp again tonight he would definitely tell them, and enlist their help in trying to escape in the dark, but they will be at Camp Medicine Bluffs in the early afternoon. The thought comes to him that even if they did camp on the trail one more night, and he did escape it wouldn't matter; the Pinkerton would just hound him until he either captured him, or one killed the other. Which would be easier, capture or death. Of course capture would probably mean death. He's sure that if the Federal government is this determined to catch him after all this time they will try him, and hang him as a spy. Probably better to call this guy out at Medicine Bluffs, and finish it once and for all; he's pretty good with a side arm. He'll have to figure out a way to make it self-defense, though. It wouldn't do to rid himself of this lawman just to saddle himself with another.

As Pug watches the last wagon fade into the dust of the road he has a decision to make. Does he just gallop in there firing away, and probably have to take on the whole train, or does he confront Principe at Camp Medicine Bluffs, and probably still have to take on the other teamsters. There is one other alternative, of course. Ride on down the road, and pick him off from ambush. It's something to think about. Congressman Butler and the committee who hired him made it perfectly clear that they didn't care whether Principe, or the others, were brought in alive or killed trying to escape. Too bad they wouldn't supply him with wanted posters on them. He likes plain, straightforward law work, not all this cloak and dagger, political, mumbo-jumbo. He's not even sure that what they are hiring him to do is legal. Who are they, after all, but a bunch of political hacks looking for revenge. They made it fairly clear that President Johnson was in favor of leniency for the rebels, but what about President Grant. Isn't he one of the Radical Republicans who is crying for accountability? Yep, he's on shaky ground, sure enough. He can't even count on assistance from the camp Provost Marshall. All he can do is show his credentials, make a credible bluff, and hope the Provost Marshall isn't a confederate sympathizer, like the U.S. Marshall in Louisiana.

When the wagon train pulls into the makeshift freight yard under the granite mountain called Medicine Bluffs you'd think the circus had come to town. Soldiers, whiskey drummers, gamblers, camp followers, Indian braves and squaws, and a passel of dogs chase after it, each yipping its own form of joyous welcome.

Now it's only a tent city with a few scattered soddies, but with these new building materials and supplies, in a few short months, it will become a new frontier fort called Fort Sill.

******

Trail Log:
Brazos Crossing

Saturday, March 14, 1869

Beast almost never stops once he's taken the trail. In fact it could be said that he attacks his responsibilities as lead steer with the pride of a professional. He allows his herd to move slow enough to graze when there's fodder, and when there's not he moves them down the trail at a fast clip, sometimes outpacing the point riders.

Charlie Goodnight boasts that he has the best lead steer in the business with his lead, Ol' Bluey, and also claims that he's never seen a better swimmer.

Well, Ol' Bluey might be a good swimmer, but he's never swum the Mississippi River. Beast has. Twice.

Yes, It is good for a trail boss to have a reliable lead steer, and I'm glad Goodnight thinks he has one, but, although Beast may be the ugliest animal I've ever seen, I wouldn't trade him for two Ol' Blueys.

True, he almost never stops once he's taken the trail, but he stopped today. Not only did he stop, uncharacteristically, he turned back into the herd, his loud bellowing causing much confusion.

I had to ride in, drop a loop over his horns, and drag him away before he caused a stampede. When I left him tied to one of the oaks along the creek he was moaning and fllingin' slobbers with every shake of his head. I said he was a great lead steer, and a good swimmer. I never said he was brave.

Sitting their horses on the ridge in front of them, there is a small party of Indians. Their long black hair is streaming in the breeze, and feathers and tufts of hair flutter from lances, shields and bows. This plus the strong scent of strange humanity blended with bear grease is enough to put uncontrollable panic into Beast's bovine heart.

Chico has ridden up from his swing position behind Andy. "Hey amigo, we got company."

"Yeah I see 'em. How 'bout going back, and alert the rest of the men. Make sure they're ready for an attack, and have them hold a tight rein on the herd. This knot head's got 'em all riled up now."

As they are talking one of the braves rides forward, holds up his hand, palm forward; sign language for friend. Andy returns the sign, and the man advances toward him.

"Howdy." The Indian grins. He's wearing a confederate forage cap, a pair of leggings cut from gray pants with a gold stripe down the leg, a breach clout covering these, and a wolf pelt covering his shoulders. The hair on top of his head is cut in a roach, but long, thick braids fall down his back.

"Name's Kilakeena Poteau." He says in a comfortable southern drawl. "Kilakeena means *the buck* in Tsa'la'gee, so most folks just call me Buck."

Andy leans forward in the saddle, extending his hand. "Andy Butler."

Buck Poteau motions toward either the U.S. brand on Barak's flank, or the blue uniform coat tied behind Andy's saddle, or both, and asks, "Yankee army?"

"Naw, I was a Rebel." Andy confirms. He pushes his lips and chin out in the Indian manner of pointing, toward the outlandish half-Confederate, half-Indian outfit Buck is wearing. "And you?"

"Confederate sergeant, General Watie's outfit." Andy knows that Stands Alone Watie was the Cherokee Brigadier General who led many Cherokee, Creek and Choctaw soldiers against the Federal army in eastern Oklahoma and Arkansas.

He motions toward the band of Indians waiting on the ridge. "They don't much look like Tsa'la'gee." He repeats the Indian name for Cherokee. He doesn't intend for his tone to sound accusatory, but to his own ear it seems to come out that way.

"No. No sir, they're not. They're Kiowa. Sir, we don't mean you no harm. It's been a real hard winter. My village is starving."

Andy turns in his saddle, and shouts to Annie, who has been waiting back by the herd. "Jita, pronto, go back, and tell Chepito to make supper for about a dozen guests, and you stay, and do what you can to help him." He turns back to Buck Poteau. Bring your band in, and then, when they've eaten, we'll cut out a few head for you to take back to your village."

Annie smiles at Buck Poteau as she piles a second helping of stew onto his plate. "There's more in the pot," she offers.

He nods a thank-you to her, and goes on with the story he is telling Andy, Ernst and Chico. "Yeah, I guess you might call me a missionary to the Kiowa. My pa was the Headmaster at the mission school at Ft. Gibson. I was gonna be a teacher there, but then the war started, and I joined up with General Watie.

While I was a student, before the war, I met, and fell in love with a Kiowa girl. When I came home, I found out she had returned to her people. It was about that time I heard the call to missions among the savages." He grins over at one of the braves. "My brother-in-law. His mother named him Hears a Loud Wind, but I say his name is Makes a Loud Wind. He still thinks it's okay to raid white settlements, take scalps, torture captives, and blow his nose with his fingers, but he doesn't think he's a savage. Isn't that so Boomer?"

The young Kiowa brave smiles, but makes a hand sign that Andy takes as an obscene gesture.

Buck shakes his head. "See what I mean. I can't learn him anything."

******

Trail Log:
Old Ft. Belknap
Monday, March 16, 1869
I allowed Buck to hold services in camp on Sunday. He asked me if that would be possible and I, of course, told him it would be great. I'm afraid I've been a little lax in holding any kind of services on Sundays, that being just another day on the trail, starting at sunrise, and ending at dusk. In my defense though, I have been diligent in beginning each day with prayer, and ending it the same way, asking God for guidance, and protection for the men and herd, and I believe that Buck showing up is an answer to prayer. Not only has he reminded me of my duties as a Christian leader, but also he has assured me that for as long as we are in his territory we will be safe from raids from

other tribes. *The Comanche, who are allies with the Kiowa, will honor his treaty with me, and the Lipan will be afraid to attack us for fear of retaliation by the Comanche or Kiowa.*

His sermon was on the 23rd Psalm this morning, and again, it helped remind me that even without the Kiowa watching over us, God's eyes are always on us. "Even though I walk through the valley of the shadow of death I will fear no evil for thou art with me." *I'm not so naïve that I don't realize that God works in mysterious ways, and that His way of protecting us, or being with us, may very well be Buck and his Kiowas. At any rate I'm happy for their presence.*

His Kiowas sat in rapt attention at everything he said, and most of my vaqueros listened attentively, but when he talked about repentance of sins Paco got up, and walked away. I fear that this is a problem I'll have to address before the drive is over. Ever since the prairie fire he seems to be getting worse. It's almost as if he's challenging God's authority over him. The day he challenges mine or Chico's authority is the day he leaves the drive.

This morning we cut out a few head of cattle here at old Ft. Belknap for the Kiowa. After we had separated them from the herd, and moved them off a bit the Kiowa rode in on their horses, killing like they were on a hunt, driving lances into their prey, and felling them with bows and arrows. When the ground was littered with their bodies the squaws moved in with their skinning and butcher knives. They have feasted all evening on beef, until they groan with being so full. What they don't eat tonight they will jerk and dry, and some of it they will pound into a mixture of berries and tallow for pemmican.

It would seem that it would be wiser to only kill a beef at a time, as they need it, and keep the rest for later, but that's not the Indian way.

Ernst pulled Buck aside, and gave him two Friesian cows and one young bull for his own family (a very pretty young squaw and 2 papooses), and made him promise not to let the braves slaughter them. He showed Slinking She Wolf, Buck's wife, how to milk the cows, and told Buck that with these starter cattle he can build a herd of their own.

I don't envy Buck his chore of taming these savages. He has shown them the light of the Gospel, but he has a long way to go to civilize them.

******

Yoni looks up at Annie's cry of outrage, watches her fist fly through the air, and strike Paco against the ear. When she rushes past him her eyes are flooded with tears. He looks from her to Paco, and then back at her as she throws herself onto her bedroll.

He ambles over to stand above her. "What's the matter querida? What did he say to you?"

She jerks around, turning her back on him. "Nothin,' leave me alone!"

"Come on, Annie. He must've said something to make you so mad." He kneels down beside her and cradles her in his arms. There has always been a familiarity between them that almost goes beyond sibling affection. "What was it? You can tell me."

She just shakes her head. "I can't."

"Annie, you an' me are tal para cual. You can tell me anything. You know that."

She sniffs loudly, but still doesn't look at him. "Not this. It's too vile."

He kisses her on top of the head, and rises. Annie has never been one to shy away from coarse language. If Paco said something to her that she won't repeat, it must be bad. He walks over to where Paco is squatting beside the fire.

"What'd you say to my sister?"

Paco looks up with contempt. "Nothing that concerns you."

"Anything that makes her cry concerns me."

"If you're so concerned go ask her."

"I did. She wouldn't tell me. She said it was too vulgar to repeat. I'm askin' you."

Paco looks around at the other vaqueros. If he refuses to tell what he said it will appear as though he is backing down before this large German boy. Even though he is fifteen, and the German boy is thirteen, they are almost the same size.

"Very well, Aleman, she's always trying to prove how grown up she is.

I told her that if she wants to be such a mujer she should meet me out on the prairie tonight, and I would give her a few free lessons on becoming a true woman."

Yoni suspects that this is pretty much what Paco conveyed to her, only, maybe in more vulgar language. He steps forward, his fists balled. "You dirty little-. I'm gonna-."

Paco reaches into his waistband, and draws a spring-blade knife. It whispers, and snicks with a metallic click when the stiletto blade flashes out. "You're gonna do what, Aleman?"

Yoni reaches down, and picks up a cedar club from next to the fire. "I'm gonna bust your calabaza, that's what."

About this time Chico steps into the firelight. "Que pasa aqui?"

Yoni drops the club into the fire. "Nothin,' just a little disagreement is all."

Chico steps between the boys, and his hand shoots out like a striking rattlesnake, grabbing Paco's wrist in a vice like grip. He twists until the knife drops to the ground. "I will tolerate no knife play in this camp, Paco. Do you understand me?"

Paco glares into Chico's eyes, but only nods.

******

Trail Log:
Near the town of Henrietta
Thursday, March 19, 1869
The Kiowa are still with us, however we seldom see them. We can usually see their dust over the rise as we move along, but they never camp with us. Buck has ridden over a couple of times to visit, and drink coffee. He left the women, children and old men back at their camp near old Ft. Belknap. It's a little sad to see a grand old fort like Belknap abandoned to the elements. Most of the buildings are still sound, but in five years some of the roofs have collapsed.

Buck says he is hoping to get them all to settle there. His dream is to establish a mission and school there, but the Kiowa are a nomadic people, used to following the buffalo herds. The term "settle down" is not in their vocabulary.

The town of Henrietta was also all but abandoned about six years ago. The Indian raids became so severe during the war that the settlers moved closer to Ft. Worth for their safety. The only residents now are a few buffalo hunters, and what looks to me like hard men on the run from the law. Even with Buck's band near by I've doubled the night watches again. I keep at least six men in the saddle all night, and Chico and I stay in the saddle for twelve to fourteen hours a day.

"Hey amigo," Eloy has ridden into an arroyo, out away from the herd, to light a cigarillo. In the dark the flare of a match can sometimes spook a resting herd. Paco rides up beside him. "Give me a soplo."

Eloy hands over the cornhusk cigarette.

"What would you say to a cerveza?"

Eloy snorts a laugh. "And where would you get a cerveza out here?"

"There. There is a town. Where there is a town there must be a cantina."

Eloy looks around nervously. "What you speak of is risky. The jefe would probably do no less than flog us if we were caught. He was willing to flog his own hija for disobeying him, and Chico may even shoot us."

"Ah! Who would miss us? We would only be gone for an hour or so. Would they miss you if you went up the arroyo to relieve yourself?"

"Still, I don't know—."

"Suite yourself. If anyone asks where I am tell them that I went over the ridge to look for some strays."

"Well, how many perdidos will you be looking for?"

"Oh, in truth, more than one man can bring back alone."

Eloy looks around again. "Well, I guess if these perdidos have wandered toward the town we must go over there to look for them."

The town is not much of a town. Most of the houses are boarded up. There is one building, however, which is still very active. Of course, it is the saloon.

Paco and Eloy walk in, and Paco slaps a coin on the counter. "Two cervezas por favor."

The bartender looks around at the three or four other men in the room, and laughs. "Where you think you're at? Ft. Worth? We ain't got no cervezas here."

"Ah well then, what about mescal. Do you have mescal?"

One of the men moves from a table in the corner, picks up the coin, and drops it into a spittoon. "I don't drink with greasers."

Eloy starts to hustle toward the door. "Come, Paco, we'd better get back to the herd."

Paco reaches into his waistband, and pulls the spring-blade stiletto out, sticking it into the plank, which serves as the bar. "I wasn't inviting you to drink with us, Señor. My friend and I were just going to have a quick drink together before we go back out to the herd."

The man looks at the stiletto, then at Paco, and then slowly and deliberately draws his side arm, and fires point blank into Paco's chest.

Eloy bangs through the batwing doors, and mounts his horse on the run.

"Cuidado! Asesinato!" He yells as he rides into camp. Andy is out riding, and Chico has just come in. "Chico, Paco has been murdered in the town."

"Murdered? Murdered in the town? What were you doing in the town?" Chico rages.

Eloy snatches off his hat, and his eyes plead for mercy. "We were searching for strays that wandered over that way, and we decided to stop at the cantina for a quick drink. We only wanted one. We weren't going to stay long."

"What happened? How was he murdered?"

Eloy shakes his head. "Paco didn't like something the man said, and pulled his knife. He didn't try to start a fight, just stuck it in the bar top, and the man shot him dead."

"Where is Paco now?"

"He's still there. I ran."

"What did the man look like who shot him?" By this time Chico is strapping on his holster, with his Walker colt and a replica of the knife that Jim Bowie made popular.

"He was white."

Chico takes in a deep breath and lets it out slow. Nobody ever said Eloy was bright. "Most of the men in this area are white, Eloy."

"No," Eloy says, "I mean he was very white, like the belly of a sapo, and he had white hair, more white than the jefe's, and his eyes were of a strange color, almost like color de rosa."

"He was an albino?"

Eloy just shrugs. He has never seen an albino, so doesn't know what one is supposed to look like. "Do you wish for me to go back with you, and identify this man?"

Chico lays a hand on his shoulder. "No primo. I wish for you to be gone when I return. If you are still here when I come back there will be sad consequences."

Eloy knew that Chico's punishment would be harsh. He drops his head, and almost sobs. "Bien Chico."

When Chico rides down the main street of what's left of Henrietta he sees Paco's horse tethered to the hitching rail, and his body lying in the road, outside the saloon.

He kneels down to touch the body, and Paco's eyes flutter. "Chico," he whispers, "they shot me, and then just threw me in the street. Am I going to d-?" His eyes go blank, his body becomes rigid, and then his bladder and bowls give way.

Chico, strolls into the bar, his spurs jingling.

"Well, would you look at that." The albino says from his table in the rear. "Another Mex. I thought we run all the Mexes out of Texas at San Jacinto."

"So, now you show your ignorance. I'm not a Mexican. I'm a Texan of Spanish decent, as was my father, and his father before him. My own father died defending the Alamo, and the son of my wife's aunt was Capitan Juan Seguin, a man decorated by none other than General Sam Houston. And where did you fight the invader of Texas, Señor?"

The albino's eyes go steely. "I did'n fight—. Anyway it ain't none o' yore business who I fit or when. But like I tol' yore friend, we don't serve greasers in here. You ain't welcome."

"Well, I didn't come here to be served." Chico strolls over to the table. "Are you the man who killed my vaquero?"

"I shot him, when he pulled a knife on me."

"So then, it was a fair fight."

The man laughs. "As fair as it gets when a stupid Mex brings a knife to a gunfight."

"Ah, then I take it you don't care for knife fights." As he says this his left hand draws the Bowie knife, and stabs it into the tabletop. Immediately the albino's hand drops to his own weapon, but he's too late. While Chico's left hand was stabbing the knife into the table, his right hand was pulling his colt, and now the barrel is against the albino's forehead. The albino slowly raises his hands, and lays them on the tabletop.

"It would seem that you don't like gunplay either, unless of course, you have the drop on your victim." He twirls the revolver on his index finger, and flips it into his holster, and in that instant of distraction his left hand shoots toward the knife, and with a downward chop he severs the first two fingers from the albino's right hand. "Maybe that will slow you down when you think about squeezing a trigger in the future. Consider yourself lucky my friend. I came here to kill you."

The other men in the room are momentarily immobilized by shock, but not so Chico. He has, again, drawn his pistol, and fires into the mirror behind the bar. "Are there any others so foolish as to try me, either with the cuchillo or the pistola?"

Most of the others in the room are buffalo hunters, not gunfighters. One man is examining the albino's maimed hand, and more than a few have just disappeared out windows and back doors.

Andy stands by the fresh mound of dirt on the prairie, and stares down into the raw hole, his old coverless bible in his hand. He has searched the scriptures for something appropriate to say over the grave, but nothing comes to mind.

Yoni takes the bible from his hand, flips through the pages, and reads, *"cursed is the ground for thy sake; in sorrow shalt thou eat of it. Thorns and thistles shall it bring forth to thee when thou hast returned unto it. For dust thou art, and unto dust shalt thou return."* He turns to Mateo and Esteban, who are standing by with shovels. "Cover him up," and he turns, and walks away. Andy just shakes his head, and wipes at a tear running down his cheek.

Annie slips her hand into his. "Why are you so sad, Dai? He wasn't a very nice boy. He said nasty things to me, and even tried to get me to go into the bushes with him."

Shock and pain register on Andy's face at the news that a young man twice her age had propositioned his eight-year-old daughter. "Oh Annie, I—!"

She misreads his concern as accusation. "I dit'n go, Dai. Honest I dit'n."

He wraps his arms around her, and hugs her to him. "Oh, I know you didn't, honey. I know you're too good a girl, and too smart to do something so stupid."

"Then why are you so sad that he got killed? He prob'ly did somethin' to make that man kill 'im."

"Annie, I'm sad because he never received God's forgiveness by believing that His son came to take away his sins. He died lost in his sins."

"Is he in hell then?"

Andy shrugs his shoulders. "Only God knows for sure, honey."

"But you think he is."

"I'm sad because I believe he might be, and that maybe I didn't do all that I could to show him the right way."

"Dai, I believe that Jesus came to take away my sins. Does that mean that I can go to heaven instead of hell, even if I'm bad sometimes?"

Andy gives her a loving smile. "Have you told God that you believe in His son, and thanked Jesus for taking away your sins?"

"Yes sir. I did it when Chepito did, after the fire, but I dit'n say it out loud, just in my head."

"Then yes, querida, you can know that you will go to heaven, and not hell when you die."

"Even If I'm still bad sometimes?"

"Yes, mi amor. Even if you're still bad sometimes, but remember what I told Paco, when you tell Jesus that you believe that he died to save you His Spirit will enter you, and then when you do bad things it will make you so sad that you won't want to do them anymore."

"But even if I don't want to be bad, and do something bad anyway, am I still forgiven?" she persists.

"Yes, you're still forgiven, but after you've done something bad you'll be very sorry that you did it, and you'll be careful not to do it again."

She nods. "Dai, how come God still loves us, even when we're bad."

He lifts her up, and holds her close to him. "Well, I guess it's like the way I love you. I love you because you're my daughter, and I know that you don't like to hurt your mom an' me, but sometimes you just think you know better than we do what's best for you."

"I'm glad you love me like that. I don't want to be bad, but sometimes I just cain't help myself."

Andy just nods. "Yeah, I know what you mean."

Chico walks up to where Yoni is standing by the chuck wagon. "That was a little harsh."

Yoni just shrugs. "Life is harsh. If he'd stayed with the herd last night, like he's s'posed to, and kept on botherin' my sister I'd o' killed 'im myself."

CHAPTER 9

With stacks of lumber, kegs of nails, and piles of other building material it's not difficult for Pug to steal through the shadows of night across the freight yard to the tall wagons. He hears the teamsters talking, and laughing around their campfire. They are beginning to break up now, and wander off to their own wagons to bed down for the night. When he hears Principe approach his oxen, and speak to them, he takes the Kerr .44 out of his pocket. Walking in the dark, Principe nearly bumps into him.

"You're a hard man to pin down, Julius; or are you someone else today?" Pug says, sticking the .44 in Principe's ribs.

"Who are you, and whadda you want with me?" Julius responds.

"Oh, come on, Julius. You know who I am, and what I want with you."

"I know you used to be Security Service, but why are you chasin' me after all this time? The war's been over five years."

"Name's Mahone. Pug Mahone. Let's just say that there's a group of powerful men in Washington who want to see you tried for treason."

"A group of powerful men; not the government."

Powerful politicians, government, it's all the same to me."

"You know alls I gotta do is yell out, and my friends will be on you in a heart beat."

Pug smiles, but in the dark it's lost on Julius. "Not your heartbeat. The minute a sound comes out of your mouth, you're dead. You see I get paid whether I bring you in dead or alive, and when your friends rush in here a few of them will go down as well. You don't want that."

Suddenly there is a loud crack, and Pug feels his hand go numb. He looks down; his Kerr is lying on the ground, and a long lash encircles his wrist. Before he can speak, or react, he is jerked off his feet by the lash, and one of the teamsters is standing above him, holding the handle of the whip like a club.

"Stay where you're at, 'n' I won't bash out your brains." Sykes says. "What's this all about?"

"He's a bounty hunter." Julius speaks up. "He says he's arrestin' me for espionage."

"You were a Reb spy in the late war?" Sykes asks.

"I worked for the Confederate government, behind enemy lines sometimes."

Sykes is thoughtful for a time. "Well, it don't matter. How much head start you need?"

"All I can get, but I'll settle for twelve hours or so."

"Okay. I'll turn him loose after he's had his breakfast in the morning. You won't mind passin' the night with us will you Mr. Mahone?" He had overheard the name when he stepped out, and let his ox whip fly.

A couple of the other teamsters have come up to see what the commotion is. "Oley, truss 'im up, an' shackle 'im to my wagon wheel. Shakespeare, I cain't pay you your wages, but here's a couple dollars, an' you can take ol' Jackrabbit. He ain't fast, but he's a sturdy mule. He can take a trail only a deer could follow."

Sykes was right. The mule named Jackrabbit isn't fast, but he has run at a lumbering gate all night, and is barely breathing hard. Julius turns, and looks back to where the sky is beginning to turn gold. He's made his way up into the Wichita Mountains, to an elevation of about two-thousand feet, and from his vantage point he can see all the way back to Medicine Bluffs, sitting like a loaf of bread on the prairie. He taps his heals into Jackrabbit's ribs, and the mule bounds upward over brush and boulders in that unique gate which gave him his name.

Julius has never been a religious man, and has never spent much time praying, but he can't help but think, *how many times can I elude this Pinkerton man?* And even though he doesn't voice it as a prayer, as such, he's thankful for his good fortune.

Pug is sitting by the morning campfire, drinking his third cup of coffee. No need getting in a hurry to chase Principe now. He's had a good fourteen hours to disappear into the mountains to the west, or possibly the Winding Stair Mountains in the east. Either way Principe is lost to him now, until Bernie can come up with more clues.

He looks up at the giant sitting across from him. "—so you ought to just leave 'im alone." Pug missed the first part of what he'd been saying.

He snorts a chuckle. "Oh, I'm gonna let 'im be for now. I got a bigger fish to fry, anyhow. One comin' right up the Chisholm Trail to me. All I gotta do is ride over to the trail an' wait on 'em to come to me."

"Another spy?" Sykes asks.

"No, this'n was a sea pirate, believe it or not."

"A sea pirate drivin' cows up the Chisholm Trail?" Smith's tone is incredulous.

Pug holds out his cup to Pork Bottom for a refill. "The other way around, I think. Rancher from Texas, named Butler, stole a ship, 'n' sailed the oceans of the world sinkin' an' burnin' any ships he come across carryin' cargo to the U.S." He turns to Sykes. "No better'n Quantrill's raiders, killin' an' burnin' in bloody Kansas." He surmises that Sykes will be sympathetic since he's from Kansas.

Sykes just frowns. "Well, there was a lot of mischief goin' on on both side I reckon. War's been over a long time now. Best to just pick up the pieces, an' start over."

"Forgive an' forget I say." Kennesaw Mountain says.

"I dunno, Forrest burned me an' my fambly out up in Kentucky. It ain't easy to forgive, an' I ain't likely to ever forget." Smith puts in his two cents worth.

Sykes scratches his beard, and looks at Pug. "Well, I guess we all got our jobs to do. Mine's to deliver freight to build the frontier, an' yore's is detectivin'. Hope you ain't sore about me holdin' you here all night."

"I s'pose I could charge you with obstructin' justice, but—." He just shrugs.

After searching Camp Medicine Bluffs from top to bottom Pug finds that the only conveyance out of there is the limber wagon portion of an artillery piece, pulled by a small jenny. Oh, he could have gone to the Indian villages up the Cashe or Wolf, and gotten a horse there, but these are about half wild, don't like white men, and, being a city boy, he never was an accomplished rider. So he settles for the army-mule, and front half of a military caisson. The box seat isn't any more uncomfortable than a regular buckboard, but the single axel and two wheels puts him in mind of a Roman chariot.

******

When Master Sergeant Jubal Hunter rides up to the hitching rail at the sutler's saloon outside of Fort Sill he has to push a big gray horse over to dismount, and immediately has a sense of dejavu. It's not really that he recognizes the horse; after all, it's not uncommon to see big gray horses branded with the US army brand at a military installation, but somehow this one jogs some long forgotten memory.

It's saddled with a big western work saddle now, but he remembers a US army saddle, one with a Union Major in command of a prison train

156

clinging desperately, swinging like a rag doll, as he is being jerked to the ground by one of the prisoners.

He sees a blue army coat tied behind the saddle, again nothing out of the ordinary, but when he looks closely he feels a churning in his gut. He unties the jacket, and sure enough, the brass US buttons have been replaced with bone buttons. An involuntary smile twitches his wide lips. What's it been, four years? No, closer to five, and yet he remembers it like it was yesterday.

He can't remember now why the Mexican prisoner, Juaquin Donavan, had aroused a sense of compassion in him, but he had. He remembers the day he took the army blouse to Donavan at Point Lookout detention camp. For some reason he had determined that he was going to get Donavan through the hard times at the prison. Maybe it was because Donavan had pleaded for a bible, and when he told his wife about it she had taken the small wooden cross from around her own throat, and asked him to deliver it, along with her father's bible, to the prisoner. He had taken one of his old uniform blouses, had her remove the chevrons and brass buttons, and replace them with these very bone buttons.

He shakes his head as he recalls guarding the prisoners at the churchyard in Virginia; how Donavan had flung the Major to the ground, and ridden the big gray horse directly at him. It hadn't occurred to him at the time that the horse would jump the gate behind him, that he *could* jump the gate behind him. At the time he only knew that he couldn't shoot Donavan out of the saddle. He couldn't even shoot the horse. All he could do was crouch, and watch, fascinated, as the horse and rider sailed over his head, and the gate. Now, here is the same horse with his army blouse tied behind a big Mexican saddle. What a small world!

It's not hard to pick out his man in the crowded saloon. He's sitting with his back to the bar, but the silver hair gives him away. Hunter remembers watching Donavan's hair turn white, almost overnight, at the prison.

"Mista Juaquin Donavan?"

Andy feels the little prickles crawl up his spine into the hair on the back of his neck. Nobody knows the name Juaquin Donavan except the crew of the Basque smuggler, Torbellino, and some of the people from Point Lookout prison camp.

Chico sees Andy's startled look at the name, and senses trouble. He reaches down, and slips the hammer-latch off his colt.

Andy remains calm though. He looks casually around the room, and then at the man speaking that long forgotten name. He looks directly into the same eyes he had looked into that fateful day at the Virginia churchyard. The day Hunter had him in his sights, but let him escape.

"Hello Mista Donavan." Hunter says with a nod.

Andy shakes his head, looking confused. "Must have me mixed up with somebody else, friend. My name is Butler. Andrew Butler."

A look of surprise flashes in Hunter's eyes, and then comprehension. "Cap'n Butler! 'Course. Now it all makes sense."

Andy's eyes narrow, but he doesn't acknowledge or deny.

Hunter glances down at the side arm on Andy's hip, and then at the other men at the table. He raises his hands in mock submission. "I ain't got no truck wid ya, Cap'n. I could o' shot you dead at that churchyard in Virginia, but I did'n.

"Course, if'n I was a mind to arrest you I got plenty o' cause: escape from a federal prison, horse stealin.' Yeah, I seen that gray horse out there an' my ol' uniform blouse on the saddle.

"Evah what you's callin' yo'self, I knows who you is. You de man dat made de most darin' escape I ever seen." He turns now to Chico and Ernst. "Dis man ever tell you about dat escape? How he snatch dat ol' Major outta de saddle, pert nigh rode me down, an' jump a six-foot wall on dat horse. I never seen such ridin' in all my days." He gives Andy a nod of admiration. "No suh, I ain't got no truck wid ya."

Now Andy smiles. "Good to see you again Sergeant. What brings you out to Indian Territory?"

Hunter grins at Andy's acceptance. "Same ol,' only now I's guardin'

Injuns 'stead o' rebels." He shakes his head. "Cain't b'lieve I'd run into you like dis. I surely never figgered on seein' you again."

Andy snorts a chuckle. If he could run into Hunter out here on the frontier, who else might he run into. "Don't suppose the Major that owned that horse is out here with you."

Hunter snickers. "Naw sah. He surely ain't. Got outta th' army I believe. It wud'n his horse nohow, borrowed it from a cavalry colonel, I recollects."

Andy laughs. "Yeah, I remember now, the colonel traded it for the majors train, the one we was prisoners on. I'd like to 'ov been around to see when the colonel brought the train back. I guess he was pretty hacked that his horse had been hijacked."

Now Hunter laughs. "Oh naw sah, you wouldn't liked to been around to see it atall. If you was around to see it then you would'n 'a' got away, an' th' horse'd 'a' still been there."

"Well, you got a point there, Master Sergeant. I did borrow the borrowed horse an' that's what got me free."

Hunter takes off his forage cap, and scratches his head. "You mought not be in de clear yet, though, Cap'n. Dey was a Pinkerton man down heah lookin' fo' a Cap'n Butler a few days ago. Nacherly, I nevah connected de names, knowin' you as Seenyor Juaquin Donavan like I did."

Andy remembers the conversation about the Pinkerton agency asking questions about his land titles. So, the U.S. Government *is* looking for him. He is sure now that they still want to bring him to trial for his activity against the Union Navy.

"Who was this Pinkerton man? Did you see 'im?" Andy asks.

"Oh yas suh. Big man. Went by de name of Malone, or Mahoney, I b'lieves. Somethin' like dat."

Andy looks around the saloon, at each man in there. "He still around?"

"Naw suh, I b'lieves he left fo' de Chisholm Trail right aftah de doins out at de freight yards. Suprised he did'n run into ya some where's on de trail between here and Red River Crossin.'"

Andy turns, and smiles at Chico.

"We didn't cross at Red River Crossin." Chico declares. "We come up through Henrietta an' crossed just above where the Wichita comes into the Red."

Hunter nods. "Makes sense I guess. De trail is somewhat east o' here, but I thought Henrietta was 'bout a ghost town now on account o' de Indian problems."

"Yeah," Andy says, "that's why we chose it. Did'n want to mess with Ft. Worth. There's still a half-breed Cherokee lives there with his Kiowa wife and kids. Nice fella, gave us safe passage through his territory."

"You're lucky. The Kiowas and Comanche been rainin' terror 'round there. Dat's how come us out heah. Gonna round 'em all up an' put 'em on reservations." He drains the dregs of his glass of beer. "Wal, ones my limit." He declares. "Guess I betah be getting' on home. My ol' lady prob'ly got my evenin' vittles ready." He turns abruptly to Andy. "Hey, you still got dat ol' bible I brung you at Point Lookout?"

"It's out in my saddlebags, why, you want it back?" He pulls out the old twig cross hanging around his neck. "Still carry this too."

Hunter reaches out, and touches the cross with his forefinger. "Why, I do declare. You knows it was God what kept me from shootin' you in Virginia don't ya?"

Andy takes the gnarled black hand, and squeezes it. "Yeah, I reckon it was."

"Dat was my father-in-law's ol' bible. He was a slave-preacher ya know."

"No, I didn't know." Andy says. "That ol' bible saw lots of action after I left your company, though. It gave comfort to many a Confederate boy just before he went into battle."

"Wal, Federal or Sesesh, I reckon if it helped some lost soul to reach Glory it served its purpose."

Andy just nods. "You say your wife is out here with you? I'd like to meet 'er, and thank 'er personally for her caring about a renegade rebel prisoner."

Hunter grasps his shoulder. His eyes are sparkling. "Yeah, I b'lieve she'd like dat too."

Andy turns to his two companions. "Why don't you guys go on back to the herd. I'm goin' with the Master Sergeant here."

Chico glares up at the black army sergeant. "You reckon that's wise, Andy?"

Andy glances up into Hunter's face. "Oh yeah, I reckon so."

The place Hunter takes Andy is a combination of a sod barn and stable, and a mud wickiup with a patched Sibley tent pitched to the side it. Andy shakes his head. It is so reminiscent of his first home at Cave Creek Ranch.

"Home sweet home," Hunter smiles. "Hey Blossom. You decent? I brung home company." A little Negro woman comes out of the wikiup, wiping her hands on a cloth towel.

Andy just holds out the old coverless bible. "Miz Hunter, I believe this is yours."

At first she just stares at it, then her hand goes to her mouth, and a tear runs down her cheek. Her eyes run from the bible up to Andy's face. "You de prisoner, ain't you?"

Andy bows. "Yes'm, and I thank you for the loan of you father's bible. It gave me much comfort during my time of imprisonment, and then, as I told your husband, it led many young soldiers to the Lord."

She touches the bible with reverence, but pulls her hand away. "No sir, it's yours. I don't take back gifts I give."

Andy pulls the cross from inside his shirt. "I don't guess you want this back either then."

She shakes her head in wonder. "Lawdy, Lawdy. I nevah thought—. Mr.—."

"Donavan. Uh, I mean Cap'n Butler." Hunter supplies.

"Cap'n Butler, I just got Jubal's vittles ready. Would you like to stay fo' supper?"

"Blossom, he don't want to eat with black folks in no hovel like this. Sorry Cap'n."

"Jubal," Andy says. "You're wrong about me. I was, and am, a southerner, but I'm not a—I'm not like that. In fact let me tell you about an old African friend of mine. His name was Salaam Hajji of a Moorish father and African mother, but everybody just called him Monk.

"He was bought from the slave pens in Ivory Coast by my old captain, Captain Donavan.

"He was born in the desert regions north of the Niger River, and tended his father's cattle and camels until his capture. He said he believed that was in his fourteenth summer.

"His name, Salaam, may have meant peace, but the only peace he knew after his capture was after he came to the Queen of Scots. In fact he had tried to escape so many times they chopped off his toes to keep him from running.

"Yep, he may have been bought as a slave, but he became Cap'n Donavan's best friend, and he became my mentor and friend as well. In fact it was Monk who led me to the Lord."

Blossom had sat quietly through Andy's story, and now she rubs away the dewiness from her eyes. "Cap'n Butler, if you don't mind, I'd like to hear that story."

Andy refills his tin cup with coffee, and leans back in his chair. He likes it when he has the opportunity to share his testimony.

"I had pulled a morning watch on board ship. It was just getting light when Monk came on deck with a hot cup of coffee for me. We were just standing there sipping our coffee, and listening to the wind singing in the shroud lines when I asked Monk something that had been bothering me for a few days."

As he begins to tell the tale he gets so engrossed it's like she was there witnessing the whole thing.

"Monk, couple of days ago Cap'n said sumpin's got me puzzled."
"Eh, what's 'at Bwana kidogo?"
Andy smiled to himself. He liked Monk's African speech. "Well, when

Cook swore and said 'Jesus Christ' the other day, Cap'n jumped on him real good an' said he didn't like it when somebody used his saviors name in vain. Said sumpin' 'bout Jesus Christ savin' his life or sumpin' like that. What you reckon he meant?"

Monk's black eyes held a compassion that Andy had never seen in anyone before. "Don't you know 'bout Jesus little Bwana?"

Andy shrugged. "Guess I all'as thought it was just sumpin' to say when you was mad about sumpin'."

Monk folded his massive hands on the rail in front of him, and searched the waves as if he were looking for an answer there. "You believe in God?" He finally asked.

Andy nodded. "Yeah, some."

"Well, Jesus was God's own son. He come down heah to earth as a mtoto kidogo, a little bitty baby, borned to the virgin Mary, to see how tings was goin,' and when he get to be a man, he find out they ain't goin' too good, so he tell his father, God. 'Somethin' got to be done to save man from his sins, 'cause dey sinnin' real bad.' You see dey jes' cain't keep all dem commandments. Dey jes ain't strong enough, but somebody got to pay for all dat sin. But Jesus, he love everybody so much, he say he take all de blame fo' evahbody."

Andy set his jaw skeptically. "So what happened? Did he take the blame?"

"Oh, yas suh, he had to pay fo' Cap'n's sins, an' mine, and yours, and everybody's."

"How'd he pay?" He was watching Monks back, and saw the broad shoulders rise in a heavy sigh.

"Dey hung him up on a big wooden cross, an' nailed spikes in his hands and feets, an' dey make a king-hat outta de thorn bush, and stick it on his head, an' make fun of him when he be dying, an' dey say if you be Gods son, just tell him to get you down off a de'ah." He turned to face Andy, and Andy could see tears in the giant Africans eyes.

"How come he didn't?" Andy asked. "Get him down, I mean, if he was God?"

"'Cause dat's the onliest way he could pay fo' all dem sins. If he didn't pay, den you an' me would have to pay. We would be sent to hell fo' all dem sins."

"An' he paid for your sins too? You don't have to go to hell to pay for your sins?"

"Oh, yas suh, he pay for slave an' massa alike. He don' know no colah Bwana Andy."

"Well, I ain't never sinned no real sins. I ain't but fourteen you know."

"You evah tell a lie?"

Andy fidgeted with wrapping a line around a belaying pin. He had told little white fibs aplenty. "Well, yeah."

"You evah do sumpin' you know you shouldn't; made somebody very unhappy?"

Again he remembered Donavan's look when he took shore leave, and drank too much rum. He dropped his eyes, and nodded.

"Dem be sins jes the same. Truth is, you be borned into sin. Dat first man, Adam, he sinned the first sin an' jes like my mama givin' me black skin, his sin be passed on to us. You cain't hep sinning Kidogo, but if you axe Jesus to take yo' sin on himself, he do it. He love you dat much."

Andy looked out, and saw several dolphins frolicking alongside the ship. "Any animals in heaven, Monk?"

Monk scratched his head. "Well suh, I doan' rightly know, but I reckon dey must be. Dey be creations of God too."

Andy thought he'd found a loophole in Monk's story. "How they gonna get to heaven if they cain't ask Jesus to save them?"

"Well," Monk said, "I reckon dey wasn't borned into sin like man 'cause dey ain't sons of Adam."

Andy shrugged. "Anyway, how can a dead man save anybody? He was probably just a man like anybody else, and got hung up like that 'cause he said he was God's son."

Monk put his hand on Andy's shoulder. *Why was it that when you tried to tell someone what Jesus had done for them, they tried to shoot holes in it?*

164

"'Cause when he been dead an' in de grave fo' tree days, he git up an' come outta de'ah, live as you an' me, an' he go around seein' his friends an' his mama."

"Aw, it was probably somebody looked like him, tryin' to fool everybody."

"Naw suh, de bible say a angel from God met his friends an' his mama at de grave, an' say why you lookin' heah fo' Jesus. He ain't dead. He alive. Besides, when he see everybody, he show 'em de holes in his hands and' feets, an' de spear hole in his side."

Andy was still a little incredulous. "So, did he die of his wounds then, or what?"

Monk beamed a smile at Andy that could only be called radiant. "De bible say God raised him into heaven while everybody watched, and Jesus say to his friends, as he go up in de clouds, 'I will go an' prepare a place for you.' Dat mean dat if you axe him to save you, an' take away yo' sins he will take you up to heaven to be with him when you die."

Andy gave him a skeptical grin, but said in a friendly way, "How you know so much about what the bible says? You cain't read."

Monk nodded gravely. "Naw suh, I cain't, an' dat's a fact. When I was in de slave pens my rafike, my friend, a monk like me, would come an' talk to me about Jesus, an' he would read me stories most evah day, an' den when de cap'n bought me from de pens, he tell me about how Jesus would take away my sins. Since den, I know I have a place in heaven. Doan' you want a place in heaven Bwana Andy?"

Andy hung his head. "If you an' the cap'n are gonna be there I do."

A big grin split the African's face. "Oh, I be deah alright, an' cap'n too, but mos' important, Jesus, he gonna be deah."

Andy looks up into the two smiling black faces. "Well, I decided right then and there that if Monk and the cap'n were going to be in heaven that's where I wanted to go too, and I've tried to be a faithful follower of Jesus ever since."

Blossom rises, goes over to Andy, and kisses him on the cheek. "I'm glad Jubal took you my pa's bible an' my cross."

"I am too, Blossom. I am too. I wouldn't have survived prison camp without them."

When there is a lull in the conversation Andy says, "So, Blossom, how do you like it out here on the prairie?"

She looks at her surroundings. "Well, it ain't what I'm used to."

"She grew up in the big house on the plantation." Hunter explains.

She shakes her head, and playfully slaps at Hunter's hand. "Oh, Jubal. He tries to make it sound like it was my house. I was house servant to de mastah's daughters. Oh, I had lots of privileges, but I's still a slave. Day an' night, Blossom, fix my hair. Blossom, do my nails. Blossom wash me. Blossom, dress me."

Hunter beams proudly. "So, tell 'im what you're doin' now."

She ducks her head shyly. "Same thing."

"Not the same thing!" He huffs. "She gots her own business, an' makes more money in a week than I do."

"Well, I jes' figgered since I had so much experience takin' care of princesses I'd open up a beauty shop fo' de officer wives. You know, washin' dey hair, paintin' dey nails, givin' 'em baths. I got me a tent in town an' I got so many ladies comin' in I have to make appointments. Jubal even got me a tub where I can offer hot baths."

Andy's eyes widen. "Miz Hunter, I think one of my cowboys is in need of your services."

"You got a cowboy dat wants pamperin'?"

"Well, I don't know about wants pamperin', but needs pamperin'."

The next morning Andy and Annie ride into Camp Medicine Bluffs. Annie is oblivious as to why she's being brought into town, but is happy to be asked to accompany her daddy.

When they walk into the salon, Blossom looks in wide-eyed amazement at this little girl, dressed in drover's clothes, high heeled boots with spurs, a wide brimmed hat covering wild, tangled hair, which is almost too dirty to tell that it's blond, and a rawhide jacket. She circles

Annie, lifting her hair off her neck, examining her chipped, dirty fingernails, looking behind her ears. "Oh my!" She exclaims. "I don't think I evah seen a white girl dis grubby befo'."

"You think you can do anything for her?"

Blossom takes a deap breath. "I can try."

At first, when Andy left her, and walked out, she was rebellious, but now, sitting in hot water with bubbles up to her chin she relaxes a little. "My mom don't usually let me get like this." She tries to explain. "It's only because of bein' on the trail. I try to bathe in the rivers, but it's awful cold yet, an' there's always the boys around. I cain't ever get much privacy."

Blossom steps back, one hand on her hip, and a dripping washcloth hanging from the other. "Well, what you doing out on de trail wid a bunch of cowboys anyhow? What's de mattah 'th yo daddy? Lettin a little thing like you go on a cattle drive. Has he lost his senses? And a mother who'd let her little girl go like dat ought to be horse whipped."

"They dit'n zakly let me go," Annie says in defense. "I run away from home an' followed 'em for two days, 'til they was to far out to take me back."

"You ran aw-. Wasn't you scared o' getting' lost out deah in dat wilderness?"

Annie chuckles. "It's kinda hard to get lost followin' three thousand steers. They make a purty good size road to follow."

"But wasn't you scared? Where'd you sleep?"

Annie gives her an incredulous look. "On the trail o' course."

"You slept out in de wilderness, by yo'self, fo' two days?"

Annie blinks, not understanding what the big deal is. "Yes'm."

"How old you say you is?"

"Eight 'n' a half."

Blossom throws back her head, and laughs. "Lawdy, Lawdy! Mz. Patricia was nineteen an' nevah even would go out to de privy by herself. Always usin' de bedpan, and den holler, Blossom, come empty dis."

Annie wrinkles her freckled nose. "I don't like usin' the pot. 'Course if I had a darkey to empty it for me maybe I wouldn't mind too much."

Blossom stares at her for a minute, and then begins to laugh again. "Mz Annie, you is sho nuff a caution, girl. You sho' is."

Annie rides into the camp with pride and self-consciousness. Her riding skirt is cleaned and pressed. Her boots have been replaced with a pair of patent leather shoes with silver buttons up the sides, and her hair has been trimmed, and hangs to her shoulders in platinum ringlets. Her blue eyes flash at Mateo when he snatches off his sombrero, and mutters, "Santa Maria! Que Linda."

She smiles at Fritz, and holds out manicured hands, to be lifted down.

Later, after supper, when all of the men are gathered around, she takes out a buttonhook, and removes her shoes. Then begins to unroll her stockings.

"Look at this!" She beams as she wiggles her toes, the nails each painted bright red.

Yoni walks over and kisses her on the forehead. "You're beautiful Annie."

She just gives him a puzzled look.

CHAPTER 10

He had never really given it serious thought, but if someone had asked Pug what he expected to find on the Chisholm Trail at the Washita Crossing he would have had to admit that he might have expected something like a game trail, or wagon road. What he didn't expect was a super highway a hundred feet wide where a couple of million cattle, thousands of horses and a myriad of chuck wagons have passed in the past five years. He had subconsciously thought that he'd just wait here, watching an empty trail until the Butler herd miraculously appeared. He was astounded when he arrived, and found that the herds were numerous, and only separated by half a mile or less.

He and the trail scout of the next herd are sitting at a campfire sharing a skillet of bacon and coffee. He produces one of Joseph McCoy's flyers begging Texas cattlemen to bring their herds to Abilene, Kansas. "Yeah," he says, "Mr. McCoy sent me down to evaluate the herds so he can estimate how many cattle to expect this season."

The scout shakes his head. "Well, we ain't goin' to Abilene. I'm takin' this herd all the way to Montana to the Snyder brothers new spread.

Maybe next season we'll be shipping cattle from both Texas and Montana."

Pug nods. "What about the herd ahead of you? You know who it belongs to?"

"Yeah," the scout says, "that's Shang's herd, Shanghai Pierce. They're going to Kansas. Got about two thousand steers I guess."

Pug makes an entry in a notebook as though he really is an agent for Joseph McCoy. "What about the herd behind you?"

"Yeah, that's Mr. Arnett, drivin' for Mr. Iliff this year. They got a herd of some thousand cows 'n' calves. Mr. Arnett says they're gonna take 'em to Mr. Iliff out of Denver, so you cain't count on them in Kansas either."

Pug shakes his head, and makes an entry. "What about the Butler herd? You know anything about them?"

The scout shakes his head. "Heard they might be bringin' a herd this year, but don't know where they'd be on the trail. Doubt they'd be too far ahead of us. It's still purty early in the season."

Pug camps by the trail through two more herds, still without any information.

C.C. Slaughter has halted his herd for the day at the Washita crossing. It is Sunday, and Mr. Slaughter won't move his herd on Sunday. He has just conducted Sunday services for his cowboys, and it is mandatory that everyone attend. Pug has waited in the hills above the herd until he sees the cowboys begin to move away from the assembly.

When he trundles into camp on his chariot Mr. Slaughter looks up. "You just missed church services Mr.—." He puts out his hand in a handshake.

"Mahone, Pug Mahone." Pug says amicably. "Sorry I missed your service, but I'm a Irish Catholic. You probably wouldn't've wanted me around kneelin' an' crossin' myself anyhow."

"Oh, a good Baptist service is for all, Mr. Mahone. Jesus wants all his children to gather in His name, Baptist, Methodist, Catholic, it don't matter. What can I do for you?"

"Well, I's hopin' you was the Butler herd."

"Naw, Butler 'n' Garza come through the Brazos country, near my ranch, two, three weeks ago. We trailed behind 'im a spell, then we kept east to Ft. Worth. Their trail cut straight north. My guess is they skipped Red River Crossin' altogether, an' that weren't an altogether unwise decision. The Red was in flood, an' they was at least four herds backed up there. Took us nigh on to a week to separate 'em. Some o' my stock is prob'ly still mixed with Shang's an' Charlie's, but then I got some o' theirs, so I guess it all comes out in the wash.

"Naw, Butler either got scalped by the Comanche, or else they're somewhere up near the Canadian by now."

******

Trail Log
Canadian River
Friday, March 27, 1869

Three days out of Camp Medicine Bluffs we are camped on the south side of the Canadian River. We lost Kilakeena (the Buck) Poteau and his band of Kiowas one day north of the Red. His Kiowas were afraid of the fort and soldiers at Camp Medicine Bluffs, and turned aside. They have good reason to be anxious; according to Master Sergeant Hunter the army is building a new frontier fort there (Ft. Sill), and will be concentrating all of its efforts to stop the Indian raids, and force the Comanche, Kiowa and Apache onto reservations. Good luck getting Quanah or Satanta onto a reservation.

The Red was in flood stage when we arrived, but we all got across safely. We crossed west of where the Wichita comes in from Texas, so it wasn't quite as bad as it would have been at Red River Crossing.

We're a little short handed without Paco and Eloy, but we're managing. Yoni, Fritz and Annie have all earned their spurs since their departure.

I'm especially proud of Annie, but am I asking too much of her? She is, after all, only a little girl, and I don't want her to lose her innocence on this drive trying to be "as good as a boy."

I blame myself for not taking her back at the Llano, but I know my daughter, and she would have made good her threat to leave again, and follow us as many times, as many days, or as many miles as it took.

She is a contradiction, though. She rides as hard as any man, but when she came back from the beauty salon the other day it came home to me that she is all girl, and beautiful girl at that. She needs the influence of other women, older women, like Ilsa, Marta or Lula. How can I protect her from boys with improper intentions when she has to attend to her toilet, and bathe around a camp full of cowboys? They try to give her some space, but it's not easy.

After the incident with Paco making lewd suggestions to her, I decided that I needed to sit her down, and have the talk that men have with their sons. I thought it would be uncomfortable, but she sat, and listened attentively. When I asked her if she had any questions she said, "Dai, I grew up around breeding stock, and I have two brothers. What questions could I have?" She's growing up so fast. I don't know what I'll do when she grows out of calling me Dai.

I have reduced the night watches back to two riders again since we left the Territory, and entered the Chickasaw Nation. There seems to be some tacit agreement between the "wild" Indians and the "civilized" tribes, and the "wild" ones don't raid in this direction. They would rather raid down into Texas it seems.

Sometimes the "Civilized Tribes" demand payment to cross their lands, but so far we haven't encountered any problems.

The weather has warmed a little, but we've been plagued with a constant drizzle since crossing the Red.

Annie wakes, stretches, and opens her eyes. It's as though someone has pulled a damp wool blanket over her head. She raises her hand, but can't see her wiggling fingers until they're only a few inches in front of her eyes. She feels for her boots, and then feels her way out from under the wagon. She stands, and stares into the gray nothingness in front of her. For a fleeting instant she feels something close to panic. "Dai?" She calls softly.

"Over here, Annie."

"Where is everybody?" She asks, reaching her hand out, seeing it disappear into the fog.

"We're all here." It's Jack's voice, but it sounds like it's coming from a far distance, and up from a well.

She takes a couple of faltering steps, feeling in front of her like a blind person. Then she sees the faint yellow glow of the fire, and ghostly figures wafting in and out of the mist. Stumbling over a root, she makes her way to the campfire, and accepts a mug of coffee with milk in it. She takes a long sip, and lays the cup on the ground. Slipping her hand into Andy's she says, "Dai, would you walk me down to the creek. I gotta pee so bad my eyeballs are floatin'."

By ten o'clock the sun has pretty much burned away the fog, and by noon only isolated patches linger in the bottoms, but on the western horizon giant thunderheads are building, and by suppertime it's clear that they are in for a storm. The air is crackling with static electricity and internal lightening lights up the insides of the black thunderheads.

The vaqueros riding herd have come up for their supper, and even though the herd is nervous, they are peaceful, some lying down to belch up their cud for a late afternoon snack.

"Andale, everybody in the saddle!" Chico commands, riding in from the prairie. "Andy, there is a dry gulch ahead about a mile." He looks up at the rolling, twisting clouds moving in their direction. "I fear we may be in for a torbellino. We need to get as many of the cows as we can down into that draw."

Just then there is an ear splitting crack as a lightening bolt blasts down through a lone cottonwood. As one, the cattle are on their feet. At the second crash they stampede into a dead run.

"Get 'em running behind me!" Chico yells, and in three jumps Mouse is in a belly-to-the-ground run.

At the sound of the lightening crash Beast's eyes bugged, and the slobbers began to flow, but now, somehow, the presence of Chico riding beside him, driving him, guiding him, gives him a sense of security. He follows Mouse in a blind run, and the rest of the herd follows him. When they reach the wide mouth of the rocky gorge the herd funnels into it, and as it narrows and steepens they slow to a trot, and then a walk. By the time they reach the box end of it the notion to stampede is out of them, and they simply mill around Beast and Chico, bawling their fear.

Andy, Annie and a few of the vaqueros have closed off the mouth of the gorge, holding back any cattle that would try to bolt back onto the prairie, but this leaves them in the open, and feeling vulnerable every time the lightening crashes.

The black cloud overhead is working, rolling, boiling; turning itself inside out, and then the sky opens, and the water descends as though someone is pumping it out of a pitcher pump. Within minutes the rain turns to pullet-egg sized hail.

Annie sees Esteban dismount, unsaddle, and hold the saddle over his head, but even though she's being pelted by the hailstones, she hesitates to follow suite. She knows it's not safe to be on the ground if the herd breaks, and stampedes. A small person like her would be trampled before she could remount.

Then a black tongue drops down, licks at the ground, and pulls itself back into the roiling mass. Several minutes pass; minutes of silence, and a strange calm that seems to suffocate; as if the retreating cloud finger had pulled the air from their lungs.

The sky turns a sea-water green, and then with a great roar of wind, rain and thunder the huge funnel drops down, tearing up trees and sod, whirling them into the air. The funnel passes directly over the chuck wagon and it just explodes; it's various pieces joining the debris inside the funnel cloud.

Annie sits spellbound, watching the funnel move directly toward her. Then when she thinks she will explode, like the wagon, Yoni's body hurtles from his saddle, and sweeps her out of hers. The crush of his body landing on hers knocks the breath out of her. Sobbing, she gasps painfully, trying to force air back into her chest. His weight is crushing her into the rocks beneath her, and then she feels the wind tugging at his body on top of hers. His arms are wrapped around her in a desperate bear hug, but the two of them are being propelled across the ground, rolling, bouncing, smashing into rocks and roots.

Finally, the roaring stops, the frantic tug of the wind stops, and all that is left is a drenching downpour, and in the distance the funnel is speeding away from them.

She sits up and looks around. Kidogos body is lying prone a hundred yards away. Parts of the wagon and most of their bedding are in the branches and limbs of the battered trees. Then, a few feet away she sees Yoni, limp on the ground, blood running from a wound on his head. A sob catches in her throat. "Oh Yoni, no! Please God, not Yoni." She rushes over to him, and cradles his head in her arms. She begins laughing and sobbing as his eyes flutter, and he looks into hers. "You okay?" he asks feebly.

The herd, and the vaqueros in the gorge all emerge unscathed, except for lumps and bruises from the hail. The ones holding the herd at the mouth of the gorge are all in fair shape, except for Fritz and Mateo. Fritz suffered a sprained shoulder when his horse threw him, and Mateo, trying to force back a young steer, was gored in the same calf that was gored during the prairie fire. This time the knife-sharp horn cut his leg from the knee to boot top.

The only one unaccounted for is Chepito. After hours of searching he cannot be found.

Annie is bent over Kidogo's still body, her hand stroking his velvety nose, tears are running down her cheeks, her shoulders jerking with emotion. She looks up at her daddy. "Dogo, Dai. Dogo's dead. What am I gonna do without him?"

He lifts her into his arms, holding her tight as she breaks into uncontrollable sobs. "I know, sweetheart. He was a good horse." He tries to console her, but he knows she is inconsolable right now. The last thing she wants to hear—needs to hear—is that she will get another horse.

Mountain sized black clouds are still boiling overhead, thunder rolls through the sky on a continuous basis, and Annie has seen lightening bouncing from cloud to cloud, and lighting up the black sky.

It's after supper now, and time to roll up in her blankets. For the first time on this drive she feels vulnerable and uncomfortable sleeping out in the open, and for the first time in her life she feels real fear. She doesn't even have the security of the chuck wagon above her now; jut the black muttering night, a threatening, fearful night.

She takes her ground sheet, and spreads it between Yoni and Fritz. Somehow Yoni has become her security. They've always been close, closer than she and Fritz, although she loves Fritz as a little sister would. But since Yoni stood up for her with Paco, and now saved her from the tornado he has become her hero.

Yoni hears her sniffling in her blankets next to him. He has never known her to cry. He reaches out from under his blanket, and drags her, blanket and all, up next to him, cradling her in his arms.

"Shhh, it's okay now. What's the matter?"

"I'm scared." She whimpers.

"What? The fearless Annie Butler is afraid? I don't believe it."

"Don't tease me!" She scolds.

"I'm not teasing you, schatze. I'm scared too."

She's silent for a minute, and then, "Yoni, whadda you reckon happened to Chepito? You think the torbellino just picked him up, and carried him up to heaven?"

He kisses her hair next to her ear. "Yeah, schatze, that's exactly what I think."

"Yeah, me too."

*****

Trail Log
Canadian River
Sunday, March 29th, 1869

I dated this Sunday March 29th, but it's probably after midnight Monday morning.

The tornado has left us all somewhat shaken. I don't think anyone is sleeping, even though they are all wrapped in their blankets—their sodden blankets.

We spent most of today (yesterday) trying to regroup, mourn our losses, and try to prepare for the remainder of the trip. We never did find any sign of Chepito.

Not only do we not have a cook now, or chuck wagon; our supplies are scattered all over the plains. We found most of our bedding hanging in the branches of the cottonwood trees along the creek, a few pots and pans, and one fifty-pound sack of flour. The flour was about a quarter of a mile from where the wagon disintegrated, and was not hurt in any manner; no seams were split, no flour was lost. It was like it had been hand carried to that place, and gently laid down, so, at least we can make biscuits and gravy. I guess we can live on biscuits and beef until I can replace the supplies.

With her talent for improvising maybe Annie can make coffee out of roasted acorns, or some other thing she finds on the trail.

Bless her heart. She lost two good friends in that storm, Chepito, and her best friend, Kidogo. Even though she tries to show a brave face she is grieving bad.

When the herd hits the trail north tomorrow, I will head back south to Medicine Bluffs. I don't like leaving the kids while they're still afraid of the weather, but there's no help for it. I couldn't do anything if there was another tornado, and we have to have supplies, and a cook.

As the sun rises over the prairie, turning the golden wheat-grass an even more brilliant shade of pink-gold, Annie is reluctant to rise and dress.

She's known that today would be difficult for her, even more difficult than yesterday in some ways. This will be the first time she's gone to the campfire, and not been greeted by the old cocinero, with a smile and a hot cup of coffee. It is also the first time since she was six years old that she won't saddle her beloved Dogo, and ride him out to the herd.

She lingers over her biscuit and cup of sassafras tea, waiting until all of the other cowboys have gone to the remuda, and selected their mounts for the day. Then she walks out to where they have covered Kidogo's body with stones.

She removes her hat, and stands beside the pile of rocks. It's easier looking at rocks than it had been seeing his lifeless body. Still, the tears roll freely down her cheeks. She kneels, and touches the stones. "Bye, my sweet boy. You rest here 'til I come for you in heaven." A little smile quivers at the corner of her mouth. "We'll ride all over heaven together, you an' me; when I come for you."

Yoni is just gathering the horses to start them on the trail when she comes up.

"Hi Annie. You want me to catch you a horse?"

"No, I'll do it." She has carried her saddle out with her. She takes her lariat loose, and walks slowly toward the milling horses, clucking her tongue as she goes, and whistling softly.

She holds the loop on her left side to make a quick hullihan toss when the opportunity affords itself.

Mancha, the buckskin-on-white paint horse, has left the tropa, and approaches her, ears forward.

With a backhand flick of her wrist the loop flies over his ears, and settles around his neck. He braces, but doesn't try to pull away. With her small body she couldn't hold him if he had.

She holds out a biscuit to him. He sniffs it, and then lips at it gently.

"Ah, you like that don't you?" She speaks soothingly to him. "You like the molasses, huh?" She had made her own brand of molasses by boiling crushed mesquite beans with Sweet gum sap. She fishes another one out of her pocket, and holds it out to him. When he stretches his neck down to get it, she slips the bit into his mouth, and the halter over his ears.

Saddling a long legged horse like Mancha is reminiscent of the early days, when she had to use the feed box at the corral to saddle Kidogo. The only problem is she doesn't have a feed box to stand in out here on the prairie.

Yoni watches with admiration as she swings the light saddle with all her might, up onto Mancha's withers, and then goes about cinching it, and tying her 22.20/410 beneath the skirt. Lastly she throws her saddlebags, ground sheet and blanket roll behind her saddle, and ties them down with the latigos. It helps that she is four feet-five inches tall. If she were a short eight-year-old she could never reach the latigos.

With all of this done she grabs a handful of mane, and leaps to get her foot in the stirrup.

******

Trail Log
Camp Medicine Bluffs
Friday, April 3rd, 1869
Life is strange. The world is small. And God does, indeed, work in mysterious ways. Who would have ever thought that my old warder at Point Lookout prison camp would become my friend and ally, but that's just what Master Sergeant Jubal Hunter has become.

I've returned to Camp Medicine Bluffs (Ft. Sill) to see if I can replace the chuck wagon, supplies, and, maybe, find a new cook.

Wagons are not easily come by out here. I have found one that belonged to the buffalo hunters, but, of course, it has been used to haul fresh hides, and I'm afraid the smell will never leave it. When I was on the Alamo we captured a ship that had been used as a slaver at one time, and although it was then in use as a cargo vessel, it still had the slaver smell.

Jubal tells me that the army might sell me an ambulance that is being surplused, but even if that's so, can I convert it for use as a chuck wagon?

He is going to take me out to the freight yard this afternoon. If there is a suitable wagon anywhere you'd think it would be at a wagon yard.

******

Sykes looks up at the two men approaching. The big one is one of those that the Indians call "Buffalo Soldiers," stationed here at Ft. Sill. The other is a cowboy. The cowboy dismounts first, and approaches with his hand stretched out.

"Howdy, Andy Butler." Sykes' eyes flicker in recognition at the name. *Cap'n Andrew Butler. So, this is the sea pirate Mahone was hunting. He just looks like any other cowboy to me. I helped Shakespeare escape. Should I warn this cowboy that a bounty hunter is looking for him?*

"I'm looking to buy a wagon suitable for a chuck wagon." Andy motions toward the Buffalo Soldier. "Sergeant Hunter thought you might have something."

"Not really." Sykes' hand waves out toward the wagon yard. "Alls we got is them freight wagons. They're prob'ly a little big for your purposes."

Andy looks at the monstrous wagons. It's no wonder they have to be pulled by three yoke of oxen, yoked three abreast.

"I got a extra wagon since one of my teamsters hightailed it out o' here a week or so ago. I's figgerin' on hiring another teamster, though; not sellin' it."

"Yeah, well, like you said it's a little big for my use anyhow. Good luck hirin' another teamster. I'm lookin' for a cook myself. Both wagons, and help seem to be in short supply around here. My fear is I might have to go all the way over to Red River Crossing to find either."

"You come up from the Crossin' did you?" Sykes' curiosity has gotten the better of his good judgment. "Bringin' a herd up the Chisholm?"

"We did'n come up the Chisholm. Did'n pick it up till the Canadian."

"So, you must not've run into a big Irishman wearin' a green bowler derby."

"Don't recall seein' anybody like that. Why?"

"Oh, you'd recall it if'n you had. If you're Cap'n Andrew Butler of the Confederate Navy that is."

Andy's eyes narrow at this statement, and his hand surreptitiously moves to rest on his hip, just above his pistol grip.

"Yeah," Sykes says, "he come in here 'bout a week ago lookin' for one of my teamsters. A man we called Shakespeare. Said Shakespeare'd been a Confederate spy durin' the war. Seems like a group of powerful men in Washington hired 'im to bring the both of you in."

"Yeah, Jubal told me he'd been askin' about me, but I heard Grant issued a pardon for all us rebels, regardless of what we did."

Hunter just shrugs, but Sykes continues. "What I gathered from Mahone, he ain't workin' for the guv'ment. Guess you might call 'im a bounty hunter. He tolt Shakespeare it did'n matter to him if Shakespeare surrendered or not. He'd get paid dead or alive."

"So, what happened to this Shakespeare?" Andy asks. "Mahone shoot 'im or turn 'im over to the army?"

Sykes waves indiscriminately towards the Whichitas. "Last I seen he was ridin' my mule, Jackrabbit, in that direction."

Andy gives him a skeptical look. "He steal your mule, or'd you help 'im get away?"

Sykes sprays a stream of tobacco juice at a wagon wheel. "Wal, let's jes say Mahone spent the night in our camp snugged up close to that wheel. Come daylight he figgered Shakespeare had too much head start on 'im to make it worthwhile to follow 'im. Said he'd jes mosey on over to the Chisholm an' wait fer you to show up. That's why I wondered if'n you'd seen 'im."

"You'd be hard to find in the Wichitas, or out there." Hunter's hand takes in all of the country to the western horizon, the land that the Comanche considered theirs.

Andy turns to him, shaking his head. "I can't run. I've got a herd to get to Abilene, an' a little girl to watch out for. I'll just have to take my chances that when he finds me, I'm smarter, or faster than him."

"You want Annie to see you in a shoot out with another man? Maybe shot down; dead an' bleedin'?" Hunter asks. "You've seen men shot up before. It ain't pretty. 'Sides Garza can get your herd to Abilene, an' what I've seen of Annie she can perty much take care of herself."

The thought of his precious, tough, independent, little Annie brings a smile to his eyes. "Naw, I need to just go back to the herd an' take my chances, but if he happens to come back through here send 'im on west, lookin' for Shakespeare." He grins at Sykes.

******

Pug sees the Indians the minute the first feathered head comes over the ridge. He hadn't stayed with the twisting river, and therefore the protection of the herds. He had, instead, gone straight north in hopes of cutting Butler's trail coming up from the southwest. He had too, and the trail was fresh; probably less than a day old, so he had felt encouraged; that is until the Indians began following him a couple hundred yards off to his left.

He knows Camp Medicine Bluffs is way too far behind him to afford any safety, and the Creek nation is a good sixty miles somewhere off to the east. His only hope is that he is close enough to Butler to make a run for it. If he was on a fast horse, and if he was a good enough rider, he might outrun them. IF, the biggest little word in the English language.

Then he remembers a story his grandfather used to tell him of an Irish prince, Cuchulainn, how he had single handedly charged his chariot into the advancing Ulstermen, scattering them, and defeating them. He removes his derby, jacket and shirt, and turns the lumbering little jenny toward the band of Indians. With his Kerr .44 in one hand, his hunting knife in the other, and the reins tied around his waist he bounces across the prairie, screaming the Celtic battle cry of *Erin go bragh*! (Ireland forever!)

At first the Indians seem bewildered, and scatter. Then the humor of the situation catches like a plague of smallpox, and they race with him, laughing, surrounding him.

An arrow catches him in the upper arm, and he loses his .44. Then one of the caisson wheels hits a rock wrong, turns the Limber over, and plummets him through the air. The jenny drags him for a few yards before the reins pull loose, leaving him stunned in the dust. He rises to his knees, and then to his feet. He holds the hunting knife out in a fighting stance. ·ain the Indians seem undecided what to do, until one races forward, ·ounts coup with a stone cudgel.

When he regains consciousness he is spread eagle on the ground, his wrists and ankles tied to stakes. The Indians are milling around him, arguing among themselves, and then the one who had counted coup steps forward, and knocks an arrow.

It feels like a red-hot poker when the flint point drives into his groin, and then another goes through his chest, and pins him to the ground.

His only vision is a red glare, and when he feels the sharp flint blade tearing at his scalp he isn't even aware that the agonized shriek filling the air is coming out of him.

******

Trail Log
Cimarron River
Tuesday, April 14th, 1869
I purchased the army ambulance from the Quartermaster at Medicine Bluffs. It was being surplused, and Jubal helped me get it at a reasonable price.

I was able to recruit an old Buffalo soldier (retired) as our cook. He wants to make his way back east anyway, and said he'd be happy to serve as our cook as far as Abilene, and then he'll take the same train that takes our cattle to market.

From the fresh cow-pies on the trail I figure we're getting close to the herd. I found one of Annie's hair ribbons tied to a Locust tree where they camped for the night. I guess that's just her way of saying, "Hurry, Dai. We went this way." It also tells me, "I'm safe, and I'm thinking about you."

Andy turns in the saddle, and looks back at Aaron James driving the ambulance some fifty feet behind him. Aaron James has already seen the buzzards circling, which Andy is pointing to, and wondered about them. When his new boss wheels the big gray horse, and gallops to the top of the ridge, Aaron James follows him. What he sees there doesn't shock him, not any more. But of all the atrocities he saw during the war, nothing equals what he has become accustomed to out here on the prairie. In the six years he served at Fort Riley, and now nearly two at Camp Medicine Bluffs he has seen every inhumane act man can do to his fellow man.

"He alive?"

Andy is kneeling over the man, staked spread eagle to the earth. "Just barely. He's got a faint pulse, but he's in pretty bad shape." He takes the bandana from around his neck, and ties it over the bleeding scalp. When he does, a black cloud of flies lifts into the air, and then settles again on the already bloody bandana.

Andy has cut the bonds holding the man to the stakes, and is trying to figure out how to remove the arrow going through the man's chest, and into the ground.

"Cut the top off the arrow, near his chest. Then just pull him straight up. The shaft will come out his back, but there's no help for it." Aaron James says.

"Well, he's not conscious, so at least he won't feel it," Andy replies. "Come down here, and help me lift him."

The two men lift Pug straight up, trying to keep him level. The flint point is embedded deep in the ground, so the shaft does pass through Pug's body, and is left sticking a foot above the ground.

"Don't you find it a little unbelievable dat de onliest wagon you could find at Medicine Bluffs was an ambulance?" Aaron James asks.

"Devine providence," Andy answers. "You savvy Devine providence?"

"If dat mean God's hand was all over it, yeah."

Andy smiles. "Yeah, that's what it means."

After the two men have Pug on the stretcher in the back of the ambulance Andy goes over to where the Limber wagon is lying on its side. In the cartouche box he finds Pug's shirt and jacket. When he lifts the jacket, he uncovers a green bowler derby.

He almost falls back in shock. *Mahone! It has to be.*

Aaron James has walked over. "You okay, Cap'n? You look like you seen a haint."

"You're a Christian man, ain't you Aaron James?"

"You know I is. Jubal tol' ya before ya hired me."

"An' he told you that there was a Pinkerton man chasin' me, did'n he?"

"You know he did." Aaron James gives Andy a dubious look.

"That man in the ambulance is him."

"You remember in Psalm fifty-nine when David prayed for deliverance from his enemies, an' even prayed for their destruction? I read Psalm fifty-nine just before we left Medicine Bluffs, an' prayed for deliverance."

Aaron James' head is shaking in disbelief. "Whooie," is his only comment.

The two men right the caisson, and with a bolt made from a post-oak sapling; they fasten it, as a trailer, to the back of the ambulance.

"I guess we gotta go back to Medicine Bluffs with 'im," Andy states. He looks up the trail; in the direction his herd went. "So close," he mutters.

"Naw suh. Ain't no need takin' 'im back to Medicine Bluffs. Dey hasn't got no real doctor back deyah. We 'bout as close to Ft. Riley as we is Medicine Bluffs now, anyhow. Gen'l Sheridan, he got a real good field hospital up deyah." He looks over at the wagon. "If he make it dat far dat is."

******

Annie has been tying hair ribbons to trees for a few of days now, hoping her daddy will find them. She's tried to put on a tough face in front of the boys, but she can't believe how much she misses him.

She has just come up from washing in a small creek when she hears Jack call her. "Hey Annie, look who's coming."

She doesn't need to identify the rider. She knows it's her daddy. Squealing she runs out onto the prairie to meet him. He grabs her outstretched hand, and swings her up behind him. She wraps her arms around his waist, and the giggles erupt out of her like a spring bubbling out of a rock.

The whole camp comes out to greet him, and look over the new chuck wagon.

"Is that the best you could do?" Chico asks, then he notices the sober look on Andy's face. "What's up, amigo?"

In his excitement Fritz has gone to the back of the ambulance, and thrown open the double doors to explore inside. "Ach, mein Gott!" He spins, and begins to wretch.

Andy swings his leg over the pommel of his saddle, drops to the ground, and runs to him. Annie guides Barak over to where she can see in, and her eyes reflect the horror she feels. "What happened to 'im Dai?" She cries.

Andy turns the sobbing Fritz over to Ernst, and goes to Annie. "Oh, Annie, I did'n mean for you to see that. I'm sorry, querida." He pulls her off the horse, and hugs her to his chest.

"But what happened to 'im, Dai?" She persists.

"Indians." He says simply.

No one wants supper. Some are trying to wash the flinty taste of bile out of their mouths with strong coffee. Others are busy in hushed conversation.

Andy, Aaron James and Chico try to take the arrow out of Pugs groin, but it is lodged too tightly between the pubic bone and the hip. They finally just cut it off at the skin. After cleaning his wounds with whiskey as best they can it's just a matter of wait and see, and push on in the morning, slowly.

Fritz has gone to bed early, and is lying shivering in his blankets with Ernst sitting by him, his hand stroking Fritz's forehead. Annie lays curled up, asleep, in Andy's lap, sucking her thumb for the first time in her life.

"Of all the people for me to find out there in that condition, it had to be the man who was hired to kill me, a bounty hunter."

"You'd 've been justified in just ridin' on." Chico says.

Andy gives him a scathing look. "You know I could'n do that."

Chico returns a tender smile. "Yeah, I've known that since the day we

TO GLORY AND BEYOND

brought frontier justice to the Mexican bandits down on the Nueces. You had no stomach for it then, and you still don't."

Aaron James brings around a fresh pot of coffee. He bends down, and strokes Annie's hair. "You want I should put her to bed, Cap'n?"

"No." Andy shakes his head. "I want to keep her close to me tonight." He turns to Yoni. "You okay, son?"

Yoni shrugs. "Yeah, I guess."

"Still," Andy says. "Bring your blankets over by me tonight. I want you close too."

CHAPTER 11

Out on the western prairie, beyond what the old timers call the Indian Meridian, the waist high Crested Wheat grass, and Little Bluestem gradually gives way to the ground hugging Buffalo and Grama grasses.

The flat, table-like land becomes broken by wide, deep gullies with huge rocky outcroppings. In the summer it can be like a blast furnace, and in the winter it can be like the Arctic Circle, but when buffalo can't be found anywhere else, they can generally be found out in this country, and this is the country that Kilakeena's band of Kiowa travel to for their spring hunt.

The meat given to them by the cattle drovers eased the hunger from the harsh winter, but now the fresh meat is gone. They still have smoked jerky and pemmican, but now they crave fresh meat again. Their desire for fresh meat, however, is only part of their need. Their greater need is to hunt. Hunting is a way of life for the Kiowa; a way of life that has been followed for generations as far back as anyone can remember.

Hears-a-Loud-Wind has seen a mixed herd before; a vast herd of buffalo, elk, antelope and mule deer, and like sheep dogs harrying their flanks, a small pack of gray wolves skirts the periphery.

Hears-a-Loud-Wind has seen one, but this is a first for Kilakeena. He turns, and grins at Kilakeena, and Kilakeena makes the sign for *good*, which is also the sign for *my heart soars like a hawk*.

They will follow this herd through the summer, killing, and eating what they need, and then, if Kilakeena gets his way, return to Old Ft. Belknap, tend and milk his Frisians, pray for a mild winter, and in the spring till the ground.

Colonel Nelson Miles leans back in his desk chair until it groans, and threatens to crash to the floor. Lieutenant Colonel Custer is sitting, slouched in an armchair, across the room, and Captain Stewart Cartwright is sitting, not at attention, but rigid, in a wooden chair in front of the desk. He is nervously turning his hat in his fingers.

Miles fastens Cartwright with a steely gaze. "Seems Satanta is on the war path again. Killed a survey party out on the Salt Fork, hit Camp Supply, and last word was he was heading down to the Palo Duro to join up with Quanah. Little Phil wants it stopped, wants him captured, and brought in." This familiarity with the nickname for General Phil Sheridan will never be repeated outside of this room, and the present company.

Custer rouses himself in the armchair. "D-d-don't capture him. A-a-annihilate him. A-a-annihilate the whole bunch of 'em. As the man says, 'the only g-g-good injun is a d-d-dead injun.'"

This slogan has variously been attributed to Chivington, Sheridan, Sherman, and all the way up to Grant. Truth be known, this, or something like it, had probably originated with Andrew Jackson.

Miles gets out of his chair, walks around to Cartwright, and lays his hand on his shoulder. He fingers the captain's bars there. "You know, a pair of gold oak leaves would look nice there. I imagine the man who brings in Satanta or Quanah would be considered somewhat of a hero."

"W-w-wouldn't have to b-b-bring in either one of 'em." Custer smirks. "J-just bring in their h-heads, something to show that they have departed this earth for g-good."

Miles gives him a scathing look. He may be Sheridan's darling, but as far as Miles is concerned he is nothing but a vainglorious, pompous braggart who stammers when he's excited or agitated.

For Custer's part, it's still a point of contention that he lost his brevetted General's stars after the war, and Miles, having been given a full colonelcy, is technically his superior.

"Stewy, Colonel Custer here has personally recommended you for this task, and I agree with him. I'd like to see you further your career. I won't order you to take this job, but if you want to volunteer—well, it would probably be very impressive to the review board."

Cartwright stands, and fidgets between a full parade rest, and attention. "Sir, I'd be more than happy to volunteer for this duty. In fact, I'm glad you considered me for it. I won't let you down, even if I have to chase them all the way to the Mexico."

Once out in the parade ground he slaps his leg with his hat. "Yes! My majority at last." He catches Master Sergeant Hunter coming from the stables. "Master Sergeant put together a couple squads of men. We're goin' after Satanta. Get that Osage scout, what's his name?"

"Cut Nose, sir." Hunter supplies.

"Yeah, Cut Nose." He knows that the Osage and the Kiowa are bitter enemies. He doesn't intend to try to bring Satanta in with two squads. Custer has already made it clear that total annihilation is preferable. He also knows that to take more than twenty men would be counter productive. They have to move fast, and secretive.

Since being posted on this western frontier he has become a student of the famous Texas Rangers, and they seldom range with more than a handful.

"Oh, and Master Sergeant, gather the toughest, meanest fighters you can find. Empty the guard house if need be."

A giant bull elk stops his grazing, lifts his head, and, with cautious suspicion, watches two very small cows approach him. He lifts his nose, and tests the air for the scent of estrus. He doesn't detect any, so he goes back to grazing.

He looks up startled when the Kiowa arrow buries itself up to the fletching, in his heart. He tries to bolt, but his legs collapse under him. His wild eyes watch for only a fading moment as one of the cows walks up to him, and cuts his throat.

Kilakeena's blood is on fire with adrenalin, and he is nearly exploding with excitement. He looks over to where Hears-A-Loud-Wind is approaching two young, fighting bulls, their five-foot antlers locked in mortal combat. Off by the edge of the herd another old bull has been watching the combat, and now he stretches out his bulging neck, and squeals his challenge.

Hears-A-Loud-Wind draws back his bow, and sends an arrow hurtling into the chest of the largest of the young bulls.

Tonight, the tribe will feast on elk heart, tongue, and brains, and tomorrow the tribe will ride into the buffalo herd with their bows and lances. This will be even more exciting than the elk hunt.

Again Kilakeena makes the sign for *my heart soars like a hawk*, and then points to the sky. This is his Christian-Indian way of saying thank you to his father in heaven.

Cut Nose rises from the sign on the trail. "Kiowa," he announces. "Today morning."

"Master Sergeant, have the men dismount. We'll make camp here. Send the scout out to locate the hostiles. When he locates them we'll move out. With any luck we can hit them before they have a chance to move again."

Hunter is already on the ground, and is checking the sign himself. This is not the trail of a war party on the run. There are definite dog and travois tracks, and the footprints of women and children.

"Cap'n, I ain't sure this is our band. This looks to me more like a hunting party, or a family on the move."

"Master Sergeant, you heard the scout. They're Kiowas. That makes 'em hostiles. Now give the order to dismount."

Hunter snaps a salute. "Patrol, dismount. No fires. Cold camp until we pursue."

It has been a long night of feasting and dancing, and Kilakeena is exhausted. He motions for Hears-A-Loud-Wind to come over. "I'm going to bed. Tell the tribe that I want to have a service in the morning before the hunt." He conveys this with hand signs, and a few grunted Kiowa words.

Hears-A-Loud-Wind gives him a dubious look. "Tomorrow's not Sunday."

Kilakeena smiles. "I know. I just want to have a time of thanks for God leading us to this great herd."

Hears-A-Loud-Wind has become a Christian, and allowed himself to be baptized, but sometimes he thinks that Kilakeena is more white than Tsa'la'gee. Still he's his sister's husband, and he loves him like a brother.

Cut nose arrives back at the army camp sometime around midnight. Some of the men are wrapped in their blankets, but most are sitting up gambling, or talking softly.

"Not too big war party. Heap big dance. Dance all night, maybe so." He reports to Cartwright and Hunter.

"Ah, yes. The hostiles always celebrate after a raid. I hope they do dance all night. They'll be too tired, or too drunk, to fight come morning." Cartwright says.

"You see any scalps on their lodge poles or lances?" Hunter asks.

Cut Nose just shrugs.

"Were you able to get a count?" Cartwright asks.

"Maybe so twenty. Maybe so thirty."

"Just right," Cartwright says. "We'll split up into two groups. Hunter you'll take eight men, and circle the camp. I'll take Cut Nose, and the remaining seventeen and—."

Cartwright is still speaking when Hunter asks, "You see Satanta?"

Cut Nose shrugs again. "Don't know he looks like, Satanta."

"Cain't miss 'im. Big man, six-two, six-three, broad shoulders," Hunter says.

His answer is another indifferent shrug.

The Kiowas are weary from dancing well into the night. This is their ancient way of celebrating their good fortune. This band has chosen to follow a new leader though, and a new way, the Christian way.

Kilakeena stands beside the dying bonfire. He has just read from Psalm 111. "The works of the Lord are great, sought out of all them that have pleasure therein. His work is honorable and glorious. He hath given meat unto them that fear him." He pauses, and then, "You thanked the Great Spirit for his great bounty by dancing and singing to him last night, and that's good. You have been faithful children, and followed his statutes, again that's good, and the Great Spirit has rewarded you with this abundance of meat. He will always provide for us, for as long as we live, as long as we're faithful."

Master Sergeant Jubal Hunter has circled the Indian camp, as ordered, and crawled up to a ridge where he can see the camp without being seen. He watches as the Indians sit in a circle around a lone figure. The figure is holding something in the air.

Is it a scalp?

No, it's a bible! Dis ain't no war party. Dis is a prayer meeting.

Suddenly he is startled by the echo of a bugle sounding charge, and gunfire.

The figure holding the bible collapses. One of the warriors jumps onto a horse nearby, and races toward the charging cavalry with his lance. He is immediately taken down by a fusillade of bullets.

"No," Hunter screams. "Dis ain't no war party. Dese is peaceful Indians." He starts running down the hill, but it's too late. His eight men have joined the charge, and are cutting down the men, women, and children who have tried to flee the attack. "Cap'n," he yells, "stop! What we doin' is murderin' peaceful Christians!" The captain can't hear him though. The blood lust has deafened his ears. All he can hear is screaming and gunfire. All he can see is running Indians, and charging cavalry. He draws a bead on a young woman, fleeing up the creek, and shoots her in the back. Another cavalryman races by, and slashes the infant in her arms.

Hunter falls to his knees sobbing. "Please Cap'n. Stop. Dis ain't right." But the carnage continues around him.

When he raises his head Cut Nose is bending over the man with the bible. He is taking the scalp. Hunter runs forward, and catches the scout under the chin with his boot.

"Get away from——."

But before he can finish the captain drives his horse into him, knocking him to the ground. He turns to one of the troopers. "Put this man under arrest. Take that Indian's head. I'll take it back to Custer in a sack." He points at Hears-A-Loud-Wind. "Get his too. He's obviously one of the chiefs."

Then turning to Hunter. "Master Sergeant, as for you. You'll answer for your cowardice in a court-martial."

******

Trail Log
Arkansas River
Sunday, April 19th, 1869
I guess we crossed over into Kansas yesterday afternoon sometime. Since there's no river crossing, and the land looks the same on both sides of the border it's hard to tell when you leave Indian Territory, and enter Kansas.

We'll rest here today, and then follow the Arkansas for another few of days. I believe we can reach Abilene by the end of the month.

We've had to take it slow because of Mahone. It's good to have the ambulance. It gives him some level of comfort, but it does have a bad spring.

Yes, he's still with us. He hasn't regained full consciousness, but he has begun to groan with the pain, and his eyes flutter occasionally.

The children, Yoni, Fritz and Annie, seem to be recovering from their initial shock of seeing him chopped up the way he was. Wednesday evening Annie asked if she could help me dress his wounds. At first I told her no, then I said, yes, I thought it was a good idea. She deals with adversity better than some adults. She's certainly dealing with this better than Fritz. He has had nightmares a few times, and he doesn't want to be out of sight of me, Ernst or Yoni.

All of this has brought to mind my old friend, Maria Victoria Guadalupe de Vargas y Villarreal les Vicomtesse D'Château dun.

I haven't thought about her in years, but now with Mahone hovering at death's door I can't help but remember how she healed Leisaola with just the touch of her hand. She had insisted that it was just her nursing, bathing his wounds, and feeding him lamb broth and wine soaked bread, but when a man is shot through the lungs (twice) it takes more than lamb broth to heal him. It takes a miracle, and God provided that through her special gift of healing.

Lupe, Mr. Mahone could sure use your healing hand right now.

******

"Andy, Mahone's awake. He wants to talk to you."

Andy climbs up into the back of the ambulance. "So, you've joined the living."

Mahone just stares at him, then in a hoarse whisper, "Are you Butler?"

Andy's nod is almost imperceptible. "Yeah."

"You know who I am?"

"Yeah, I know."

"Why'd you do it?"

Andy thinks a minute before answering. "What? Fight against the Union navy, or save you?"

"You haven't saved me yet, just prolonged my agony."

Andy just shrugs at this. There is no answer.

"Did they scalp me? My skull is killin' me."

"They tried, but they made a poor job of it. My guess is they were just youngsters on their warrior quest. You were prob'ly their first victim."

"Couldn't get the arrow out of my thigh, could you?"

"No. It's pretty well imbedded. We broke off the shaft, but had to leave the arrow head in there."

"Which'un 'll kill me? The one you left in me, or the one through my chest?"

Andy hesitates for only a minute. "Prob'ly the one in your chest."

"You don't sugar coat it, do you? I like that in a man." He doubles over, coughing, and coughs up blood.

"The men I work for say you're guilty of piracy on the high seas. Are you?"

"I sank and burned ships, but I never made any of my victims walk the plank, if that's what makes a pirate."

"But you killed men."

"Men died. It was a war. Men die in war."

"You know, I never got into the politics of it. I just tried to do my job."

"And your job is to bring me in, or kill me trying."

Pug doesn't answer the question. "Is there a girl here?"

Andy looks up surprised. "Yeah, my daughter. Why?"

"I heard her talking. I think she sang me a song at some point."

"Yeah, that sounds like my Annie."

"I want to see her, and thank her."

"Okay. I think I can arrange that."

"You never answered my question. Why'd you do it?"

"I couldn't just leave you there, or put a bullet in your brain. Would you've just ridden on, and let me die?"

Pugs eyes close, and he is silent so long Andy fears that he has slipped back into a coma.

Then with his eyes still closed Pug says, "You know what my name means in the Irish?"

"Mahone? I did'n know it meant anything."

"Pug Mahone. The spelling's a little different, but it sounds the same. It means kiss my keester." He chuckles, and the effort starts the coughing to the point that the blood is running down his chin. "My grandfather Dougherty thought it was a great joke on me to call me Pug. I've found it a great joke on society to be know as 'kiss my keester,' an' most people don't even know it."

Wiping the blood off his chin and neck Andy thinks, *He can't last long now. Certainly not to Ft. Riley.* "Yeah, I can see where it might give you a grin or two, when people ask you your name an' you smile 'n' say Pug Mahone."

Pug starts to chuckle again. "Don't make me laugh. Laughin' kills me."

"No," Andy says. "That would be the arrow that passed through your lung."

Pug opens his eyes, and looks directly at Andy. "I like you Butler." He's silent for a minute. "Would you do me a favor? Two really."

I s'pose. What is it?"

"Well, first, after I'm gone I want you to wire Bernie Goldblatt at the Pinkerton Agency in Chicago, and tell her this. Say, 'found Butler and Principe. Both cases closed.' Then, when you plant me out here on this God forsaken prairie put up a marker on my grave that says, 'Pug Mahone.' Maybe someday some other Irishman will see it, and get a laugh."

Time has lost all meaning for Pug. He doesn't know whether it's been one day or a week since Butler found him. He has slipped in and out of consciousness several times, but last night was rough. To begin with it feels like someone is trying to drive nails into his skull. Then, on top of that, he can't breathe. Several times during the night he was afraid he would drown in his own blood. He's glad when the first rays of dawn steal into the wagon. For some inexplicable reason he's afraid to die at night, alone.

He opens his eyes when he feels someone climbing up onto the back step, and then the rising sun blinds him with the opening door. At first all he can make out is the silhouette of unruly curls springing from a small head; the sunrise creating the glow of a halo around it. "Is this an angel come to carry me off, or is this, Annie, the girl with the beautiful voice?" He remembers Andy calling her Annie.

As the door closes behind her he can now make out platinum curls framing a well shaped, triangular face, and the most brilliant blue eyes he's ever seen.

"Well, I sure ain't no angel, that's for sure. Anybody on this drive can tell you that." Annie giggles. "How're ya feelin'?"

"I'm feeling better now that you're here." Pug says. "How many times did you come to visit me when I was—asleep?"

Annie shrugs. "I dunno, maybe twice with Dai, an' a couple more by myself."

"Were you by yourself when you sang to me?"

She dips her head in embarrassment. "I dit'n know you could hear me."

"What was the song? It was pretty, but I couldn't make out the words."

"It was a German lullaby my mom taught me."

"Mmmm, Ulainne used to sing me Irish lullabies, but I liked the German one too."

Annie giggles her funny little adolescent giggle again. "That's a funny name, Ulainne."

"Actually I think it's the Celtic name for Annie." He just makes that up on the spur of the moment.

Annie is beginning to fidget. "Well, I jus' came by to see how you was doin.' I guess I better go fetch my horse an' get into place. They're about to start the drive."

"Let some light in, and let me get a good look at you." Pug says after a coughing fit. Annie takes off her bandana, wipes the blood off his chin, and then opens the back door a crack to let a little light in. What Pug sees is a skinny, long legged, young girl clad in leather riding britches, high topped boots, spurs, a rawhide jacket, and a flat crowned hat hanging down her back. "How old are you Annie?"

"Eight 'n' a half." She answers.

He just nods. "Will you come back and see me again?"

She gives him a questioning look. "Sure. Would you like me to bring you some willow bark tea? It's s'posed to take away some o' the pain I think. At least that's what my cocinero tol' me."

"Yes, thank you. I would like that very much."

It seems like a hundred hours of bouncing and rocking, instead of seven, from the time that Annie left him until the noon stop. When he feels the wagon tilt he can tell that someone heavier than Annie has stepped on the step, and his spirits sag just a little. He's never had anyone affect him like she does. Well, maybe his sister Ulainne, but that was so long ago he can barely remember it.

Andy sticks his head in the back door. "How you holdin' up?"

"I ain't dead yet. Where's Annie?"

Andy chuckles. "She's out fixin' your lunch. She shot a pheasant; shot it, cleaned it, plucked it, and is now roasting it. I did'n even know we had pheasant in America."

Pug's eyes show the smile through his pain. "Yeah, some Polack or Austrian count, or somebody, brought 'em in. You say Annie shot it?"

"Yeah, she carries a 410 shotgun under her saddle skirt. She's a pretty good shot too."

"Did you find my handgun?"

"Yeah, it was a few yards from the overturned caisson. It's over there with your hat."

"I want you to give it to Annie."

Andy studies him a minute. "Don't you think a .44 is a little much gun for a little girl? I only carry a Walker thirty-five."

"A Walker Colt is too heavy for her. My Kerr is a pocket pistol. It'll fit her just right, and the .44s 'll also fit the 410 bore. It's perfect for her."

"I'll think about it," Andy responds.

"She's quite a gal. You should really be proud of her."

"Yeah. She's a handful though. She gets into more mischief than the boys ever thought of."

"You wouldn't change her though. Would you?"

Andy studies on this question before answering. "You mean would I trade her for a sissy-girl? No, I like her pretty much like she is."

"Have you told her that?" Silently Pug remembers a father who had little time for his children, and never told them he liked them just as they were, faults and all.

Again Andy thinks about the question. "Not near enough I s'pose."

There is a long pause in the conversation, and then Pug asks, "How long'll we be stopped for?"

"We'll stop here for the night. We've pushed pretty hard for the last couple o' days. I reckon you an' the herd could use a rest."

"Well, I thank you for that. By the way, what day is it?"

"I b'lieve it's Tuesday the twenty first. Why?"

"Just tryin' to figure out how long I been a burden to you."

"Me an' Aaron James found you on the seventeenth. To be truthful I never figured you'd last this long. You must have a constitution like a Longhorn bull. You know, I knew a boy once who survived two bullet holes through the lungs. He was built like an Andalusian bull." Andy grins. "Andalusian 'cause he was from Spain."

"Does Annie know I was gonna take ya back to hang ya?"

"I haven't told her."

"Good. I don't want her to know." He is silent for a long time, and then, "Can you forgive me for that?"

"I guess if Jesus can forgive you, I can."

"Has Jesus forgiven me? I ain't been to confession for a long time."

"Sure you have. You confessed to me."

"So, then, you're a priest now, are you?"

Andy lifts Pug's hand, and squeezes it. "I am. In the bible Saint Peter says all believers are."

"I guess you'll do as good as the next, then." Pug bows his head, "Forgive me Father for I have sinned. It's been well over three years since my last confession. I've hounded two good men into the ground, for no good reason other than monetary gain." He looks up at Andy, and then closes his eyes again. "Oh yeah, on the boat to Memphis I led a poor young woman into sin."

Andy doesn't consider himself a Catholic, he doesn't really consider himself any denomination, he's never even been to a Catholic service, but he knows what Pug needs to hear.

"You're forgiven."

"What's my penance, priest?"

"Your penance is to pray to Jesus, and thank Him for His sacrifice. That's all."

Pug feels like laughing out loud when he feels Annie's light tread on the back step. It seems like hours since Andy's visit.

"Mister Pug?" She whispers, sticking her head in the door. "You awake?"

"I've been waiting for you." He answers.

"I wasn't sure if you was awake or not. Are you hungry? I brought you some Fuzznent. You like Fuzznent?"

The suppressed chuckle hurts his chest. "I don't know. I don't think I ever had any."

"It's good. I tasted it while I was cookin' it. I brought you a leg and' some white meat. My brothers pestered the life out o' me to let 'em taste it, so I let 'em have what was left. I hope you don't mind."

"No, that's fine. I'm sure you brought me more than I'll be able to eat."

"Well, you need to eat a lot to make you strong again."

His eyes fill with tears. If he could make himself well, just for this little girl, he'd do it.

She holds the leg up to his mouth, and he nibbles at it.

He protests, but she makes him eat all she brought, and then drink the willow bark tea.

When she wipes his mouth with her shirttail he asks, "So then, have you got a lovely song for us?"

She ducks her head shyly. "I been practicin' on one. I could try to sing it for you if you want."

"I want very much."

Her clear, sweet voice sings out softly: "Hush a bye, don't you cry. Oh, the pretty little baby.

"When you wake you shall have all the pretty little horses. Blacks and bays, dapples and grays, all the pretty little horses.

"Hush a bye, don't you cry, oh, the pretty little baby. When you wake we'll have sweet cake, and all the pretty little horses. A brown and a bay, a black and a gray and a coach and six a little horses.

"Go to sleep you pretty little baby." His eyes are closed, and she thinks he has fallen asleep, so she begins to tiptoe out.

"Annie," he calls. "Don't leave me. I don't like bein' alone at night."

She thinks it's strange for a grown man to be afraid of the dark, but she looks over to where the other stretcher is hanging on the opposite wall. "I s'pose I could let the other bed down, and sleep here tonight."

"Could you? It'd make me feel a lot easier."

"Yeah," she says brightly, "just let me go tell Dai where I'm at."

Sometime during the night she hears him strangling, and gets up to turn his head so he can spit out the blood.

"Is that you Ulainne? Where were you? I been waitin' for you." He says in a childish, plaintive voice.

"No, it's Annie. I'm sleepin' over there, 'member?"

"Ulainne, you shouldn't leave me so long. I been scared."

She lets out a long sigh. "It's okay, I'm here now. I won't leave you." She strokes his forehead, and feels the burning fever.

"Ulainne, did Pa come home drunk again?" His voice is a hoarse whisper. "Did he hit Momma? Is she crying?"

She leans over, and kisses his burning cheek. It's all she can do to force the words out. "Hush a bye, don't you cry, all the pretty little horses."

******

Trail log

Abilene, Kansas

Monday, April 27th, 1869.

We lost Mahone five days ago. Annie was with him until the last. She came, in the middle of the night, to tell me he was burning up with fever, and talking to someone named Ulainne.

He slipped into a coma during the night, and never came out of it. I stayed with him until the end, and made Annie stay away. She gave him some comfort during the last days of his life. I'm glad of that, but I saw no reason for her to have to witness his passing. She has already witnessed more tragedy than any eight year old should. She's sad, but she's handling it well.

I left the herd in Chico's care, and Aaron James and I drove the ambulance, non-stop, on into Abilene. It took us thirty-four hours.

Chico thought we should just bury him on the trail, but I wanted to ship his body back to Chicago. I don't know what family he has, but at least he has the family of the Pinkerton Detective Agency in Chicago.

I wired Ms. Goldblatt telling them when to expect the train. I didn't put any details of his death in the wire. I wrote her a personal letter instead, telling her about the Indian attack, and how I found him; and sent it along with Aaron James. He will accompany the body to Chicago before he goes on to Philadelphia.

I'm praying that this warrant for my arrest will die along with Pug. He said to tell Ms. Goldblatt that both cases were closed. I did.

I've made an excellent deal for the cattle with Mr. McCoy. It seems I'm the first to arrive this spring.

I won't go so far as to say it made us rich, but I can pay off the men, split the profits with Chico, give Ernst enough to get him started on his own ranch at Willow Creek, and still have enough to put in the bank in San Antonio.

POST LOG

Annie stomps out of the general store on the main street of Abilene, her spurs jingling, onto the boardwalk. It's drizzling rain so she pulls her hat down tight, and tightens the strap under her chin. She's wearing Mahone's little Kerr .44 on one hip and her hunting knife on the other. She takes a plug of licorice out of a sack, and bites off a chaw.

"Mommy," a little girl cries, scurrying behind her mother's skirts, "is that a girl?"

"Come away dear. Don't go near her," the mother answers, pushing the little girl into the store.

Like a drowning man, Annie's life, of the last few months, flashes before her minds eye; the look on Ilsa's face when she told her not to worry about her, camping out by herself in Willow Creek canyon, watching from the rim of the canyon with the eyes of God himself as the herd made up, and disappeared down the trail, the flames of the prairie fire as it lapped at the tailgate of the wagon, Paco's vulgar remarks to her when he tried to get her to go into the woods with him, and then his subsequent death, the tornado, her beloved Dogo resting beneath a pile of rocks out there on the prairie, and then Mr. Pug being scalped by Indians.

It doesn't really occur to her that she's seen, and done, more than most adult men, and she's only nine.

She gives a grim smile, and then the laughter bubbles up out of her like an artesian well.

She hooks her thumbs in her cartridge belt, and steps out into the rain. She tosses her head, and shouts back over her shoulder. "Don't worry—dear. I ain't got tick fever or nothing."

******

Aaron James is standing away from the rest of the funeral party. He has joined the two gravediggers, who will cover up the grave when the funeral is over.

He's never seen a funeral quite like this. His first shock was when an honor guard from the Chicago Police Department met the train, and escorted the coffin to the cemetery. Now, it seems, all of Pinkerton Detective Agency has turned out, and there is an Irish pipe and drum corps beating on their drums, and wailing away on their bagpipes. He flinches a little when the honor guard fires their twenty-one-gun salute.

He notices Ms. Goldblatt, the woman he gave Cap'n Butler's letter to, linger over the casket, and then dabbing her eyes with a handkerchief, slowly walk away.

When the funeral party has gone he follows the gravediggers to the grave. There is a massive marble headstone with a Celtic cross on the top, and the words below:

Calvin A. Mahone,
Born December 25, 1823
Died April 22, 1869
Rest in Peace.

206

He takes the wooden plaque that Cap'n Butler hand carved, and asked him to place at the grave.

"Can I put this here?" he asks.

The workers look at each other, and shrug. "Sure."

He drives it into the soft dirt at the foot of the grave.

It reads simply:

> Here lies a Pinkerton man.
> Pug Mahone

******

"The defendant will rise. Master Sergeant Jubal Hunter, on the charge and specification of cowardice under fire this court martial finds you not guilty. "Notwithstanding your belief that the Indian band in question was peaceful you still raced, unarmed, and on foot into the fray. We find this action inconsistent with cowardice.

"On the charge of insubordination, and failure to follow an order we find you not guilty. While your action of attacking one of your own troopers might be ill advised we are in agreement that it would only be insubordination if you had attacked your superior officer."

Colonel Nelson Miles directs his stern look on Captain Cartwright.

"Captain, while no charges will be filed against you," he flicks a smoldering glance at Custer, "or any who may have incorrectly advised you, I must say that your actions in this campaign were reprehensible.

"Officers in the army of the United States do not mutilate the enemy fallen, or allow the men under them to do so.

"We will never know whether this particular band of Kiowa were hostiles or not, but if I had my way you would be stripped of rank, and suffer forfeiture pay.

"Further, this court martial has decided that in the best interest of the army you will be transferred to the 7th cavalry under command of Lieutenant Colonel Custer."

Cartwright tries to look repentant, but his smug attitude shows through. He knows that Colonel Miles would have stripped him of rank, and caused him forfeiture of pay, except for the intervention of Custer, and General Sheridan, and his transfer to Custer is in the best interest of Miles, not the army.

Now Miles returns his gaze to Hunter. "Also in the best interest of the army, Master Sergeant, you will report to Fort Apache in the Arizona Territory on or before June first, instant.

"This court-martial is convened."

******

The big man steps from his cabin, sixty miles north west of Skagway, in Yukon Territory, and starts down the hill to the river, where his partner is already panning for gold.

"Hey Shakespeare, you found anything yet?"

Julius Principe looks up, fishes a couple of nuggets, about the size of number 10 buckshot, out of his pan, and holds them up. "Yeah, Mountain. We're showing a little color this morning."

******

Andy raises his head from his saddlebag pillow, and watches the gray overcast break up, and float away. *Maldiciones, no rain again.* He replaces Nancy's journal back in the saddlebag pocket, saddles Blue, and begins the ride back to the homestead.

Ilsa looks up, and shifts the baby straddling her hip when she sees the man riding down the trail from the mesa. She turns to the little boy, racing his stick horse around the yard, trying to lasso a rooster. "Juaquin

Donavan Butler, you better stop tryin' to rope that rooster! Your daddy's gonna skin you alive."

The boy stops, looks up at the man at the yard gate, and pushes his flop hat back with his thumb. "Hidy, 'migo. I gonna catch dis bird fer supper."

Andy pulls the boy off his stick horse, throws him into the air, catches him under the arms, and amid squealing giggles, kisses the baby fat under his chins.

Then smiling at the woman with the baby girl on her hip, and wrapping his arm around her waist, he says. "Hello Mother. What *is* for supper? I'm starving."